Y0-BBY-635

please pass the guilt

other books by rex stout

NOVELS

How Like a God • Golden Remedy • Seed on the Wind
O Careless Love! • Mr. Cinderella • Forest Fire
The President Vanishes

NERO WOLFE MYSTERIES

Fer-de-lance • The League of Frightened Men
The Rubber Band • The Red Box
Some Buried Caesar
Over My Dead Body • Black Orchids
Where There's a Will • Not Quite Dead Enough
Too Many Cooks • The Silent Speaker
Too Many Women • And Be a Villain
Trouble in Triplicate • The Second Confession
Three Doors to Death • In the Best Families
Curtains for Three • Murder by the Book
Triple Jeopardy • Prisoner's Base • The Golden Spiders
Three Men Out • The Black Mountain
Full House: A Nero Wolfe Omnibus • Before Midnight
Three Witnesses • Might as Well Be Dead
Three for the Chair • If Death Ever Slept
And Four to Go • All Aces: A Nero Wolfe Omnibus
Champagne for One • Plot It Yourself
Three at Wolfe's Door • Too Many Clients
Five of a Kind: The Third Nero Wolfe Omnibus
Homicide Trinity: A Nero Wolfe Threesome
The Final Deduction • Gambit • The Mother Hunt
Trio For Blunt Instruments • A Right to Die
The Doorbell Rang
Royal Flush: The Fourth Nero Wolfe Omnibus
Death of a Doxy • The Father Hunt
Kings Full of Aces: The Fifth Nero Wolfe Omnibus
Death of a Dude
Three Aces: The Sixth Nero Wolfe Omnibus
Three Trumps: The Seventh Nero Wolfe Omnibus

TECUMSEH FOX MYSTERIES

Double for Death
The Broken Vase • Bad for Business

MYSTERIES

The Hand in the Glove • Mountain Cat
Alphabet Hicks • Red Threads

please pass the guilt

A NERO WOLFE NOVEL

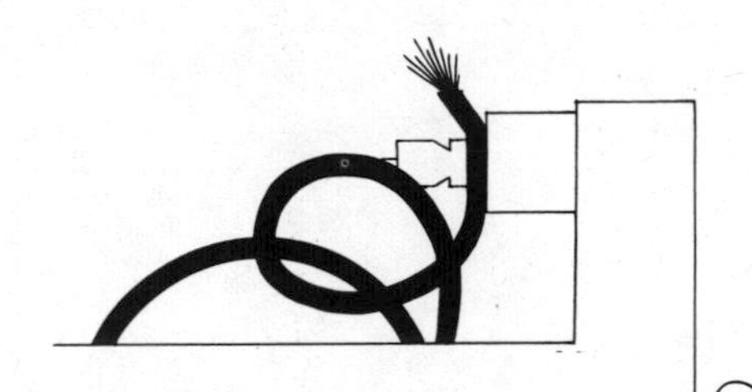

rex stout

THE VIKING PRESS NEW YORK

First published in 1973 by The Viking Press, Inc.
625 Madison Avenue, New York, N.Y. 10022
Published simultaneously in Canada by
The Macmillan Company of Canada Limited
SBN 670-55994-6
Library of Congress catalog card number: 73-5112
Printed in U.S.A.

please pass the guilt

1

HE GRUNTED—the low brief rumble that isn't meant to be heard—turned his head to dart a glance at me, and turned back to Dr. Vollmer, who was in the red leather chair facing the end of Wolfe's desk.

It wasn't just that he was being asked for a favor. If there was a man alive who could say no to a request for a favor easier than Nero Wolfe, I hadn't met him. The trouble was that it was Dr. Vollmer, whose house and office was only a few doors away, who had said he wanted one, and the favor score between him and us was close to a tie. So Wolfe was probably going to be stuck, and therefore the grunt.

Vollmer crossed his long, lean legs and rubbed his narrow, lean jaw with a knuckle. "It's really for a friend of mine," he said, "a man I would like to oblige. His name is Irwin Ostrow, a psychiatrist—not a Freudian. He's interested in a new approach to psychiatric therapy, and he's working at it. Crisis intervention, they call it. I'll have to explain how it works. It's based on—"

"First aid," Wolfe said. "Emotional tourniquet."

"How—you know about it?"

"I read. I read for various purposes, and one of them is to learn what my fellow beings are up to. There are several thousand emergency-treatment centers now operating in this country. The Detroit Psychiatric Institute has a Suicide Prevention Center. The crisis center at Grady Memorial Hospital in Atlanta is staffed by psychiatrists, nurses, social workers, lay therapists, and clergymen.

The director of clinical psychiatry at San Francisco General Hospital has written and spoken at length about it. His name is Decker."

"What's his first name?"

"Barry."

Vollmer shook his head. "You know," he said, "you are the most improbable combination of ignorance and knowledge on earth. You don't know what a linebacker does. You don't know what a fugue is."

"I try to know what I need to know. I make sure to know what I want to know."

"What if it's unknowable?"

"Only philosophers and fools waste time on the unknowable. I am neither. What does Dr. Ostrow want to know?"

Vollmer slid back in the red leather chair, which was deep. "Well. I don't want to bore you with things you already know. If I do, stop me. The Washington Heights Crisis Clinic is on 178th Street, near Broadway. It's a storefront operation; people can just walk in, and they do. A woman who can't stop beating her two-year-old daughter. A man who keeps getting up in the middle of the night and going outdoors in his pajamas. Most of them are on the way to a mental hospital if they're not headed off quick, and the clinic—but you know all that. Eight days ago, a week ago yesterday, a young man came and told a nurse he needed help and she sent him in to Irwin—Dr. Ostrow. He gave the nurse his name, Ronald Seaver."

Vollmer looked at me with his brows up. "I hope *they* don't have to go to a crisis clinic," I said, and turned to Wolfe. "One of your ignorance areas, baseball. Ron Swoboda is an outfielder and Tom Seaver is a pitcher. 'Ron Seaver' is obviously a phony, but it might help to know he's a Met fan, if a clue is needed."

"It is," Vollmer said. "Of course Irwin knew it was an alias, but people often do that their first visit. But he came back five days later, Saturday morning, and again the next day, Sunday, and he not only hasn't told his real name, he won't give any facts at all except what his crisis is. It's blood on his hands. His hands get covered with blood, not visible to anybody else, and he goes and washes them. The first time, ten days ago—no, twelve—it was in the middle of the night and he had to go to the bathroom and wash his hands. It happens any time, no pattern, day or night, but usually when he's alone. A nurse there says it's the Lady Macbeth syndrome. He says he knows of no event or experience that could have caused it, but Irwin is sure he's lying."

He turned a palm up. "So that's his crisis. Irwin says he really has one, a severe one; the possibility of a complete mental breakup is indicated. But they can't get through to him. One of Irwin's colleagues there is a woman, a lay therapist, who has had remarkable success with some tough ones, even catatonics, but after two hours with him—that was Sunday, day before yesterday—she told him he was wasting his time and theirs. Then she said she had alternative suggestions: either he could go to a surgeon and have his hands amputated, or he could go to a detective, perhaps Nero Wolfe, and try to dodge his questions. And do you know what he said? He said, 'I'll do that. I'll go to Nero Wolfe.' "

My brows were up. "He tried to," I said. "So that was Ron Seaver. He phoned yesterday around noon and said he wanted to come and pay Nero Wolfe a hundred dollars an hour to ask him questions. He wouldn't give his name and didn't mention bloody hands. Naturally I thought he was a nut and said no and hung up."

Vollmer nodded. "And he phoned Irwin and Irwin phoned me." To Wolfe: "Of course the hundred dollars an hour wouldn't tempt you, but I didn't come to tempt you, I came to ask a favor for a friend. You said you make sure to know what you want to know. Well, Dr. Ostrow thinks it's possible that this man *did* have blood on his hands, and he wants to know if he can and should be helped. I admit I do too. I've dealt with people in crises myself, any doctor has, but this is a new one to me."

Wolfe looked at the wall clock. Twenty minutes to seven. "Will you dine with us? Shad roe Creole. Fritz uses shallots instead of onion and no cayenne. Chablis, not sherry."

Vollmer smiled, broad. "Knowing how few people get invited to your table, I should beam. But I know it's only compassion for my—"

"I am *not* compassionate."

"Hah. You think my meals are like the one Johnson described to Boswell: 'ill-killed, ill-dressed, ill-cooked, and ill-served,' and you feel sorry for me. Thank you, but I have things to do before I eat. If I could come tomorrow and bring that man . . ."

Wolfe made a face. "Not for dinner. I suppose he'll see Dr. Ostrow tomorrow, or telephone. If he does, tell him to come tomorrow evening at nine o'clock. There will be no fee. And no compassion."

2

THAT WAS Tuesday, the third of June. The next morning there was a little problem. When we haven't got a job or jobs going, I usually get out for a walk after breakfast, with or without an excuse like a trip to the bank, but that Wednesday I didn't. I don't know if I have ever mentioned that the three employes of the Midtown Home Service Corporation who come once a week are always male because Wolfe insists on it. That Wednesday Andy and Sam came at nine o'clock as usual, but they had a woman along, a husky coal-black female with shoulders nearly as broad as mine. Andy, who was white but broad-minded, explained that it was tougher than ever to get men, and repeated one of his favorite remarks, "Goddam it, TV men and carpet layers work in homes." He called the woman Lucile and started her on the dining room, across the hall from the office on the ground floor of the old brownstone. Of course Wolfe, up in the plant rooms on the roof for his morning session with the orchids, hadn't seen her. I went back to the kitchen, sat at my little breakfast table for my second cup of coffee, and told Fritz, "We'll tell him it's a man in disguise because he's wanted."

"There's batter for another cake, Archie."

"No, thanks. They're extra good, they always are, but I've had five. He's wanted for peddling pot. Or maybe acid."

"But his front? The *monts*?"

"Part of the disguise. King-size bra. Is this the Brazilian coffee?"

"No, Colombian. Of course you're just talking. If he sees her—" He threw his hands, and aimed his eyes, up.

"But he probably will. He often comes to the kitchen while you're giving them lunch." I sipped hot coffee. "I'll tell him when he comes down. Have your ear plugs in, he may let out a roar."

So I didn't go for a walk. Anything could happen; Lucile might know about the orchids and sneak up for a look. I was at my desk in the office when the sound of the elevator came at eleven o'clock, and when Wolfe entered and told me good morning and went to put a cluster of Acampe pachyglossa in the vase on his desk, I said, "There's an amendment to the by-laws. Andy is here with Sam and a woman, a black one named Lucile. She is now up in your room with Andy. He says that more and more men think housework isn't manly, which is silly since Fritz and Theodore and I work in your house and we're as manly as they come. It looks like a case of circumstances beyond our control, but if you don't agree, control it."

He sat, got his nineteen stone (it looks better in stone than in pounds) arranged in his made-to-order chair, glanced at his desk calendar, and picked up the stack the mailman had brought. He looked at me. "Are there female Black Panthers?"

"I'll look it up. If there are, Lucile isn't one. She would be a black mare, Clydesdale or Percheron. She can pick up the vacuum cleaner with one finger."

"She is in my house by invitation. I'll have to speak with her, at least a nod and a word."

But he didn't. He didn't go to the kitchen while they were there at lunch, and Andy, who knew Wolfe's habits, kept their paths from crossing. Their regular leaving time was four o'clock, but that was also the time for Wolfe's afternoon turn in the plant rooms, and Andy waited until he was in the elevator on his way up. With them gone, I relaxed. In view of Wolfe's basic attitude on women, there's no telling what will happen when one is in that house. I was making entries, from notes supplied by Theodore, on the germination and performance cards, when Dr. Vollmer phoned to say that

Ronald Seaver would come at nine o'clock. The only preparation needed took about six minutes—going to a cabinet for a fancy glass-and-metal jar with the sharpened ends of a dozen pencils protruding at the top, and placing it at a certain spot and a certain angle near the right edge of my desk, and putting a certain plug in a certain hidden outlet.

He was nearly half an hour late. It was 9:23, and we had just finished with after-dinner coffee in the office, when the doorbell rang and I went. Going down the hall, what I saw on the stoop through the one-way glass panel was commonplace for anyone who knows midtown Manhattan: a junior executive, medium-sized, with a poorly designed face tired too young, in a dark gray suit that had been cut to fit, no hat. I opened the door and invited him in, and added as he entered, "If you had told me on the phone you were Ron Seaver I would have asked you to come and discuss the outlook."

He smiled—the kind of smile that comes quick and goes quicker —and mumbled, "They're doing better."

I agreed and ushered him down the hall. In the office, he stopped about three steps in and one foot backed up a little. I thought that at sight of Wolfe he was deciding to call it off, and so did he, but when I indicated the red leather chair, he came to Wolfe's desk, muttered something, and put out a hand, and Wolfe said, "No, there's blood on it. Sit down."

He went to the red leather chair, sat, met Wolfe's eyes, and said, "If you could see it, if *you* could actually *see* it."

As I went to my chair at my desk I glanced at the jar of pencils; it was in position.

Wolfe nodded. "But I can't. If Dr. Vollmer has described the situation accurately it must be assumed that you are either obtuse or deranged. In your right mind, if you have one, you couldn't possibly expect the people at the clinic to help you unless you supplied some facts. Are you going to tell me your name?"

"No." It wasn't a mumble.

"Are you going to tell me anything at all? Where you live, where you work, where you have seen blood that other people saw or could have seen?"

"No." His jaw worked a little. "I explained to Dr. Ostrow that I couldn't. I knew that that clinic had done some remarkable things for people. I had been—I had heard about it. I thought it was just possible—I thought it was worth trying."

Wolfe turned to me. "How much did his suit cost?"

"Two hundred or more. Probably more. The shoes, at least forty."

"How much would a magazine or newspaper pay him for an article about that clinic?"

"My god," Ronald Seaver blurted, "that's not—" He bit it off and clamped his jaw.

"It's merely one of the valid conjectures." Wolfe shook his head. "I don't like to be imposed on, and I doubt if Dr. Ostrow does. The simplest way to learn if you are an impostor is to discover who and what you are. For Mr. Goodwin to follow you when you leave would take time and trouble, and it isn't necessary. —Archie?"

I picked up the jar and told Ronald Seaver, "Candid camera inside." I removed a couple of the pencils and held them up; they were only two-inch stubs. "Leaving room for the camera below. It now has eight shots of you. Tomorrow I'll show them to people I know—a newspaper man, a couple of cops—"

When you are sitting in a chair and a man comes at you, your reaction depends on what he has in mind. If he has an idea of hurting you, with or without a weapon, you get on your feet fast. But if he merely intends to take something from you, for instance a jar of pencils, and if you have decided that you are stronger and quicker than he is, you merely pull your feet back. Actually he didn't even come close. He stopped three steps short, turned to Wolfe, and said, "You can't do that. Dr. Ostrow wouldn't permit it."

Wolfe nodded. "Of course he wouldn't, but this office is not in his jurisdiction. You have presumed to take an evening of my time, and I want to know why. Are you desperately in need of help, or are you playing some silly game? I'll soon know, probably tomorrow, depending on how long it takes Mr. Goodwin to get you identified from the photographs. I hope it won't be prolonged; I am merely doing a favor for a friend. Good evening, sir. I'll communicate with Dr. Ostrow, not with you."

With me it had been a tossup whether the guy was in some kind of bad jam or was merely on a complicated caper. His long, pointed nose, which didn't go well with his wide, square chin, had twitched a couple of times, but that didn't prove anything. Now, however, he gave evidence. His half-closed, unblinking eyes, steady at me, with a deep crease across his forehead, showed that something was really hurting.

"I don't believe it," he said, louder than necessary, since he was only two arm's lengths away.

Without letting my eyes leave him, I reached for the jar, which I had put back on my desk, stood, removed the top that held the pencil stubs, tilted the jar to show him what was inside, and said, "Autophoton, made in Japan. Electronic control. One will get you ten I'll have you tagged by sundown tomorrow."

His lips parted to let words out, but none came. His head turned to Wolfe, then back to me, and then he turned clear around and took a slow, short step, and another, and I thought he was heading out. But he veered to the right, toward the big globe near the book shelves, stopped halfway to it, and stood. Apparently he wanted his face to himself while he decided something. It took him a good two minutes, maybe three. He turned, got a leather case from his breast pocket, took things from it, selected one—a card—went to Wolfe's desk, and handed it to him. By the time Wolfe had given it a look, I was there, and he passed it to me. It was a New York driver's license: Kenneth Meer, 5 feet 11, age 32, 147 Clover Street, New York 10012.

"Saving you the trouble of asking questions," he said, and extended a hand. I gave him the card and he put it back in the case and the case in his pocket; and he turned and went. Not slow short steps; he marched. I followed out to the hall, and when he had opened the front door and crossed the sill and pulled the door shut, not banging it, I went back to my desk, sat, cocked my head at Wolfe, and spoke:

"You told Doc Vollmer yesterday that you read to learn what your fellow beings are up to. Well?"

He scowled. "I have told you a dozen times that 'Doc' is an obnoxious vulgarism."

"I keep forgetting."

"Pfui. You never forget anything. It was deliberate. As for Kenneth Meer, there has been no picture of him in the *Times.* Has there been one in the *Gazette*?"

"No. His name several times, but no picture. Nor any report that he got blood on his hands, but of course he saw plenty. I suppose, since it's a favor for a friend, I'll have to see a couple of people and find out—"

"No. Get Dr. Vollmer."

"But shouldn't I—"

"No."

I swiveled and swung the phone around. Of Vollmer's three numbers, the most likely one at that hour was the unlisted one on the third floor of his house, and when I dialed it he answered himself. Wolfe got at his phone and I stayed on.

"Good evening, doctor. That man came, half an hour late, and has just left. He refused to give us any information, even his name, and we had to coerce him by a ruse with a concealed camera. Under constraint he identified himself by showing us his motor vehicle operator's license, and then departed without a word. His name has recently been in the news in connection with a murder, but only as one of those present at the scene; there has been no published indication that he is under suspicion or is likely to be. Do you want his name, for Dr. Ostrow?"

"Well." Silence for at least ten seconds. "You got it by—uh—coercion?"

"Yes. As I said."

"Then I don't think—" Another silence, shorter. "I doubt if

Irwin would want it. He never uses coercion. May I ask him and let you know?"

"Certainly."

"Do you intend— Are you interested in the murder? Professionally?"

"Only as a spectator. I am not involved and don't expect to be."

Vollmer thanked him for the favor, not enthusiastically, and they hung up. Wolfe looked at the wall clock—five past ten—and reached for his current book, *Grant Takes Command,* by Bruce Catton. I went to the hall and up the two flights to my room, to catch the last inning or two at Shea Stadium on television.

3

We keep both the *Times* and the *Gazette* for three weeks, sometimes longer, and even if the bank balance had been at a record high I would probably have had another go at the accounts of the Odell murder just for curiosity, since I had now met one of the cast of characters. But we needed a job. In the past five months, the first five of 1969, we had had only six cases, and the fee had gone to five figures in only one of them—getting a damn fool out of a nasty mess with a bunch of smoothies he should have been on to at the first contact. So the checking account balance had lost a lot of weight, and to meet the upkeep of the old brownstone, including the weekly payroll for Theodore and Fritz and me, by about the middle of July Wolfe would have to turn some documents into cash, and that should be prevented if possible. So it wasn't just curiosity that sent me to the basement Thursday morning for old newspapers.

The murder was two weeks old, but what had happened, and how, had been plain and clear in the first reports and had not been substantially revised or amended. At 3:17 P.M. on Tuesday, May 20, a man named Peter J. Odell had entered a room on the sixth floor of the CAN building on West Fifty-fourth Street, pulled open the bottom drawer of a desk, and died instantly. The bomb that shredded him was so powerful that it not only blew the metal desk up to the ceiling but even buckled two of the walls. CAN stood for Continental Air Network, which occupied the whole building, and Peter J. Odell had been its vice-president in charge of development.

The room and desk were not his; they belonged to Amory Browning, the vice-president in charge of programming.

All right, that was what happened, but in addition to the main question, who had put the bomb in the drawer, there were others that had still not been answered, at least not for publication. It wasn't unheard of for a vice-president to enter another vice-president's room, but why had Odell opened that drawer? *That* drawer. It was known to enough people at CAN to get into both the *Times* and the *Gazette* that that drawer had rarely, possibly never, been opened by anyone but Browning himself because nothing was kept in it but a bottle or bottles of twelve-year-old Ten-Mile Creek bourbon. It had almost certainly been known to Odell.

No one had admitted seeing Odell enter Browning's room. Helen Lugos, Browning's secretary, whose room adjoined his, had been down the hall in a file room. Kenneth Meer, Browning's chief assistant, had been down on the ground floor in conference with some technicians. Browning himself had been with Cass R. Abbott, the president of CAN, in his office—the corner office on that floor. If anyone knew why Odell had gone to Browning's room, he wasn't saying. So the answer to the question, Who put the bomb in the drawer? depended partly on the answer to another question: Whom did he expect to open the drawer?

Rereading the accounts in fifteen copies of the *Times* and fifteen of the *Gazette,* I was impressed by how well I had absorbed the details of an event we had not been involved in, and by nothing else. There was nothing to give me a nudge on a start of what I had in mind. It was after eleven o'clock when I finished, so Wolfe had come down from the plant rooms, and I went up to the phone in my room to dial a number—the switchboard of the *Gazette.* It was an afternoon paper and Lon Cohen's line was usually busy from 10 A.M. to 4:20 P.M., but I finally got him. I told him I wanted thirty seconds and he said I could have five.

"Then," I said, "I won't tell you about the steer that grew the Chateaubriands that Felix is saving for us. Can you meet me at Rusterman's at a quarter past six?"

"I can if I have to. Bringing what?"

"Just your tongue. And of course plenty of lettuce for later."

The "later" meant the poker game at Saul Panzer's apartment which started at eight o'clock Thursday evenings. Lon made an appropriate retort about lettuce and hung up, and I dialed another number I didn't have to look up and got Felix, and told him that this time my request for the small room upstairs was strictly personal, not on behalf of Wolfe, and that if he was short on chateaubriands, tournedos would be fine. He asked what kind of flowers would be preferred, and I said my guest would be a man from whom I hoped to get some useful information, so instead of flowers make it four-leaf clovers for luck.

An announcement to Wolfe that I wouldn't be there for dinner was not required, since I never was on Thursdays. Since his dinner time was 7:15, I couldn't eat at his table and be at Saul's poker table at eight. I merely mentioned casually, after we had finished with the morning mail, that I would be leaving around a quarter to six, before he came down from the plant rooms. I did not mention Kenneth Meer, and neither did he, but around the middle of the afternoon Vollmer phoned to say that Dr. Ostrow didn't want to know what Ronald Seaver's name was. Which of course was a polite lie. Dr. Ostrow would certainly have liked to know the name, but not from Wolfe if he had got it by a trick.

The small room upstairs at Rusterman's had many memories for me, back to the days when Marko Vukcic was still alive and making it the best restaurant in New York, with frequent meals with his old friend Nero Wolfe helping to keep it the best. It was still better than good, as Lon Cohen remarked that evening after his third spoonful of Germiny à l'Oseille, and again after his second bite of Chateaubriand and his first sip of the claret.

With about his fourth sip he said, "I'd be enjoying this more—or less, I don't know which—if I knew the price. Of course you want something, or Nero Wolfe does. What?"

I swallowed meat. "Not Nero Wolfe. Me. He doesn't know about it and I don't want him to. I need some facts. I spent two hours this morning reading everything two great newspapers have printed about the murder of Peter J. Odell and I still don't know enough for my personal satisfaction. I thought a chat with you might be helpful."

He squinted at me. "How straight is that? That Wolfe doesn't know you're feeding me."

"As straight as from a ten to an ace."

His eyes aimed about a foot above my head, as they often did when he was deciding whether to call or raise, stayed there while I buttered a bite of roll, and leveled down to mine. "Well, well," he said. "You could just put an ad in the *Gazette.* Of course with a box number since Wolfe mustn't know you're drumming."

Just looking at Lon you would never guess, from his neat little face and his slick black hair, how sharp he is. But people who know him know, including the publisher of the *Gazette,* which is why he has a room to himself two doors down the hall from the publisher's room.

I shook my head. "The kind of people I want to reach don't read *Gazette* ads. To be perfectly frank, I'm going stale and I need exercise. There must be plenty about that crowd that isn't fit to print. This room isn't bugged and neither am I. Have Cramer and the DA got a lead that they're saving?"

"No." He forked peas. "Almost certainly not. Of course the hitch is that they don't know who the bomb was intended for." He put the peas where he wanted them. "Probably no one does but the guy who planted it. It's reasonable to suppose it was meant for Browning, but after all it was Odell who got it. A fact is a fact. Did Browning plant it *for* Odell? He did have a motive."

"Good enough?"

"Apparently. Of course you know that Abbott is retiring the last of August and the board of directors was going to decide on his successor at a meeting scheduled for five o'clock that afternoon, and it would be either Browning or Odell. Odell certainly didn't plant the bomb for Browning and then open the drawer himself, but did Browning plant it and somehow get Odell to open it?"

I sipped claret. "Of course your best men are on it, or have been. What do they think?"

"They've quit thinking. All they have is guesses. Landry's guess is that Mrs. Browning put the bomb there for Helen Lugos, her husband's secretary, knowing, or thinking she knew, that Helen checked the bourbon supply every morning."

"Did she? Check the bourbon supply every morning?"

"I don't know and I doubt if Cramer does. Helen isn't speaking to reporters and it is said that she isn't wasting any words with the law. Also I don't know for sure that Helen and Browning were bedding, but Landry thinks he does. Ask Inspector Cramer, he may know. Another guess, Gahagan's, is that Odell was setting the bomb for Browning and fumbled it. He has been trying for a week to trace where and how Odell got the bomb. Perlman's guess is that Abbott did it because he thought they were going to pick Browning for the new president and he was for Odell. He has three theories on why Odell went to Browning's room and opened the drawer, none of them much good. Damiano's guess is that Helen Lugos did it, to get Browning, but he is no better than Perlman on why Odell horned in."

"Why would Helen want to get Browning?"

"Sex."

"That's not responsive."

"Certainly it's responsive. When sex comes in by the window, logic leaves by the door. When two people collaborate sexually, either one is capable of doing anything and nobody can be sure he knows why he did it. I think Damiano's guess is based on something a man named Meer, Kenneth Meer, told him. Meer is Browning's chief of staff. Damiano got him talking the day after it happened—they had been choir boys together at St. Andrew's—and Meer said that anyone who wanted to know how it happened should concentrate on Helen Lugos. Of course Damiano kept at him then, but Meer backed off. And as I said, Helen isn't doing any talking."

"Has Damiano told Inspector Cramer what Meer said?"

"Of course not. He didn't even tell us until a couple of days ago. He was hoping to earn a medal."

"Does anybody guess that Meer did it?"

"No one at the *Gazette* does. Naturally he has been considered, everybody has, but even for a wild guess you've got to have a motive. Meer certainly wouldn't have wanted to get Browning; if Browning is made president, Meer will be right up near the top. And how could he have got Odell to go to Browning's room and open that drawer? Of course guesses are a dime a dozen. If the bomb was intended for Browning, there are at least a dozen possible candidates. For instance, Madeline Odell, now the widow Odell. She had been expecting her husband to be the CAN president ever since she married him, twenty years ago, and it looked as if Browning was going to get it instead. Or Theodore Falk, the Wall Street Falk, old friend of the Odells and a member of the CAN board of directors. Of course he didn't do it himself, but millionaires don't have to do things themselves. Or Sylvia Venner. You know?"

I nodded. " 'The Big Town.' "

"Right. She had that program for two years and Browning bounced her. Now she does chores, and she hates Browning's guts. I could name more. Of course if the bomb was intended for Odell, there are candidates for that too, but for them there's the problem of getting Odell to enter that room and open that drawer."

I swallowed my last bite of Chateaubriand and pushed the button for Pierre. "You said Odell's wife had been expecting him to be president ever since she married him. Had she been doing anything about it?"

"Plenty. She inherited a big block of CAN stock from her father, Carl Hartig, along with a lot of oil wells and miscellaneous items, and she's been on the board of directors for ten years. She would probably have given half of her seventy or eighty million to have Browning removed from competition, but if she had known that bomb was in that drawer she would have made damn sure that her husband wouldn't go near that room that day. That's why she's not *my* guess—or anybody else's as far as I know."

"Seventy or eighty *million*?"

"At least that. She's really loaded."

"Huh. What kind of sauce do you want on your soufflé? Brandy ginger or mocha rum?"

"Mocha rum sounds better."

Pierre had come and was removing empty dishes. I told him what we would have and waited until he was gone to resume with Lon. You never know. Abbott or Browning or Madeline Odell might be one of Pierre's pet customers.

When, at a quarter to eight, out on the sidewalk, we decided to walk the eleven blocks to Saul Panzer's instead of scouting for a taxi, I had collected around a hundred more facts and guesses, but it would be a waste of paper and ink to list them for you since none of them was any help to my program. Also I will not report on the course of events at the poker table, except to say that having a complicated operation on my mind was no help to my wallet. I lost sixty-eight bucks.

4

THE FIRST problem was how to get to her, and the second one was what to say when I did. "Her" was of course Madeline Odell, the widow. She was almost certainly in the clear on the bomb, she had the best reason for wanting the bomber to be caught and nailed, and she had the biggest stack. It was those two problems trying to take over that had caused me to make three big mistakes and several small ones at the poker game, and cost me money. They did not keep me from getting a good eight hours' sleep, nothing ever does, and they didn't affect my appetite at breakfast, but I skipped things in the *Times* that I usually cover, and I guess I was short with Fritz. In the office I actually forgot to put fresh water in the vase on Wolfe's desk.

I still hadn't decided at lunchtime. Of course any one of a dozen dodges would have got me to her; no one is inaccessible if you put your mind on it; but then what? If possible the approach should lead naturally to the proposition. After lunch I went for a walk with a couple of unnecessary errands for an excuse, and didn't get back until after four o'clock, so Wolfe was up in the plant rooms and I had the office to myself. I swung the typewriter around and rolled paper in and gave it a try.

> *Dear Mrs. Odell: This is on Nero Wolfe's letterhead because I work for him and am writing it in his office, but it is strictly personal, from me, and Mr. Wolfe doesn't know I am writing you. I do so because I am an experi-*

enced professional detective and it hurts me to see or read about poor detective work, especially in an important case like the murder of your husband. Mr. Wolfe and I have of course followed the published accounts of the investigation, and yesterday he remarked to me that apparently the most crucial fact was being ignored, or at least not getting the priority it deserved, and I agreed with him. Such a criticism from him to the police or the District Attorney would probably have no effect, but it occurred to me this morning that it might have some effect if it came from you. If you wish to reach me the address and telephone number are above.

I read it over twice and made five improvements: I took out "strictly" and "professional," changed "poor" to "inferior," "crucial" to "important," and "priority" to "attention." I read it again, changed "an important case like" to "such a vital case as," typed it on a letterhead with two carbons, signed it, and addressed an envelope to a number on East Sixty-third Street. I went to the kitchen to tell Fritz I was going out for air, and walked to the post office on Eighth Avenue.

Since it was a Friday afternoon in June, it was possible, even probable, that she wouldn't get it until Monday, and nothing would interfere with my weekend pleasures at Shea Stadium, but a little after eleven o'clock Saturday morning, when Wolfe was dictating a long letter to an orchid collector in Malaysia, the phone rang and I swiveled and took it.

"Nero Wolfe's office, Archie Goodwin speaking."

A businesslike female voice: "This is Mrs. Peter Odell's secretary. She has received your letter and wishes to speak to Mr. Wolfe."

Of course I had known that might happen, with Wolfe right there. "I'm sorry," I said, "but Mr. Wolfe isn't available and won't be until Monday. Anyway I made it clear that the letter was personal."

She covered the transmitter and I heard nothing. In a couple of minutes she was back: "Mr. Goodwin?"

"Here."

"Mrs. Odell wishes to see you. Will you be here promptly at three o'clock?"

One of my basic opinions is that people who take things for granted should be helped to a better understanding of democracy, and at three o'clock it would be about the fourth inning, but I hadn't been asked to write that letter. "Yes," I said, "I'll be there," and hung up, and swiveled.

"Someone using your name in vain," I told Wolfe. "People should read letters at least three times." I looked at my notebook. "The last I have is 'in spite of all the crosses hybridizers have tried.' "

It took another full page of the notebook.

My intention had been to get to Shea Stadium a little after one and enjoy a couple of hot dogs and a pint of milk while watching batting practice. Instead, I got to Sam's diner on Tenth Avenue a little after one and enjoyed rye bread and baked beans, two items that never appear at Wolfe's table, and then walked the nearly two miles from West Thirty-fifth Street to East Sixty-third. The people you see on midtown sidewalks Saturday afternoons are completely different from other days.

It was a five-story, forty-foot-wide stone mansion, between Fifth and Madison, and I was stopped at the entrance to the vestibule by a broad-shouldered husky with a Lathrop Protective Service badge on his buttoned-up jacket. Apparently after more than two weeks, pests—for instance, journalists—were still a problem, or Mrs. Odell thought they were. He said grimly, "Well, sir?"

I pronounced my name and said I was expected, and produced evidence of my identity from my card case. He entered the vestibule and pushed the button, and the door was opened by a woman in a neat gray uniform with a skirt that reached a good four inches below her knees who accepted my name without evidence. She crossed the marble floor to an intercom on a marble table and told it Mr. Goodwin was there, and in a couple of minutes there was the sound of an elevator about one-tenth as noisy as Wolfe's. A door at the far end of the large entrance hall slid open, and a woman stuck her head out and invited me to join her. We went up past two doors and stopped at the third, and she led me down the hall to an open door at the front and stood aside for me to enter.

It was a big room, the whole width of the house, and my sweeping glance saw desks, working chairs and easy chairs, two couches, oil paintings, filing cabinets, a color television—and my glance stopped there because a ball game was on, Ralph Kiner was talking, and his audience was a woman propped against a bank of cushions on an oversized couch. Even if it hadn't been her house I would have recognized her from pictures in the *Times* and *Gazette:* a face bulged in the middle by wide cheek bones, and a wide full-lipped mouth. Her loose, pale blue dress or robe or sack was zippered shut in front, top to bottom. I crossed over to her and asked politely, "What's the score?"

Her brown eyes darted to me and back to the game. "Mets two, Pirates four, last of the fourth. Sit down."

I went to a chair not far from the couch that faced the TV set. Ed Kranepool was at bat. He went to three and two and then grounded out, ending the inning, and a commercial started yapping. As I looked around for the secretary and saw she wasn't there, the sound quit and I turned back to Mrs. Odell. Remote control; she had pushed a button.

"I'll leave the picture on," she said. She sized me up head to foot, taking her time. My pants were pressed. "That was a poor excuse for a letter you sent me. 'The most important fact,' you said, but you didn't say what it is."

"Of course I didn't."

"Why 'of course'?"

The commercial had finished and a Pirate was coming to bat. She left the sound off but sent her eyes back to the game, so I sent mine, too. "I work for Nero Wolfe," I told the Pirate as he swung and missed. "He makes a living solving problems for people, and part of what they pay him pays my salary. It would be pretty dumb for me to tell people for free what he has said about their problems. I wrote that letter only because I hate to see a case bobbled."

"Oh, come off it." Her eyes darted to me and back to the game. "You invited me to reach you and wouldn't put him on when I phoned. How much do you want?"

"You might try a million. No one has ever bid high enough to make it tough for me. But I did invite you to reach me, didn't I? Do you know what I suspect? I'll bet that at the back of my mind, down in the subconscious, there was a sneaking idea that after two weeks and three days of the cops and the DA getting nowhere, you might want to discuss it with Nero Wolfe. Do you know anything about him?"

"Personally and definitely, no. I know his reputation, certainly."

One Pirate had watched a third strike go by and another one had popped up to the infield. Now a third one lofted a major-league blooper out to left center and both Cleon Jones and Tommy Agee were on the gallop. It would fall in . . . but it didn't. Jones stretched an arm and one-handed it, and kept it. A good inning for Koosman. As the picture of the commercial started, I turned to the couch. "To be honest," I said, "I may as well admit that that letter *was* dumb. How could you needle the police or the District Attorney about neglecting the most important fact if I didn't tell you what it is? I apologize, and I not only apologize, I pay a forfeit. The most important fact is that your husband entered that room and opened that drawer, and the most important question is, why? Unless and until they have the answer to that the ten best investigators in the world couldn't possibly solve the case. Tell Inspector Cramer that, but don't mention Nero Wolfe. The sound of that name riles him." I stood up. "I realize that it's possible that you know why he entered the room and opened the drawer, and you have told the DA and he's saving it, but from the published accounts I doubt it, and so does Mr. Wolfe. Thank you for letting me see Cleon Jones make that catch."

I turned and was going, but she raised her voice. "Damn it, sit down!"

I did so, and as I sat Jerry Grote lined a double to the right-field corner. Bud Harrelson beat out a bunt and Grote moved to third, and Mrs. Odell pushed the button and the sound came on. More action and two Mets crossed the plate. When Ed Charles made the third out the score was tied, and as the commercial started she pushed the button, looked at me, and said, "Call Wolfe and tell him I want to see him. Now." She aimed a finger. "The phone on that desk. How long will it take him?"

"Too long. Forever. You certainly don't know him 'definitely.' He leaves his house only for personal errands no one else can do, never on business. I suppose you'd rather not discuss it on the phone, so you'll have to go to him. The address is on the letterhead. Six o'clock would be a good time, he'll be available then, and the game will be—"

"My god, what a nerve," she said. "You think I would?"

"No, I think you wouldn't. But you said you want to see him, and I—"

"All right, all right. Forget it." She pushed the button. Bob Murphy had replaced Ralph Kiner and he talks louder. She had to raise her voice: "Miss Haber will take you down. She's in the hall."

I got up and went. I hadn't the slightest idea, as I was escorted to the elevator and down, and to the entrance, by Miss Haber, and as I walked to Madison Avenue and turned downtown, headed for a bar where I knew there was a TV, whether or not I had wasted a letterhead and a postage stamp and most of an afternoon. On a bet I would have taken either end. But after all, she had said she wanted to see him, and if I know women one-tenth as well as Wolfe pretends to think I do, she was strongly inclined to get what she wanted. By the time the game ended, which the Mets won 7 to 5, I would no longer have taken either end. Two to one I had hooked her. That was how it looked as I used my key on the door of the old brownstone a little before six o'clock.

Of course I couldn't leave the house that evening. When I'm not there Fritz usually answers the phone, but sometimes Wolfe does, and she might call any minute. She *might.* She didn't. It was also possible that she would tell either Cramer or the DA about it and he would call. He didn't. When I went to bed around midnight the odds were no longer two to one. But there was still an off chance, and when I went to the office after breakfast Sunday morning, I rang Lily Rowan and told her I was stuck for the day and would send the tickets for the ball game by messenger, and I hoped she could find someone who could yell at the umpire as loud as I did. And then, about eight minutes after the messenger had come and taken the tickets, the phone rang, and it was Mrs. Odell in person, not the secretary. She said she wanted to speak with Wolfe and I said no, that he didn't even know I had written her and seen her.

"My god," she said, "you might think he's the President. I want to see him. Bring him."

"I can't and he wouldn't. Honestly, Mrs. Odell, I wish he would. It would do him good to get out more, but not a chance. If there was a way of scoring pigheadedness it would be interesting to match him with you. I think he'd win."

"Of course I'm pigheaded. I always have been."

"I'm perfectly willing to make it 'strong-minded' if you prefer."

Silence. It lasted so long that I thought she had quit without bothering to hang up. Then she said, "I'll be there at six o'clock."

"Today? Sunday?"

"Yes." She hung up.

I took a deep breath and enjoyed it. So far so good, but the highest hurdle was still ahead. The Sunday household routine was different. Theodore didn't come on Sunday and Wolfe's morning with the orchids could be anything from twenty minutes to four hours. Also Fritz might leave for the day right after breakfast, or he might not. That day not, he had said. The question was when to spring it. Going up to the plant rooms with it was of course out of the question; I wasn't welcome there even for a real emergency.

I decided not to decide until he came down and I saw what his mood was like.

When he showed, a little after eleven, he had the Sunday *Times* under one arm and a fourteen-inch raceme of Peristeria elata in the other hand, and his "Good morning" was a greeting, not just a growl. So when the flowers were in the vase and his bulk was satisfactorily arranged in the made-to-order chair he wouldn't swap for its weight in uranium, I spoke.

"Before you get started on the *Review of the Week,* I have an item you won't like. A woman is coming to see you at six o'clock today. Mrs. Peter J. Odell, whose husband opened a desk drawer and died. I had to ignore the rule on consulting you before making an appointment."

He was glaring at me. "I was here. I was available."

"Sure, but it was an emergency." I opened a drawer of my desk and took out a paper. "This is a carbon of a letter I sent her Friday afternoon." I rose, handed it to him, and returned to my chair. "She phoned yesterday morning, or her secretary did, and I went to see her yesterday afternoon, at her house on Sixty-third Street. She asked me to phone you to come, which of course wasn't discussable. I told her the only place she could see you was your office. She phoned this morning, an hour ago, and said she would be here at six o'clock.

He had read the letter. He read it again, with his lips pressed tight. He dropped it on his desk and looked at me. Not a glare or a scowl, just a hard, straight look. "I don't believe it," he said. "It would be insufferable, as you well know."

I nodded. "Of course that's the reaction I expected. But she'll be here at six. The emergency I referred to is in the safe. Your checkbook. You have of course noticed that since May first I have been giving you a memo of the condition every week instead of twice a month. Of the hundred and fifty-eight days this year you have worked about ten and I have worked less than twenty, not counting office chores. I happened—"

"Not 'less' than twenty. 'Fewer.' "

"Thank you. I happened to learn that Mrs. Odell's pile goes to eight figures, maybe even nine. The alternatives were (a) quit this job and make her an offer, or (b) get her to make you an offer. I tossed a coin and you won. So I wrote her that letter."

"Now," he said through his teeth with his lips barely moving, "*I* have alternatives."

"Certainly. Fire me, or go to work. If you fire me I won't expect severance pay. I would have to draw the check, and for more than a month every time I have drawn a check I have had to set my jaw. In deciding, please remember that at least twice you have yourself put out a hook when the bank balance got too low for comfort. The last time was when you sent me to see a woman named Fraser. The only difference is that this time I did it without consulting you. I like to earn *part* of my pay."

He cupped his hands over the ends of the chair arms, leaned back, and shut his eyes. But his lips didn't start to work in and out, so he didn't really have a problem; he was just looking at it. He may have thought I was holding my breath, but probably not, because he knows me nearly as well as I know him.

I was about to swivel and resume with my copy of the *Times* when he opened his eyes and straightened up and spoke. "Regarding my remark to you about the most important fact that is not getting the attention it deserves. She will of course want to know what it is, and so do I. Have you a suggestion?"

"Sure. I have already told her, yesterday. It's that Odell entered Browning's room and opened the drawer of his desk that everybody knew had only bourbon in it. Why? That's the most important question. You have only read the newspaper accounts, but I have also discussed it for an hour and a half with Lon Cohen and learned a few things that haven't been printed."

"Confound it." He made a face. "Very well. Talk. From Mr. Cohen, the substance. Your conversation with that woman, verbatim."

I talked.

5

MOST OF THE people who enter that office for the first time have something eating them, but even so they often notice one or more of the objects in view—the fourteen-by-twenty-six Keraghan rug or the three-foot globe or the floral display in the vase on Wolfe's desk. Mrs. Peter J. Odell didn't. When I escorted her to the office, her eyes fixed on Wolfe and stayed there as she crossed the rug and stopped just short of his desk. Of course he stayed put in his chair, as usual.

"Charlotte Haber is my secretary," she said. "I brought her because I may need her." She went to the red leather chair, sat, and put her handbag on the little stand at her elbow. Meanwhile I had moved up one of the yellow chairs for the secretary. From the look Miss Haber had given me at the door, and the one she was now giving Wolfe, it was a good guess that she would rather have been somewhere else. The crease in her narrow forehead made it even narrower, and the way she was puckering her mouth, which was too small anyway, made it almost invisible.

"I have asked three men about you," Mrs. Odell told Wolfe. "You're highhanded and opinionated, and you charge high fees, but you're dependable."

Wolfe grunted. "You should have inquired further. Competence?"

"Oh, apparently you're smart enough. I'll decide that myself. Your man told me that you said the police are neglecting the most important question, why did my husband go to Browning's room and open that drawer? I want to know why that is so important." She got her bag and opened it and took out a checkfold. "How much for telling me that?"

He shook his head. "I discuss details only with clients and you haven't hired me. But since Mr. Goodwin has presumed to quote me to you—without my prior knowledge—I'll make an exception. On trial for murder, a man may be convicted without proof of motive. Establishment of motive of course helps with a jury, but it is not requisite. But in an *investigation* of a murder, motive is of first importance. The question was first asked in an ancient language many centuries ago: *Cui bono?* To try to learn who put that bomb in that drawer without knowing whom it was intended for is close to hopeless, and to learn whom it was intended for it is essential to know why your husband entered the room and opened the drawer, and who knew he was going to. Actually that's the most important question: Who knew he was going to? Did anybody? If it were my problem I would begin by concentrating on that question to the exclusion of all others. I give you that, madam, with my compliments, since Mr. Goodwin quoted me without bothering to get permission."

She still had the checkfold in her hand. "The police think it was intended for Amory Browning."

"No doubt. A reasonable assumption. But if it was actually intended for your husband, they're wasting their time and they'll get nowhere."

"Why do you think it was intended for my husband?"

"I don't. But I think it might have been—and I repeat, I would want first to learn if anyone knew he was going to enter that room and open that drawer, and if so, who."

She sat and looked at him. Then she turned her head to look at me, and turned it further to look at Charlotte Haber. I don't know if that was any help, but probably she had already made up her mind and didn't even know she was doing it. She opened the checkfold, slid a pen out of its loop, wrote, on both the stub and the check, and tore the check out. "You said I haven't hired you," she said. "Now I have. This twenty thousand dollars is for a retainer. I'm going to tell you something and ask you what to do, with the understanding that it is in confidence and you will never tell anyone about it—under any circumstances."

Wolfe shook his head. "I can't accept it on those terms."

"My god, why not? A lawyer would."

"I am not a member of the bar. What a client tells me is not a privileged communication. Archie. Your notebook."

I got it from a drawer, and a pen.

"One carbon," he said. "I acknowledge receipt of a check for twenty thousand dollars from Mrs. Peter J. Odell as a retainer for my services. Period. I guarantee that any information she gives me will be revealed to no one, comma, either by me or by Archie Goodwin, comma, without her consent, comma, unless circumstances arise that put me or him under legal compulsion to reveal it." He turned to her. "I assure you that we do not invite or welcome legal compulsion. Will that do?"

"I don't—I'll look at it."

I put paper in the typewriter and hit the keys. On the wall back of my desk is a mirror four feet high and six feet wide, and in it I could see that Miss Haber was looking surprised. No female secretary thinks a man can use eight fingers and two thumbs on a typewriter. I rolled it out, kept the carbon, and got up to hand Wolfe the original. He signed it and handed it back, and I took it to Mrs. Odell. She read it, pursed her lips, read it again, folded it and put it in her bag, and handed me the check. I gave it a look and took it to Wolfe, and without even a glance at it he dropped it on his desk.

He looked at the client: "I signed that receipt, madam, but I shall not consider myself definitely committed until I learn what you want me to do. I hope it won't be necessary for me to return your check, but I can if I must. In any case, what you tell me will be held in confidence if possible. What do you want?"

"I want advice. I want to know what *I* can do. I know why my husband went to Amory Browning's room and opened that drawer.

So does Miss Haber. That's why she's here. I know the bomb was intended for him, and I know who put it there."

I suppose Wolfe has been surprised by things people have said as often as you or me, but his ego has arranged with him not to show it and he rarely does. But that got him. His eyes stretched wide, as wide as I have ever seen them, then they narrowed at her, half closed, and he cleared his throat.

"Indeed," he said. "Have you told the police?"

"No. I have told no one. No one knows about it except Miss Haber and me. I have hoped the police would get him. Why haven't they found out where and how he got the bomb? My god, are they any good at all? It has been more than two weeks. Now, after what you have said, I have got to do something and I want you to tell me what. How much do you know? Do you know that there was to be a directors' meeting at five o'clock that day to decide who would be the new president of CAN?"

"Yes. And that it would be either your husband or Mr. Browning."

She nodded. "And they were both to be at the meeting, and give their ideas about policy and what they thought should be done, and answer questions, and then leave, and we would discuss it and then vote. Did you know that?"

"No."

"Well, that's how it was. If you have read the papers, you know that Amory Browning kept a certain brand of whiskey in that bottom drawer of his desk."

"Yes."

"And that every afternoon around four o'clock he took a drink of it."

"That has been said, yes."

"Well, he did. Every afternoon, between four and five o'clock. Everybody knew it. All right, now I'm telling you what you have guaranteed not to repeat. My husband went to that room and opened that drawer to put something in the whisky. It was my idea. Do you know what LSD is?"

"Yes. Lysergic acid diethylamide."

"My god, you can pronounce it. Well, I got some. You don't need to know how I got it. Miss Haber knows. I got some, it was a powder, and I put it in a little plastic container, and I persuaded my husband to use it. The police know he had it. It was in a pocket of his jacket. You didn't know about *that.*"

"No."

"They haven't told about it. I think they haven't told anyone but me, and I told them I knew nothing about it. He was going to put it in the whisky. Almost certainly Browning would take a drink before he went to that meeting at five o'clock. We didn't know what that amount of LSD would do to him—of course we didn't know how full the bottle would be. But there was a good chance it would do enough for him to make a bad impression at that meeting, and it was understood and agreed that we would make a final decision that day. All right, now you know why he went to that room and opened that drawer."

Wolfe nodded. "I probably do. It isn't likely that you would trump up a tale of such an exploit—and the police have the LSD. You said that Miss Haber knows how you got it. Did she also know how you planned to use it?"

"Yes."

"Did anyone else know?"

"Yes. Amory Browning."

Wolfe shook his head. "My credulity will stretch only so far, madam. Obviously you are going to tell me that Mr. Browning murdered your husband."

"That's right. He did." Her head turned. "Charlotte?"

Miss Haber's mouth opened, and closed. She lifted a hand, and dropped it. "Please, Mrs. Odell," she said. "I don't think—You tell him. Please?"

"Well, you're here." Mrs. Odell went back to Wolfe. "There are strong people," she said, "and there are weak people, and Miss Haber is one of the weak ones. She's extremely competent, but weak. She found out for me how to get some LSD, and in fact she got it for me, about a month ago. Then she found out what I was going to do with it by eavesdropping on us—my husband and me. Then she phoned Amory Browning and told him what we were going to do. I didn't know that until three days after my husband died. So she was weak three times—getting the LSD for me without knowing what I wanted it for, and phoning Browning, and telling me. You said the most important question is who knew my husband was going to that room and open that drawer. All right, three people knew: Miss Haber and me, and Amory Browning. And she told Browning four days before it happened, so he had plenty of time to get the bomb."

Wolfe was frowning at her with his chin down. "A remarkable performance," he said. "Extraordinary. You seem not to be aware that—"

She cut in. "I'm not through. About Browning getting the bomb. Do you watch television?"

"Rarely."

"About three months ago, CAN had a one-hour special they called 'Where the Little Bombs Come From.' Did you see it?"

"No."

"Lots of people thought it told too much about what bombs are made of and who makes them, but it really didn't, because they changed all the names and didn't give any addresses. That program was Browning's idea and his staff did all the research, so getting one would have been easy for him. If you mean it would have been remarkable for him to get a bomb in four days and know how to use it, it wouldn't."

Wolfe was still frowning. "I didn't mean that. I meant *your* performance. That is of course one detail to be considered, but before considering details I must know if I'm going to be concerned with them. If I take the job, what do you expect me to do?"

"I expect you to tell *me* what to do, and I suppose help me do it. I want Amory Browning indicted and tried and convicted, but I do *not* want what I have told you to be known. I am not going to sit in a witness chair and tell what my husband and I did and answer questions about it. How many things have *you* done that you wouldn't want everyone to know about?"

"Perhaps a thousand. Adulterating a rival's whisky is not one of them, but tastes and methods differ." Wolfe's head turned. "Miss Haber. Do you corroborate what Mrs. Odell has told me of your share in this affair?"

The secretary swallowed. I had her in profile, but apparently her eyes were straight at him. She said "Yes," but it was barely audible, and she repeated it louder, "Yes, I do."

"You got some LSD at her request?"

"Yes, but I'm not going to tell how I got it."

"I don't need to know, at least not now. And you learned how she was going to use it by overhearing conversations she had with her husband?"

"Yes. I thought I had a right to know. LSD is illegal. It can't be sold legally and you can't even have it in your possession."

"And you decided to tell Mr. Browning about it? Why?"

"Because I was afraid it might kill him. The amount I got and gave Mrs. Odell—it was about four tablespoons—I didn't know what it would do. If the whisky bottle was only half full, or even less, and Mr. Odell put all that LSD in it—from the little I knew I thought it *would* kill him. I would be an accessory to a murder, and anyway I didn't want to help kill a man. It may be what Mrs. Odell said, that I'm one of the weak ones—anyhow, I didn't want to be a murderer."

"How did you communicate with Mr. Browning? Did you write to him?"

"I phoned him. I phoned him Friday evening, from a booth, at his place in the country. I didn't tell him my name. I didn't tell him *any* names. I just told him that Tuesday afternoon someone was going to put a dangerous drug in the whisky in his desk drawer and he had better not drink it. He wanted to ask questions, but I hung up. Of course I supposed he would suspect it would be Mr. Odell, but I certainly didn't suppose he would do what he did."

"Where is his country place?"

"In Connecticut. Westport."

"You say you phoned him Friday evening. Which Friday?"

"The Friday before it happened. Four days before."

"That was May sixteenth."

"Was it?" It took her only a moment, not a long one, to figure it. "That's right, May sixteenth."

"You phoned him at what hour?"

"Around nine o'clock. A little after nine. When I thought he would have finished dinner."

"How sure are you it was Mr. Browning?"

"Oh, *quite* sure. He answered the phone himself, and I know his voice. I have heard him on the phone at least a dozen times, when he has called Mr. Odell at home."

Wolfe regarded her. "And you didn't tell Mrs. Odell you had warned him."

"Of course not."

"But you did tell her, three days after Mr. Odell died. Why?"

"Because—well, I *had* to. I said I didn't want to be a murderer, but I *was* one. If I hadn't made that phone call, Mr. Odell would still be alive, and maybe Mr. Browning would too. The LSD might not have hurt him at all. To go right on being with Mrs. Odell every day—I *had* to tell her."

Wolfe turned to the prospective client. "That was two weeks ago. Why haven't you dismissed her?"

"That's a silly question," Mrs. Odell said. "She might tell anyone. She might tell the police. I'm not hiring you to analyze what Miss Haber has done—or what I have done. I want to know how we can make Browning pay for what *he* did without telling what *we* did."

Wolfe closed his eyes, and the forefinger of his right hand started making little circles on his desk blotter. But he wasn't tackling a tough one; his lips didn't move. So he had made his decision and was merely considering whether he should ask more questions before announcing it. In half a minute he quit making circles, lifted his hand to give his forehead a rub, and swiveled to look at me. If they hadn't been there he would have put it into words: "You got me into this. I concede the desirability of a fee, but you got me into *this.*"

Having looked it, long enough to count ten, he swiveled back to her. "Very well. It's an impossible job, but I'll accept the retainer. My fee will be based on effort and risk, not on accomplishment. I'll need facts, many facts, but it's nearly dinner time, and anyway I want them at first hand. Archie, list these names: Mr. Browning. Mr. Abbott. Mr. Falk. Mr. Meer. Mrs. Browning. Miss Lugos. Miss Venner." Back to the client: "Will you have those people here tomorrow evening at nine o'clock?"

She stared at him. "I will not. How can I?"

"I don't know, but it shouldn't be too difficult. They were associates of your husband, who was murdered. They should be willing to help you learn who murdered him, and you are concerned at the lack of progress in the official investigation and have engaged my services. Shouldn't they sacrifice an evening at your request?"

"They might. I don't want to ask them. And I won't."

Wolfe picked up the check and held it out. "Take it. You have wasted your time and mine. You want a miracle, and miracles are not in my repertory. Give me the receipt."

"My god," she said, "you *are* highhanded. What can *they* tell you?"

"I don't know, and I need to know. If there is a fact that will help me do what you want done, I want it. If you think I may inadvertently disclose what you have told me, even a hint of it, if you think me capable of such ineptitude, you were a ninny to come to me at all."

She was chewing her lip. "Is this the only—do you *have* to do this?"

"If I take the job as you defined it, yes."

She looked at me, and saw only an open, intelligent, interested, sympathetic phiz.

"Damn it," she said. "Give me the list."

6

SINCE THE state of the bank account had been responsible for the state of my nerves for at least six weeks, it might be supposed that ten o'clock Monday morning would find me at the door of the Continental Bank and Trust Company, waiting for it to open so I could deposit the check, but I wasn't. I knew darned well that Wolfe would not be firmly and finally committed until Mrs. Odell came through, and I couldn't blame him. Of the people on the list I had given her, there wasn't one that he could tell me to go and bring with any right or reason to expect me to fill the order, and if he expected to fill *her* order, he had to get some questions answered, and not just by her and Miss Haber. So it was possible that the twenty grand would have to be returned, and if so, it would be neater to return her check than to deposit it and then have to draw one of Wolfe's.

And at four o'clock Monday afternoon, it became about ten to one that she was going to get her check back. She had done fine with the invitations; she reported by phone that all of them had said yes. The hitch was that when she told me she would come a little early, around half past eight, I had to tell her, as instructed by Wolfe, that he had decided she shouldn't come at all. She wasn't invited and wouldn't be admitted. So she blew her top. I tried to explain why, but she wouldn't listen. She commanded me to get Wolfe to change his mind and ring her, and if she hadn't heard from me by four-thirty, she would tell them not to come. I went to the kitchen to tell Fritz I was going on an errand, ran, not walked, to the garage on Tenth Avenue where the Heron sedan that Wolfe owns and I drive is kept, made it to Sixty-third and Madison in nineteen minutes, probably a record for that time of day, and was inside the Odell mansion at 4:28. If I reported that conversation verbatim you would think I was tooting my horn, so I'll merely say that I sold her. I explained that when Browning told lies, as he surely would, if she was there she would almost certainly horn in, and if she expected Wolfe to get results she would have to let him do it his way. Also, of course, if she told them not to come, the deal was off and she would have to find someone who would do it her way, and obviously she didn't have any or she wouldn't have gone to Wolfe and given him a check for twenty grand. She didn't like it, but she lumped it.

Then, leaving, I got a break. I had had to double-park, on Sixty-third Street, and it was a pleasant surprise to see that no city employee had happened by to put a ticket on the windshield. The return trip took thirty-one minutes. When Wolfe came down at six o'clock and I reported, he didn't even say "Satisfactory." He merely scowled and rang for beer. His outlook was bleak. It was now settled that he was going to have to work, and with an obstreperous female for a client.

They all came. The first to arrive, Sylvia Venner, showed a little before nine, and the last, Kenneth Meer, at 9:08. Cass R. Abbott rated the red leather chair on two counts: he was the president of CAN, and, being close to seventy, he had seniority. So I put him there. For the others I had placed two rows of yellow chairs facing Wolfe's desk. I have a sort of rule that when there is company and one of them is, or is supposed to be, a murderer, the place for him or her is the front row nearest to me, so that was where I put Amory Browning. Next to him was his wife, and then Theodore Falk. In the back row Kenneth Meer was in the middle, with Helen Lugos on his right and Sylvia Venner on his left. The only one I had ever seen before was Kenneth Meer. When I let him in, he had looked me in the eye and asked, "More tricks?" and I said, "No, and we have made no use of that one. If anyone here knows about your bloody hands, he didn't learn it from us."

Since you're meeting them, you should see them. Cass R. Abbott, the president, looked like one. The mop of well-tended white hair, which he had a right to be proud of and probably was, was a good cap for the well-arranged, long, pale face. Amory Browning, who would soon be president if he wasn't otherwise engaged, didn't rate it on looks. If he was fifty-two, which would have been my guess, he had probably been pudgy for about five years, and he would be bald in another five. Theodore Falk, the Wall Street Falk, was about the same age, but he had kept himself lean and limber and had a deep tan. He probably played tennis. You have already seen Kenneth Meer's long, pointed nose and wide, square chin.

As for the females, I would have recognized Sylvia Venner from the dozen or so times I had seen her do "The Big Town," the program Browning had bounced her from. She was easy to look at, especially when she was using certain muscles to show her dimples, but TV girls, like all actresses, are always working at it and if you get really interested you have to make allowances. I don't want to be unfair to Mrs. Browning merely because our client had her husband tagged for murder, but the truth is she was scrawny. I could give details, but why rub it in? She was about her husband's age, and she was scrawny, and facts are facts. Helen Lugos, Browning's secretary, was the one you would have to see with your own eyes, because she was the kind with whom details like color of eyes and hair, and shape of face, and kind of mouth don't really tell it. She was probably three or four years under thirty, but that was only another unimportant detail. The point was that I had put her in the back row chair the other side of Kenneth Meer because that was where I could see her best and oftenest without turning my head much. I would have liked to put her in the red leather chair where I would have had her full face, but of course that was the president's place. Hers was the kind of face that is different from any two angles.

I had invited orders for liquids, but they had all been declined, and when Kenneth Meer was in and seated, I went to Wolfe's desk and gave the kitchen button three stabs, and in a moment he came, detoured between the red leather chair and the wall to his desk, sat, and sent his eyes around. As I pronounced the seven names, he gave each of them a nod—*his* nod, about an eighth of an inch.

"On behalf of Mrs. Odell," he said, "I thank you for coming. She intended to be here, but she conceded my point that her presence would make our discussion more difficult, both for you and for me. I know, of course, that you have all been questioned at length by officers of the law, and I shall not try to emulate them, either in pertinacity or in scope. I frankly admit that I strongly doubt if I'll get what Mrs. Odell wants. She hired me to learn who killed her husband, and the prospect is forlorn. Apparently no one knows whether his death was premeditated, or fortuitous—except the person who put the bomb in the drawer."

His eyes went right, then left. "What information I have has come from three sources: the newspapers, Mrs. Odell, and four or five journalists who have worked on the case and with whom Mr. Goodwin is on friendly terms. There is no agreement among the opinions they have formed. One of them thinks that Mr. Odell went to that room and opened that drawer, and put the bomb in it, in order to—"

"Oh for god's sake." It was Theodore Falk. "That kind of crap?"

Wolfe nodded. "Certainly. In the effort to solve any complex problem, there are always many apparent absurdities; the job is to find the correct answer and demonstrate that it is *not* absurd. Another of the journalists thinks that Mr. Abbott put the bomb in the drawer because he didn't want Mr. Browning to succeed him as president of CAN. Still another thinks that Mrs. Browning did it, or arranged to have it done, because she didn't want her husband to continue to enjoy the favors of Miss Lugos. He hasn't decided whom it was intended for, Mr. Browning or Miss Lugos. And another thinks that Miss Lugos did it because she did want Mr. Browning to continue to enjoy her favors but he—"

"Tommyrot!" Cass R. Abbott, in the red leather chair, blurted it. "I came because Mrs. Odell asked me to, but not to hear a list of idiotic absurdities. She said you wanted to get some facts from us. What facts?"

Wolfe turned a palm up. "How do I know? All of you have been questioned at length by the police; you have given them thousands of facts, and in assembling, comparing and evaluating a collection of facts they are well practiced and extremely competent. It's possible that from the record of all the questions they have asked, and your answers to them, I might form a surmise or reach a conclusion that they have failed to see, but I doubt it. I confess to you, though I didn't to Mrs. Odell, that I have little hope of getting useful facts from you. What I needed, to begin at all, was to see you and hear you. It seems likely that one of you put the bomb in the drawer. There are other possibilities, but probabilities have precedence. A question, Mr. Abbott: Do you think it likely that the person who put the bomb in the drawer is now in this room?"

"That's absurd," Abbott snapped. "I wouldn't answer that and you know it."

"But you *have* answered it. You didn't give me a positive no, and you're a positive man." Wolfe's eyes went right. "Mr. Falk. Do you think it likely?"

"Yes, I do," Falk said, "and I could name names, three of them, but I won't. I have no evidence, but I have an opinion, and that's what you asked for."

"I don't expect names. Mrs. Browning. The same question."

"Don't answer, Phyllis," Browning said. A command.

"Of course not. I wasn't going to." Her voice didn't match her scrawniness; it was a full, rich contralto, with color.

Wolfe asked, "Then you, Mr. Browning? Are you going to answer?"

"Yes. I'll tell you exactly what I have told the police and the District Attorney. I not only have no evidence, I have no basis whatever for an opinion. Not even an opinion as to whether the bomb was intended for me or for Odell. It was my room and my desk, but the fact remains that it was Odell who got it. I'll also tell you that I am not surprised that Mrs. Odell has engaged you, and I don't blame her. After nearly three weeks the official investigation is apparently completely stymied."

Wolfe nodded. "I *may* have better luck. Miss Lugos? The same question."

"The same as Mr. Browning," she said. I acknowledge that her voice wasn't as good as Mrs. Browning's; it was thinner and pitched higher. "I have no idea. None at all." Also she wasn't a good liar. When you have asked about ten thousand people about a million questions you may not be able to spot a lie as well as you think you can, but you're right a lot oftener than you're wrong.

"Mr. Meer?"

Naturally I was wondering about Kenneth Meer. Like everybody who reads about murders in newspapers, I knew that he had been the fourth or fifth person to enter Browning's room after the explosion, so he had seen blood all right, but that alone wouldn't account for the blood-on-his-hands crisis that had sent him to the clinic, unless he had bad kinks in his nervous system, bad enough to keep him from working up to such an important job at CAN and hanging onto it. There was the obvious possibility that he had planted the bomb, but surely not for Browning, and if for Odell, how did he know Odell was going to the room and open the drawer? Of course Mrs. Odell had made the answer to that one easy: Browning had told him. Now, how would he answer Wolfe's question?

He answered it with a declaration which he had had plenty of time to decide on: "I think it extremely likely that the person who put the bomb in the drawer is now in this room, but that's all I can say. I can't give any reason or any name."

"You can't, or you won't?"

"Does it matter? Just make it I don't."

"But I ask you if—no. That will come later, if at all. Miss Venner?"

She wasn't showing the dimples. Instead, she had been squinting at Wolfe, and still was. "I don't get it," she said. "I don't think you are dumb, but *this* is dumb, and I wonder why you're doing it. Even if I thought I could name the person who put the bomb in the drawer, would I tell you with them here? Mr. Abbott is the head of the company that employs me, and Mr. Browning is going to be. I can't, but even if I could . . . I don't get it."

"You haven't listened," Wolfe told her. "I said that I had little hope of getting any useful facts from you, and I could have added that even if I do, you probably won't know it. For instance, the question I ask you now. About three months ago CAN had a special program called 'Where the Little Bombs Come From.' Did you see it?"

"Yes. Of course."

"Then you know that the preparation for that program required extensive research. There had to be numerous contacts between members of the CAN staff and people who knew about bombs and had had experience with them. Call them the *sources.* Now I ask you regarding three weeks ago—Friday, May sixteenth, to Sunday, May eighteenth—where and how did you spend that weekend? It may help to remember that the Tuesday following, two days later, Mr. Odell died."

"But why do you—" She wasn't squinting; her eyes were wide in a stare. "Oh. You think I went to one of the 'sources' and got a bomb. Well, I didn't."

"I don't 'think' anything. I'm trying to get a start for a thought. I asked where and how you spent that weekend. Have you a reason for not telling me?"

"No. I have no reason for telling you either, but I might as well. I've told the police four or five times. I took a train to Katonah late Friday afternoon and was a house guest of friends—Arthur and Louise Dickinson. They know nothing about bombs. I came back by train Sunday evening."

I had got my notebook and a pen and was using them. Wolfe asked, "Mr. Meer? Have you any objection to telling me how you spent that weekend?"

"Certainly not. I drove to Vermont Friday evening and I hiked about forty miles in the mountains Saturday and Sunday, and drove back Sunday night."

"Alone, or with companions?"

"I was alone. I don't like companions on a hike. Something always happens to them. I helped some with the research for that program, and none of the 'sources' was in Vermont."

"I am hoping that Mr. Browning will tell me about the sources. Later. Miss Lugos?"

Her face was really worth watching. As he pronounced her name, she turned her head for a glance at Browning, her boss. It was less than a quarter-turn, but from my angle it wasn't the same face as when she was looking at Wolfe. Her look at Browning didn't seem to be asking or wanting anything; evidently it was just from habit. She turned back to Wolfe and said, "I stayed in town all that weekend. Friday evening I went to a movie with a friend. Saturday afternoon I did some shopping, and Saturday evening I went to a show with three friends. Sunday I got up late and did things in my apartment. In a file at the office we have a record of all the research for that program, all the people who were contacted, and I didn't see any of them that weekend."

Wolfe's lips were tight. In his house, "contact" is not a verb and never will be, and he means it. He was glad to quit her. "Mr. Falk?"

Falk had been holding himself in, shifting in his chair and crossing and uncrossing his legs. Obviously he thought it was *all* crap. "You said," he said, "that you wouldn't try to emulate the police, but that's what you're doing. But Peter Odell was my best and closest friend, and there may be a chance that you're half as good as you're supposed to be. As for that weekend, I spent it at home —my place on Long Island. We had four house guests—no, five —and none of them was a bomb expert. Do you want their names and addresses?"

"I may, later." As Wolfe's eyes went to Mrs. Browning, her husband spoke: "My wife and I were together that weekend. We spent it on a yacht on the Sound, guests of the man who owns it, James Farquhar, the banker. There were two other guests."

"The whole weekend, Mr. Browning?"

"Yes. From late Friday afternoon to late Sunday afternoon."

I put my eyes on my notebook and kept them there. With all the practice I have had with my face, I should of course always have it under control, but I had got two jolts, not just one. First, was that why Wolfe had started the whole rigmarole about that weekend, to check on Browning, and second, had Browning heard it coming and got set for it, or had he just given a straight answer to a straight question? I don't know how well Wolfe handled *his* face, since my eyes were on my notebook, but otherwise he did fine. There were two or three other questions he must have wanted to ask Browning, but he didn't. He merely remarked that he doubted if Mr. Farquhar or the other guests were in the bomb business and then said, "And you, Mr. Abbott?" and my eyes left the notebook.

"I resent this," Abbott said. "I knew Pete Odell for twenty years and we worked together for ten of them, and I have a warm and deep sympathy for his wife, his widow, but this is ridiculous. I assumed you would have some new angle, some new approach, but all you're doing, you're starting the same old grind. Each of us has spent long hours with the police, answering questions and signing statements, and while we want to oblige Mrs. Odell, naturally we do, I certainly don't think she should expect us to repeat the whole performance with you. Why doesn't she ask the police to let you see their files? In one of them you'll find out how I spent that weekend. I spent it at home, near Tarrytown. There were guests. I played golf all day and bridge at night. But I repeat, this is ridiculous."

A corner of Wolfe's mouth was up. "Then it would be fruitless to continue," he said—not complaining, just stating a fact. He put his hands on the edge of his desk for purchase, pushed his chair back, and rose. "I'll have to contrive a new approach. On behalf of Mrs. Odell, I thank you again for coming. Good evening." He moved, detoured again between the wall and the red leather chair, and, out in the hall, turned left.

"I'll be damned," Theodore Falk said.

I think they all said things, but if any of it was important, that will be a gap in this report. I wasn't listening, as I went through the appropriate motions for godspeeding a flock of guests. I had heard enough, more than enough, for one evening. I didn't even notice who went with whom as they descended the seven steps of the stoop to the sidewalk. Closing the door and sliding the chain-bolt in its slot, I went to the kitchen. Fritz, who had kept handy to fill orders for refreshments if called for, was perched on the stool by the big center table with a magazine, but his eyes weren't on it. They were on Wolfe, who was standing, scowling at a glass of beer in his hand, waiting for the bead to settle to the right level.

"It's going on eleven o'clock," I said. "I would love to start on it right now, but I suppose I can't."

"Of course not," he growled. He drank beer. "Do we need to discuss it?"

"I don't think so." I went and got a bottle of scotch from the cupboard. There are times when milk will not do. "I have a suggestion. Do you want it?"

He said yes, and I gave it to him.

7

AT FIVE minutes past eleven Tuesday morning, I was seated in a comfortable chair at the end of a big, expensive desk in a big, expensive room on the thirtieth floor of a big, expensive building on Broad Street, near Wall, facing a man whose tan was much deeper than Theodore Falk's—so deep that his hide might have been bronze.

Getting to him had been simple, but first I had had to confirm that he existed and owned a yacht. At one minute past nine I had dialed the number of the magazine *Fore and Aft;* no answer. Modern office hours. Half an hour later I got them, and was told by a man, after I held the wire while he looked it up, that a man named James J. Farquhar had a fifty-eight-foot Derecktor cruiser named *Prospero.* So it was a yacht, not just a rowboat with a mast or an outboard motor. Next I dialed the number of the Federal Holding Corporation, and via two women and a man, which was par, got through to Avery Ballou. He sounded as if he still remembered what Wolfe and I had done for him three years ago, and still appreciated it. I told him we needed a little favor and asked if he knew a banker named James Farquhar.

"Sure," he said. "He's next to the top at Trinity Fiduciary. What has he done?"

"As far as I know, nothing. It isn't another paternity problem. I want to ask him a couple of questions about something that he's not involved in—and he won't be. He's the best bet for a piece of information we need, that's all. But the sooner we get it, the better, and Mr. Wolfe thought you might be willing to ring him and tell him that if I phone him for an appointment, it would be a good idea for him to tell me to come right away and get rid of me."

He said he would, and ten minutes later his secretary phoned and said Farquhar was expecting a call from me. She even gave me the phone number, and I dialed it and got *his* secretary.

So at 11:05 there I was, at his desk. I was apologizing. "Mr. Wolfe didn't want to bother you," I said, "about a matter that you will consider trivial, but he sort of had to. It's about something that happened more than three weeks ago—Friday, May sixteenth. A lawyer has a client who is being sued for damages, fifty thousand dollars, and he has asked Mr. Wolfe to check on a couple of things. The client's name is O'Neill, Roger O'Neill, and a man named Walsh claims that around half past eight that evening he was in his small boat, fishing in the Sound, near Madison, about a mile off shore, and O'Neill's big cruiser came along fast, doing at least twenty, he says, and hit his boat right in the middle—cut it right in two. The sun had set but it wasn't dark yet, and Walsh says he had a light up. He wasn't hurt much, but his twelve-year-old son was; he's still in the hospital."

Farquhar was frowning. "But where do I come in? I have a busy morning."

"I'm keeping it as brief as possible. Walsh says there were witnesses. He says a bigger boat, around seventy feet, was cruising by, about two hundred yards farther out, and there were people on deck who must have seen it happen. He tried to see its name, but he was in the water and the light was dim. He thinks it was *Properoo.*" I spelled it. "We can't find a boat with that name listed anywhere, but your yacht, *Prospero,* comes close to it. Friday, May sixteenth. Three weeks ago last Friday. Were you out on the Sound that day?"

"I'm out *every* Friday. That Friday . . . three weeks . . ." He shut his eyes and tilted his head back. "That was . . . No. . . . Oh, sure." His eyes opened and his head leveled. "I was across the Sound.

Nowhere near Madison. Before nine o'clock we anchored in a cove near Stony Brook, on the other shore."

"Then it wasn't you." I stood up. "Have you ever seen a boat named *Properoo?"*

"No."

"If you don't mind—Mr. Wolfe always expects me to get everything. Who was on board with you?"

"My wife, and four guests. Mr. and Mrs. Percy Young, and Mr. and Mrs. Amory Browning. And the crew, two. Really, damn it —"

"Okay. I'm sorry I bothered you for nothing, and Mr. Wolfe will be too. Many thanks."

I went.

In the elevator, going down, a woman moved away from me, clear away. I wasn't bothering to manage my face, and probably its expression indicated that I was all set to choke or shoot somebody. I was. Down in the lobby I went to a phone booth and dialed the number I knew best, and when Fritz answered I said, "Me. I want him."

It took a couple of minutes. It always does; he hates the phone.

"Yes, Archie?"

"I'm in a booth in a building on Broad Street. I have just had a talk with James J. Farquhar. At nine o'clock Friday evening, May sixteenth, he anchored his yacht in a cove on the Long Island shore. The four guests aboard were Mr. and Mrs. Percy Young and Mr. and Mrs. Amory Browning. I'm calling because it's nearly eleven-thirty, and if I proceed as instructed I couldn't have her there in less than an hour, which would be too close to lunch. I suggest that I phone her instead of going to get her, and—"

"No. Come home. I'll telephone her. The number?"

"On my yellow pad in the middle drawer. But wouldn't it—"

"No." He hung up.

So he too was set for murder. He was going to dial it himself. He was going to risk keeping lunch waiting. As I headed for the subway, which would be quicker than scouting for a taxi in that territory, I was trying to remember if any other client, male or female, had ever equaled this, and couldn't name one.

But when I entered the old brownstone, and the office, a few minutes before noon, I saw that he wasn't going to choke her or shoot her. He was going to slice her up. At his desk, with his oilstone and a can of oil on a sheet of paper, he was sharpening his penknife. Though he doesn't use it much, he sharpens it about once a week, but almost never at that time of day. Evidently his subconscious had taken over. I went to my desk and sat, opened a drawer and took out the Marley .38, and asked, "Do I shoot her before you carve her, or after?"

He gave me a look. "How likely is it that Mr. Browning telephoned him last night, or saw him, and arranged it?"

"No. A hundred to one. I took my time with a phony buildup and watched his face. Also at least seven other people would have to be arranged: his wife, the four guests, and the crew. Not a chance. You got Miss Haber?"

"Yes." He looked at the clock. "Thirty-five minutes ago. I made it—"

The doorbell rang. I put the Marley in the drawer and closed it, and went. But in the hall, I saw more than I expected. I stepped back in and asked Wolfe, "Did you invite Mrs. Odell too?"

"No."

"Then she invited herself. She came along. So?"

He shut his eyes, opened them, shut them, opened them. "Very well. You may have to drag her to the front room."

That would have been a pleasure—preferably by the hair with her kicking and screaming. She performed as expected. When I opened the front door, she brushed past me rudely and streaked down the hall, with Miss Haber at her tail, trotting to keep up. Thinking she might actually scratch or bite, I was right behind as she entered the office and opened up, heading for Wolfe's desk. I'm not sure whether the five words she got out were "If you think you can" or "If you think you're going," before Wolfe banged a fist on the desk and bellowed at her:

"Shut up!"

I don't know how he does it. His bellow is a loud explosion, a boom, as a bellow should be, but also it has an edge, it cuts, which doesn't seem possible. She stopped and stood with her mouth open. I was between her and him.

"I told Miss Haber to come," Wolfe said in his iciest tone. "Not you. If you sit and listen, you may stay. If you don't, Mr. Goodwin will remove you—from the room and the house. He would enjoy it. I have something to say to Miss Haber, and I will not tolerate interruption. Well?"

Her mouth was even wider than normal because her teeth were clamped on her lower lip. She moved, not fast, toward the red leather chair, but Wolfe snapped, "No. I want Miss Haber in that chair. Archie?"

I went and brought a yellow chair and put it closer to my desk than his. She gave me a look that I did not deserve, and came and sat. I doubted if Charlotte Haber would make it to the red leather chair without help, so I went and touched her arm, and steered her to it.

Wolfe's eyes at her were only slits. "I told you on the telephone," he said, "that if you were not here by twelve o'clock, I would telephone a policeman, Inspector Cramer of Homicide South, and tell him what you told me Sunday evening about your telephone call to Mr. Browning on May sixteenth. I'll probably find it necessary to tell him anyway, but I thought it proper to give you a chance to explain. Why did you tell me that lie?"

She was making a fair try at meeting his eyes. She spoke: "It wasn't—" Her tongue got in the way and she stopped and started over: "It wasn't a lie. It was exactly like I told you. If Mr. Browning won't admit it, if he denies—"

"Pfui. I haven't discussed it with Mr. Browning. The conclusive evidence that you couldn't have made that call did not come from him. Even candor may not serve you now, but certainly nothing else will. Unless you tell me what and who induced you to tell me that lie, you're in for it. You'll leave here not with your employer, but with a policeman, probably for detention as a material witness. I will not—"

"You can't!" Mrs. Odell was on the edge of her chair. "You know you can't! You guaranteed in writing!"

"Remove her, Archie," Wolfe said. "If necessary, drag her."

I rose. She tilted her head to focus up at me and said, "You don't dare. Don't dare to touch me."

I said, "I dare easy. I admit I'd rather not, but I have bounced bigger and stronger women than you and have no scars. Look. You tried to steal home and got nailed, and no wonder. You didn't even have sense enough to check where Browning was that Friday night. As for that guarantee in that receipt you got, it says, quote, 'Unless circumstances arise that put me or him under legal compulsion to reveal it.' End quote. Okay, the circumstances are here. The cops have spent a thousand hours trying to find out why your husband went to the room and opened the drawer, and who knew he was going to. Now *I* know. So I'm withholding essential evidence in a murder case, and there's a statute that puts me under legal compulsion to reveal it. Also, I'm not just a law-abiding citizen, I'm a licensed private detective, and I don't want to lose my license and have to start a new career, like panhandling or demonstrating. So even if Mr. Wolfe got big-hearted and decided just to bow out, there would still be me. I feel responsible. I *am* responsible. I started this by writing you that letter. Mr. Wolfe told Miss Haber that unless she comes clean he will open the bag. I may or may not stay with him on the *unless.* I am good and sore, and for a dirty crinkled dollar bill with a corner gone I would go now to the drug store on the corner and ring a police sergeant I know. I also know a man on the *Gazette* who would love to have a hot item for the front page, and I could back it up with an affidavit. And would."

I turned to Wolfe. "If I may offer a suggestion. If you still want her bounced, okay, but from her face I think she has got it down."

I turned back to her. "If you get the idea that you can say it was *all* a lie, that you wanted to fasten it on Browning and made it *all* up, nothing doing. They found the LSD in your husband's pocket and they've got it. You're stuck, absolutely, and if you try to wriggle you'll just make it worse."

She had kept her eyes at me. Now they went to her right, clear around past Wolfe to Miss Haber, and they certainly saw nothing helpful. Below the crease in the narrow forehead, the secretary's eyes weren't aimed anywhere. They could have been seeing her hands clasped on her lap, but probably they weren't seeing anything.

Mrs. Odell aimed hers at Wolfe. "You said you haven't discussed it with Browning. The—the LSD. Who have you discussed it with?"

"Mr. Goodwin. No one else."

"Then how did you—How can you—"

"Mr. Goodwin talked this morning with a man who owns a yacht. At nine o'clock in the evening of Friday, May sixteenth, when he anchored in a cove on the Long Island shore, two of the guests aboard were Mr. and Mrs. Amory Browning. In all my experience with chicanery, madam, I have never encountered a more inept performance. A factor in our animus is probably the insult to our intelligence; you should have known that we would inquire as to Mr. Browning's whereabouts that evening, and therefore *you* should have. By the glance you just gave Miss Haber I suspect that you are contemplating another inanity: saying it was some other evening. Pfui. Don't try it. Look at Miss Haber."

She didn't have to; she already had. And she proceeded to demonstrate that she was by no means a complete fool. She cocked her head at me for a long, steady look, and then cocked it at Wolfe. "I don't believe," she said, "that you have really decided to tell the police about it. If you had, you wouldn't have phoned Miss Haber and—"

"I haven't said I have decided. I said, to Miss Haber, 'Unless you tell me what and who induced you to tell that lie.' "

"*I'll* tell you. *I* induced her."

"When?"

"Three days ago. Saturday evening. And Sunday morning, before I called Goodwin. *What* induced her was money. She needs money. She has a younger brother who has got himself into—but that doesn't matter, what she needs it for. And anyway, I think Browning put that bomb there. I'm *sure* he did. I don't know how he knew Peter was going to open that drawer, but I'm sure he did. Maybe Peter told somebody. You didn't know Peter, you don't know what a wonderful man he was. He married me for my money, but he was a wonderful husband. And Browning killed him, and with all the money I have, now there's only one thing I want to do with it. I don't think the police will ever get him, and you know something they don't know. Can you handle Goodwin?"

"No." He was scowling at her. "No one can 'handle' Mr. Goodwin. But he handles himself reasonably well, and he wouldn't divulge information he got as my agent without my consent. My problem is handling me. Your fatuous attempt to hoodwink me relieves me of my commitment, but I too am a licensed private detective. If Mr. Cramer learns that those seven people were here last evening, as he probably will, and if he comes to see me, as he almost certainly will, I'll be in a pickle. I have many times refused to disclose information on the ground that it was not material, but the fact that your husband went to that room and opened that drawer in order to put LSD in the whisky is manifestly material. Confound it, they even have the LSD—that is, you *say* they have it."

"They do. They showed it to me." She opened her bag and took out the checkfold. "I've made one idiotic mistake with you and I don't intend to make another one. I'm going to give you a check for one hundred thousand dollars, but I have sense enough to know that I have to be careful how I do it. If you think that I think I can pay you and Goodwin for not telling the police about the LSD, I don't. I know I can't. But I do think they will never get Browning, and I think you might. I think the only chance of getting him is if you do it. I don't care what it costs. The hundred thousand dollars is just to start. You may have to give somebody twice that much for something." She slid the pen out and started to write on the check stub.

"No," Wolfe said. "You can't pay me at all on the terms you imply. I certainly would not engage to demonstrate that Mr. Browning killed your husband. I might engage to try to learn *who* killed your husband and to get evidence that would convict him. As for withholding information from the police, that must be left to my discretion. Mr. Goodwin and I are disinclined to share with others information that gives us an advantage."

"It *was* Browning. Why do you think it wasn't?"

"I don't. He is as likely a candidate as anyone—much the most likely, if he knew of your husband's intention to drug the whisky." He swiveled to face the red leather chair. "Miss Haber. You didn't tell Mr. Browning about it, but whom did you tell?"

"Nobody." It came out louder than she intended, and she repeated it, lower. "Nobody."

"This is extremely important. I *must* know. This time you are expected to tell me the truth."

"I *am* telling you the truth. I *couldn't* have told anyone because I didn't know myself. I didn't know what the LSD was for until last Saturday evening, three days ago, when Mrs. Odell told me . . . When she asked me . . ."

Wolfe turned to Mrs. Odell with his brow up.

"*I* believe her," she said, and he turned back to the secretary. "Do you go to church, Miss Haber?"

"Yes, I do. Lutheran. Not every Sunday, but often."

He turned to me. "Bring a Bible."

On the third shelf from the bottom, at the left of the globe, there were nine of them, four in different editions in English and five in foreign languages. I picked the one that looked the part best, in black leather, and crossed to the red leather chair.

"Put your right hand on it," Wolfe told her, "and repeat after me: With my hand on the Holy Bible I swear."

I held it at her level and she put her hand on it, palm down, flat, the fingers spread a little. "With my hand on the Holy Bible I swear."

"That I did not know what Mr. Odell intended to do."

She repeated it.

"With the LSD I had procured for Mrs. Odell."

She repeated it.

"Until Saturday, June seventh."

She repeated it.

Wolfe turned to the client. "You can suspect Mr. Browning only if you assume that he knew what your husband was going to do. Miss Haber didn't. I don't suppose you or your husband told him. Whom did you tell?"

"I didn't tell anybody. Absolutely nobody. So Peter must have. I wouldn't have thought—but he *must* have. Of course there were people who wanted Peter to be the new president, not Browning, and he must have told one of them. For instance, Ted Falk, but Ted wouldn't have told Browning. I can give you names. Sylvia Venner. Then there's a man in public relations—"

"If you please." He had turned his head to look at the wall clock. "It's my lunch time. You can make a list of the names, with relevant comments. But there must be no misunderstanding about what you expect me to do. My commitment is to try to learn who killed your husband and get evidence that will convict him. Just that. Is that clearly understood?"

"Yes. But I want to be sure . . . No. I suppose I can't be." She opened the checkfold. "But if it wasn't Browning . . . Oh, damn it. *God damn it.*" She wrote the check.

8

AT TWENTY minutes to seven, Theodore Falk, in the red leather chair with his legs crossed, told Wolfe, "It would depend on what it was he was going to do."

In the four and a half hours since lunch, much had been done but nothing visible had been accomplished. We had discussed the Cramer problem. If and when he came, I could open the door only the two inches the chain on the bolt allowed and tell him Wolfe wasn't available and there was no telling when he would be, and I was under instructions to tell nobody anything whatever. He probably couldn't get a warrant, since all he could tell a judge was that some of the people involved in a murder case had spent part of an evening in the house, but if he did, and used it, we would stand mute—or sit mute. Or I could open the door wide and let him in, and Wolfe would play it by ear, and we voted for that. There was always a chance that he would supply one or more useful facts.

We had also decided to spend thirty-one dollars an hour, for as long as necessary, of the client's money, on Saul Panzer, Fred Durkin, and Orrie Cather—eight each for Fred and Orrie, and fifteen for Saul. If no one had known that Odell intended to go to Browning's room, the bomb couldn't have been intended for him, and it was going to take more doing than having people come to the old brownstone for some conversation. I had phoned Saul and Orrie and asked them to come Wednesday at ten o'clock, and left a message for Fred. And I had phoned Theodore Falk, Odell's best and closest friend, and told him that Wolfe wanted to have a talk with him, without an audience, and he said he would come around six o'clock.

By a couple of phone calls—one to a vice-president of our bank and one to Lon Cohen—I had learned that Falk was way up. He was a senior member of one of the oldest and solidest investment firms and sat on eight boards of directors. He had a wife and three grown-up children, and he and they were also solid socially. Evidently a man the race could be proud of, and from personal observation the only thing I had against him was his buttoned-down shirt collar. A man who hates loose flaps so much that he buttons down his collar should also button down his ears.

He came at 6:34.

Wolfe told him that he needed all the information he could get about Odell. Specifically, he needed the answer to a question: If Odell decided to do something secretly, some shabby deed that would help him and hurt someone else, how likely was it that he would have told anyone? And Falk said, "It would depend on what it was he was going to do. You say 'shabby'?"

Wolfe nodded. "Opprobrious. Mean. Furtive. Knavish. Tricky."

Falk uncrossed his legs, slid his rump clear back in the red leather chair, which is deep, recrossed his legs, and tilted his head back. His eyes went left and then right, in no hurry, apparently comparing the pictures on the wall—one of Socrates, one of Shakespeare, and an unwashed coal miner in oil by Sepeshy. (According to Wolfe, man's three resources: intellect, imagination, and muscle.)

In half a minute Falk's head leveled and his eyes settled on Wolfe. "I don't know about you," he said. "I don't know you well enough. A cousin of mine who is an assistant district attorney says you are sharp and straight. Does he know?"

"Probably not," Wolfe said. "Hearsay."

"You solicited Mrs. Odell."

I cut in. "No," I said. "I did."

Wolfe grunted. "Not material." To Falk: "Mr. Goodwin is my

agent, and what he does is on my tally. He knew my bank balance was low. Does your firm solicit?"

Falk laughed, showing his teeth, probably knowing how white they looked with his deep tan. "Of course," he said, "you're not a member of the bar." He lifted a hand to rub his lip with a finger tip. That helped him decide to say something, and he said it. "You know that the police have a vial of LSD that was in Odell's pocket."

"Do I?"

"Certainly. Mrs. Odell has told me that she told you. Has she told you what he was going to do with it?"

"I'm sharp, Mr. Falk."

"So you are. Of course you'll tell her what I say, but she already knows that I think she knew what Pete was going to do with the LSD, though she won't admit it, and no wonder, not even to me."

"And you knew."

"I knew what?"

"What he was going to do with the LSD."

"No, I didn't. I don't know even now, but I can make a damn good guess, and so can the police. So can you, if Mrs. Odell hasn't told you. Going to Browning's room and opening that drawer, with LSD in his pocket? Better than a guess. You would call it shabby and opprobrious for him to dope Browning's whisky? And knavish?"

"Not to judge, merely to describe. Do you disagree?"

"I guess not. Not really. Anyway another good guess is that it was her idea, not his. You can tell her I said that, she already knows it. Of course your question is, did I know about it, did he tell me? He didn't. He wouldn't. If he told anybody it would have been me, but a thing like that he wouldn't tell even me. The reason I'm telling you this, I'm beginning to doubt if the police are going to crack it, and you might. One reason you might, Mrs. Odell will probably tell you things she won't tell them. Another reason is that with people like these, like us, the police have to consider things that you can ignore."

"And you want it cracked."

"Hell yes. Pete Odell was my favorite man."

"If no one knew he was going to open that drawer, he died by inadvertence."

"But whoever planted that bomb killed him." Falk turned a palm up. "Look, why am I here? This will make me an hour late for something. I wanted to know if you were going to waste time on the idea that the bomb was *intended* for Odell. The police still think it could have been and there's not a chance. Damn it, I *knew* him. It just isn't thinkable that he would have told anyone he was going to try to bust Browning by doping his whisky."

"If he had told you, would you have tried to dissuade him?"

Falk shook his head. "I can't even discuss it as a hypothesis. If Pete Odell had told me that, I would just have stared at him. It wouldn't have been him. Not his doing it, his telling me."

"So the bomb was for Browning?"

"Yes. Apparently."

"Not certainly?"

"No. You told us yesterday that the journalists have different ideas, and we have too—I mean the people who are involved. They are all just guessing really—except one of course, the one who did it. My guess is no better than anybody else's."

"And no worse. Your guess?"

Falk's eyes came to me and returned to Wolfe. "This isn't being recorded?"

"Only in our skulls."

"Well—do you know the name Copes? Dennis Copes?"

"No."

"You know Kenneth Meer. He was here last evening. He's Browning's man Friday, and Copes would like to be. Of course in a setup like CAN, most of them want someone else's job, but the Copes-Meer thing is special. My guess is that Meer had a routine of checking that drawer every afternoon and Copes knew it. Copes did a lot of work on that program about bombs and getting one would have been no problem. That's my best guess partly because

I can't quite see anyone going for Browning with a bomb. A dozen people *could* have, but I can't see any of them actually doing it. You said one of the reporters thinks it was Browning's wife, but that's absurd."

"Did Kenneth Meer check the drawer every day?"

"I don't know. I understand he says he didn't."

I could fill three or four pages with the things Theodore Falk didn't know, but they didn't help us, so they wouldn't help you. When I returned to the office after going to the hall to let him out, we didn't discuss him, for two reasons: the look we exchanged showed that we didn't need to, and Fritz came to announce dinner. The look was a question, the same question both ways: How straight was Falk? Did we cross him off or not? The look left it open.

The fact was, Wolfe hadn't really bit into it. It was still just batting practice. He had taken the job and was committed, but there was still the slim chance that something might happen—the cops might get it or the client might quit—so he wouldn't have to sweat and slave. Also in my book there was the idea that I had once mentioned to him, the idea that it took a broil with Inspector Cramer to wind him up. Of course when I had offered it, he had fired me, or I had quit, I forget which. But I hadn't dropped the idea, so when the doorbell rang at 11:10 Wednesday morning and I went to the hall and saw who it was on the stoop through the one-way glass, and stepped back in the office and said "Mr. Fuzz," I didn't mind a bit.

Wolfe made a face, opened his mouth and then clamped his jaw, and in five seconds unclamped it to growl, "Bring him."

9

THAT WAS A FIRST—the first time Inspector Cramer had ever arrived and been escorted to the office in the middle of a session with the hired hands. And Saul Panzer did something he seldom does—he stunted. He was in the red leather chair, and when I ushered Cramer in I expected to find Saul on his feet, moving up another yellow chair to join Fred and Orrie, but no. He was staying put. Cramer, surprised, stood in the middle of the rug and said, loud, "Oh?" Wolfe, surprised at Saul, put his brows up. I, pretending I wasn't surprised, went to get a yellow chair. And damned if Cramer didn't cross in front of Fred and Orrie to *my* chair, swing it around, and park his big fanny on it. As he sat, Saul, his lips a little tight to keep from grinning, got up and came to take the yellow chair I had brought. That left the red leather chair empty and I went and occupied it, sliding back and crossing my legs to show that I was right at home.

Wolfe didn't merely turn his head left to face me; he swiveled. "Was this performance arranged?" he demanded.

"Not by me," I told him. "This chair was empty, that's all."

"I guess I was just too surprised to move," Saul said. "I didn't know the Inspector was coming."

"Balls," Cramer said. "No one knew I was coming." He focused on Wolfe. "I hope I'm not interrupting anything important."

"I hope you are," Wolfe said, not thorny. "We are discussing the prospect of making an important contribution to the investigation of a murder."

Cramer nodded. "Yeah. I thought you would be."

Actually the discussion had barely begun. Saul Panzer, who looks like a guy who was trying to sell encyclopedias but gave up and quit, and is actually the best operative alive; and big-footed, heavy-set Fred Durkin, who looks as if he wouldn't know what an encyclopedia is but actually bought a Britannica for his kids; and good-looking, six-foot Orrie Cather, who would trade an encyclopedia for a full-length mirror if he didn't already have one, but can handle a tough assignment when he needs to, had come in at ten o'clock, and I had briefed them good. On some jobs they are called in on, some details have to be reserved, but not that one. I had given them the whole picture, and Wolfe, coming down from the plant rooms at eleven o'clock, had just got started.

When Wolfe faced Cramer in my chair with me in the red leather chair, I had his profile from his left instead of his right, and I had to adjust to it. I don't know why it made so much difference, but it did. His chin looked more pointed and his hair thicker. He asked Cramer politely, "You have questions?"

"Nothing specific." Cramer was leaning back, comfortable, also polite. "Don't mind me. Go right ahead." Saul's stunt had cued him.

Wolfe's eyes passed Orrie and Saul to Fred. "I was asking," he said, "if Archie covered the ground to your satisfaction. Do you need more?"

"I hope not." Fred riffled the pages of his notebook. "No room for more."

"What do you suggest?"

That routine was nearly always just talk, but now and then it led to something. "Well," Fred said, "You can't just walk up to the counter at Macy's and say one Number Four gelignite bomb and charge my account and don't bother to wrap it." He looked straight at Cramer. "What the hell."

Wolfe nodded. "No doubt the police have made every effort. Twenty-two days. Three weeks yesterday. You suggest . . . ?"

"I need time to sort it out."

"Yes. Orrie?"

"I need more," Orrie said. "For instance, I need to know if Odell had gloves on. One theory is that he was putting the bomb in the drawer to get Browning, and if so, he would have used gloves if he wasn't a moron. I suggest that you ask Inspector Cramer if he was wearing gloves; and if not, that will narrow it. Also you can ask him about fingerprints."

"Anything else?"

"Maybe. After I know that."

"Saul?"

"I may as well say it, " Saul said. "Maybe it wasn't just surprise. I had a suggestion ready and the Inspector coming flipped me. I was going to say that if you asked for a look at the files, both Homicide and the DA, they might want to cooperate. After three weeks they must have quite a stack of stuff that—"

"Shove it," Cramer growled. "Who the hell are you, Panzer? Do you think you're Goodwin?" His eyes stopped at me a second on their way to Wolfe. To Wolfe he said, "It's you. It's always you."

A corner of Wolfe's mouth was up a thirty-second of an inch. For him a broad grin. He asked politely, "Does that mean something?"

"You know damn well—" Cramer bit it off. "Skip it. I don't want to interrupt. I have all day. Go right ahead. I might learn something."

"We haven't even started."

"*That* would be something. How you start."

"Well . . . " Wolfe shut his eyes. In ten seconds he opened them, looked at Saul, then at Fred, and then at Orrie. Then at me. "Get Mr. Abbott."

It didn't seem necessary to pretend I had to look up the number, so instead of going to my desk, where Cramer was, I went around to the other end of Wolfe's desk, reached for his phone, and dialed. It took four minutes to get the president of CAN—first an operator and then his secretary, and I had to say it was urgent. Since it was Wolfe's phone and I didn't go to mine, I heard only him.

"Good morning, Mr. Abbott. . . . Yes, I'm busy too, this won't take long. You said Monday evening that you have a warm and deep sympathy with Mrs. Odell and you want to oblige her; and this request is from her through me. I have just given three men the known facts about Mr. Odell's death. Their names are Saul Panzer, Fred Durkin, and Orrie Cather. They are experienced and competent. I ask you to give them permission to talk with people who are employed by your company—to move freely about the premises and talk with anyone who is available and willing. Only those who are willing. The police can do that without permission, but these men can't. They need a letter from you, and I want to send them to your office to get it. They will be considerate; they will not impose. They will not ask to talk with anyone who was here Monday evening. If you have a complaint about one of them, he will be withdrawn. May they come now for the letters? . . . No, of course not. No compulsion. . . . No, there will be no difficulty about that. Inspector Cramer is here hearing me, and . . . Yes, Inspector Cramer of Homicide South. He is here in my office. . . . No, there is nothing official about this request. Mr. Cramer came to talk with me and interrupted my talk with these men. He has neither approved this request nor objected to it. . . ."

There was some more, mostly about interrupting people at work. When Wolfe hung up I was back in the red leather chair. He leaned back and sent his eyes to Fred and across Orrie to Saul. To them: "So you are going fishing. First to Mr. Abbott for credentials, and then scatter. As usual, anything whatever may or may not be significant. If any single question has precedence, it is who, if anyone, knew that Mr. Odell was going to that room and open that drawer. If you get no answer to that or any other question, you may at least get hints. Report to Archie daily as usual. I doubt if any bribing will be necessary or desirable, but the available funds are unlimited." He turned to me. "Five hundred?"

I said that should do for a start and went and opened the safe. From the supply in the cash box, always used bills, I got thirty twenties, sixty tens, and sixty fives, and split them three ways.

Wolfe was telling them, "You heard me say that you will exclude those who were here Monday evening. Saul, you will try Dennis Copes. The question you want answered, did he know or think he knew that Kenneth Meer habitually inspected that drawer, is of course the one you won't ask. Orrie, you will try Dennis Copes's secretary if he has one. We want that question answered. Fred, you will follow your nose. Smile at people. Your smile is admirably deceptive. All of you, don't push and don't impose. There is no urgency.—Mr. Cramer. Have you a question or a comment before they go?"

Cramer said, "No," louder than necessary, and with the used lettuce, distributed by me while Wolfe was talking, in their wallets, they got up and went. I gave Cramer a deceptive smile and said, "Let's trade," and he rose and crossed to the red leather chair and I took the one I belonged in.

Wolfe swiveled to face him. "Obviously," he said, "you are not in armor. Perhaps you will answer one question. Who told you about my Monday evening visitors?"

"Kenneth Meer. He phoned Lieutenant Rowcliff yesterday morning."

"Indeed."

"Yes." Cramer got a cigar from a pocket, stuck it in his mouth, and clamped his teeth on it. "You have Goodwin report verbatim, so I will. When Rowcliff told me about Meer's call, he said, 'Of course when they left, that fat son-of-a-bitch leaned back in his goddam tailor-made chair and shut his goddam beady eyes and worked his lips a while, and then he sat up and told that smart-ass Goodwin who the murderer was and told him to have him there at six o'clock when he came down from nursing his goddam orchids. So we'll put a man there to see who comes at six o'clock and then all we'll have to do is dig up the evidence and the motive.' Well, we did put a man there, and he reported that Theodore Falk came at half-past six. I thought it would save time and trouble to come and ask you, at least for the motive. That will help, getting the evidence."

Wolfe shook his head. "This isn't like you. Wasting your breath on clumsy sarcasm. And sitting here hearing me send those men on their errands you said nothing to them, or to me, about interference by private investigators in a murder case. How many times have you threatened to take my license? Are you desperate?"

"Yes."

"Oh." Wolfe's eyes opened wide. He shut them and opened them again. "Shall we have beer?"

"Yes."

Wolfe reached to the button to give Fritz the beer signal. Cramer took the cigar from his mouth, inspected the teeth marks, started it back toward his mouth, changed his mind, and laid it on the little table at his elbow. Fritz came with a bottle and glass on a tray and was told to bring another.

Cramer aimed a frown at me and then switched it to Wolfe. "I didn't come to ask for help. I'm not down that low. But it looks close to impossible. Of course lots of murder cases are impossible and have to be put on the open list, which means they're closed actually, but that won't do when the victim is a Peter Odell. But look at it. How can we get a murderer when we don't know who he wanted to kill? After three weeks we don't even know *that.* Durkin thinks we should have traced the bomb. Nuts. Seventeen people had a hand in getting the dope for that goddam program, and they have named nine sources that were contacted, and God knows how many others there were that they haven't named and won't name. And some of them learned enough to make their own bombs, and who did they tell? Of course we're still on that, but it looks worse now than it did a week ago."

He turned his palms up, the fingers spread. "You told them that the first question is who knew Odell was going to that room and open that drawer. Yeah? Sure. They'll bring you a list of names? Like hell they will. I don't suppose you already know who knew? That you told them that because I was here?"

"Nonsense. If I knew that, I probably wouldn't need those men."

Fritz had come with another bottle and glass, and Wolfe got the opener from the drawer and used it, and I got up and served Cramer. Wolfe poured, and as he waited for the foam to reach the right level, he told Cramer, "Of course you know *why* Odell went there and opened that drawer."

"I do?"

"Certainly. With a powerful drug in his pocket, opening the drawer where Browning kept his whisky? You are not a nincompoop."

"Naturally Mrs. Odell has told you."

"She told me that you showed her the LSD. I don't suppose it was flour or sugar, supplied by you. Why would you? Was it?"

"No." Cramer drank, emptied the glass, put it down on the table, picked up the bottle, and poured. He picked up the cigar, put it in his mouth, and took it out again. He looked at Wolfe, whose head was tilted back to drink, and waited for Wolfe's eyes to meet his.

"Why I came," he said. "Not to ask for help, but I thought it was possible that an exchange might help both of us. We have collected a lot of facts, thousands of facts, some established and some not. Mrs. Odell has certainly told you things that she hasn't told us, and maybe some of the others have too. We might trade. Of course it would hurt. You would be crossing your client, and I would be giving you official information that is supposed to be withheld. You don't want to and neither do I. But I'm making a straight offer on the square. I haven't asked you if this is being recorded."

"It isn't."

"Good." He picked up his glass. "That's why I came."

Wolfe swiveled, not his chair, his head, to look at me. The look said, as plain as words, "I hope you're appreciating this," and my look said, "I am." He turned back to Cramer and said, just stating a fact, "It won't do, Mr. Cramer."

"It won't?"

"No. There is mutual respect between you and me, but not mutual trust. If I gave you every word spoken to me by Mrs. Odell, and by the others, you would think it possible, even probable, that

I omitted something. You say you have thousands of facts. If you gave me ten thousand, I would think it likely that you had reserved at least one. You know as well as I do that in the long record of man's make-believe, there is no sillier formula than the old legal phrase, 'the truth, the whole truth, and nothing but the truth.' Pfui."

"So you *would* omit something."

"Perhaps. I could add that if I did give you every word, you would know nothing helpful that you don't know now, but you wouldn't believe me."

"You're damn right I wouldn't." He looked at the glass in his hand and squinted at it as if he wondered how it got there. "Thanks for the beer." He put the glass, not empty, on the table, saw the cigar, and picked it up. I expected him to throw it at my wastebasket and miss as usual, but he stuck it in the beer glass, the chewed end down. He stood up. "I had a question, I had one question, but I'm not going to ask it. By God, you had the nerve—those men—with me sitting here—" He turned and walked out.

I didn't go to see him out, but when I heard the front door open and close, I went to the hall to see that he *was* out. Back in, I went to the safe to enter the outlay in the petty cash book. I don't like to leave things hanging. As I headed for my desk, Wolfe said, "I thought I knew that man. Why did he come?"

"He said he's desperate."

"But he isn't. So healthy an ego isn't capable of despair."

I sat. "He wanted to look at you. Of course he knew you wouldn't play along on his cockeyed offer. He thinks he can tell when you've got a good hand, and maybe he can."

"Do *you* think he can? Can you?"

"I'd better not answer that, not right now. We've got a job on. Am I to just sit here and take calls from the help?"

"No. You are to seduce either Miss Lugos or Miss Venner. Which one?"

I raised one brow. He can't do that. "Why not both?"

We discussed it.

10

WHEN I had a chance, after lunch, I looked up "seduce" in the dictionary. "1. To persuade (one) as into disobedience, disloyalty, or desertion of a lord or cause. 2. To lead or draw (one) aside or astray, as into an evil, foolish, or disastrous course or action from that which is good, wise, etc.; as, to be *seduced* into war; to *seduce* one from his duty; to tempt or entice; as, pleasures that *seduced* her from home. 3. To induce to evil; to corrupt, specif., to induce to surrender chastity; to debauch."

Even on the 3 I couldn't charge him at some appropriate moment with having asked me to go too far, since we had no evidence that either of them had any chastity to surrender.

The best spot in the metropolitan area at four o'clock on a Saturday afternoon in June is an upper box at Shea Stadium, but I wasn't there that Saturday. I was sitting in the cockpit of a thirty-foot boat, removing a flounder the size of my open hand from the hook at the end of Sylvia Venner's line. The object I enjoy most removing from a hook is a sixteen-inch rainbow or Dolly Varden or cutthroat, but there aren't any in Long Island Sound. We had spent a couple of hours trying for stripers or blues without a bite and had settled for salmon eggs on little hooks. The name of the boat was *Happygolucky.* I had borrowed it from a man named Sopko, who had once paid Wolfe $7,372.40, including expenses, for getting his son out of a deep hole he had stumbled into.

It was from Sylvia Venner herself, on the telephone Wednesday afternoon, that I had learned that she didn't care for baseball, didn't like dancing, had seen all the shows in town, and wouldn't enjoy dining at Rusterman's because she was on a diet. The idea of a boat had come from her. She said that she loved catching fish, all except actually touching one, but the soonest she could make it was Saturday.

In fifty-six hours Saul and Fred and Orrie had produced nothing that would need help from me during the weekend. Friday evening I assembled the score for the two and a half days on a page of my notebook and got this:

> *Number of CAN employes who thought or guessed or hinted*
>
> *—that Odell was putting the bomb in the drawer to get Browning* 4
>
> *—that Browning planted the bomb to get Odell and somehow got Odell to go and open the drawer* 1
>
> *—that Dennis Copes planted it to get Kenneth Meer* 2
>
> *—that no one had planted it; the bomb was a left-over from the research for the program and was supposed to be de-activated* 2
>
> *—that Sylvia Venner had planted it to get Browning* 1
>
> *—that Helen Lugos had planted it to get Kenneth Meer* 2
>
> *—that Kenneth Meer had planted it to get Helen Lugos* 1
>
> *—that some kind of activist had planted it to get just anybody* 3
>
> *—that it would never be known who had planted it for whom* 8

If you skipped that I don't blame you; I include it only because I didn't want to waste the time I spent compiling it. It adds up to twenty-four, and they spoke with a total of about a hundred people, so some seventy or eighty were keeping their thinking or guessing or hinting to themselves. Wolfe and I agreed, Friday evening, to ignore the favorite guess. The idea that Odell had himself supplied the bomb was out. His wife would have known about it, and she would not have given Wolfe a hundred grand to start digging. Also why the LSD in his pocket? Because he was on the stuff and had it with him in case his nerves needed a boost? Cramer and the DA had certainly included that in their tries and had chucked it. So no. Out. One of the four who liked it was Dennis Copes, but that didn't prove anything. Saul's description of Copes was "5 feet 9, 160 pounds, brown hair down to his collar, sideburns that needed trimming, showy shirt and tie, neat plain gray Hickey-Freeman suit, soft low-pitched voice, nervous hands." He had chatted with him twice and learned nothing useful. Of course he hadn't asked if he knew or thought he knew that Kenneth Meer had the habit of checking on the whisky in the drawer, and though he is as good as Wolfe at the trick of getting an answer to an unasked question, it hadn't worked with Copes.

Actually nothing worked with anybody. I have just looked over my notes, and since there is nothing in them that helped us they certainly wouldn't help you.

At four o'clock Saturday afternoon it looked as if I wasn't going to get anything helpful from Sylvia Venner either. She had stopped bothering about the dimples. In blue shorts and a white sleeveless shirt with big blue plastic buttons she was showing plenty of nice smooth skin with a medium tan, and her well-arranged face was the kind that looks even better in bright outdoor light than inside. While we were eating the broiled chicken supplied by Fritz, and yogurt and thin little tasteless crackers supplied by her, and pickles and raw carrots and celery, and she was drinking something called Four-Root Juice and I was drinking milk, she had suddenly said, "I suppose you know what etymology is."

"Hah," I said. "I work for Nero Wolfe."

"Why," she said, "is that relevant?"

"Certainly. He knows more words than Shakespeare knew."

"Oh. I don't really know anything about him except what he

does. They tried to get him on my program once, but he wouldn't, so I didn't have to research him. Are you up on words too?"

"Not really. Just enough to get along on."

"I think words are fascinating. I was thinking, looking at you while you were dropping the anchor, take words like 'pecker' and 'prick.' In their vulgar sense, or maybe I should say their colloquial sense."

Without batting an eye I said, "You mean 'prick' as a noun. Not as a verb."

She nodded. "Yes, a noun. It means 'a pointed instrument.' 'Pecker' means 'an instrument for pecking,' and 'peck' means 'to strike repeatedly and often with a pointed instrument.' So the definition of 'pecker' and 'prick' is identical."

"Sure. I've never looked them up, but evidently you have."

"Of course. In Webster and in the OED. There's an OED at the office. Of course the point is that—well, well, there's a pun. 'Point.' The point is that they both begin with *p,* and 'penis' begins with *p.*"

"I'll be damned. It certainly does."

"Yes. I think that may be relevant to that old saying, 'Watch your p's and q's.' *But.* But two other words, 'piss' and 'pee'—*p*-double-*e*—they start with *p* too. What it is, it's male chauvinism."

"I'm not sure I get that."

She sipped Four-Root Juice. "It's obvious. Women urinate too. So they have to call it 'piss' or 'pee' just because 'penis' begins with *p.* What if they called it 'viss' or 'vee,' and they made men call it 'viss' or 'vee' too? Would men like that?"

"Viss," I said. "Vee. I don't . . ." I considered it, sipping milk. "Oh. Vagina."

"Certainly. Virgin too, but that may be just coincidence."

"I admit it's a point. A voint. You may not believe this, but personally I wouldn't object. It even appeals to me. 'Excuse me while I viss.' 'Turn your back while I vee.' I rather like the sound of it."

"I don't believe it, and anyway not many men would. It's male chauvinism. And another point, 'poker' begins with a *p* too. Why didn't they make it 'poker' instead of 'pecker'? Because a poker is three feet long!"

"It is not. I've never seen a poker three feet long. More like two feet. Possibly thirty inches."

"You're just quibbling. Even two feet." She put her open hands out, apparently she thought two feet apart, but it was about twenty-eight inches. She picked up a pickle. Vickle. "So they couldn't very well call it 'poker.' Take another letter, take *f.* 'Female' begins with *f.* What is one of men's favorite four-letter colloquial words that begins with *f?*"

"Offhand I couldn't say. I'd have to think."

"All right, think."

So there I was, on a borrowed boat on Long Island Sound, alone with a Women's Libberette who was majoring in etymology. If you think that in the above exchange she was making a roundabout approach to a pass at me, I appreciate the compliment, but I doubt it. If so, my reaction cooled it. Even in such an ideal situation as a boat with a cabin at anchor in smooth water, I refuse to be seduced by quotations from Webster and the Oxford English Dictionary.

She was not a nitwit. Soon after we got our lines out she said, "What are you waiting for? You haven't asked me a single question about the murder."

"What murder?"

"Oh, come off it. Do you think I think my dimples took you?"

"No. I have never seen better dimples, and there's nothing wrong with other parts of you either, but a newspaperman I know thinks you planted the bomb to get Browning, and I wanted to get a close-up of you. With a good look and some talk with a woman, I can tell if she is a murderer. The way they eat helps too. For instance, do they lick their fingers."

She was frowning at me. "Do you really—no, of course you don't. All right, I'll play. Have you decided about me?"

"Not to cross you off, but ten to one you didn't plant the bomb. But three to one, make it five to one, you have a pretty good idea who did. You've been there four years, you know everybody, and you're smart."

"I am not smart. If I was smart I would have hooked that skunk Browning instead of letting Helen Lugos take him. Do you know who I could love?"

"No, but I'd like to."

"All right, I'll tell you. I could love the man who can prove I'm not dumb. I simply can't persuade myself I'm not dumb. Browning is going to be it, he's going to be the top cock, and where will I be? No, I didn't plant the bomb, but I could have."

"Who did?"

"I don't—*now* what have I done?"

She had snarled her line. Not purposely, to change the subject, because half an hour later, after we had unsnarled her and quit on stripers and were trying for blues, she said, "I've got a pretty good idea who might have. The bomb. But not for any signed statement. They always want signed statements. I'm not *that* dumb."

I made a cast. "Not me. I just want an idea to play with."

"Play? My god, you should have seen that room. Browning's office. When I got there Helen Lugos and Ken Meer were trying to keep people out. Ken's hands were bloody. When I heard what had happened—that was later—my first idea was that Ken had done it."

"How did he know Odell would come and open—"

"Not Odell. Browning. To kill Browning. Of course he—"

"Isn't Meer with Browning? His right hand?"

"Yes, but he hates him. No, that's wrong, it's not hate, it's—what, jealousy? It's worse than jealousy. It kills him that Helen does it with Browning. He got an itch for Helen when she came, two years ago, and he's got it bad. I've seen him look at her with that sick look—you know?"

I nodded. "Male chauvinism upside down."

"What? Oh. It is at that. But I dropped that idea. Ken certainly wants Helen, but he wants to move up even more, and if Browning was president he would be in a very good spot. So I still think he probably planted the bomb, but not for Browning, for Odell. So Odell couldn't be president. He knew Odell was going to come and open that drawer."

"How did he know that?"

"You'll have to ask *him.* I can't wrap it up for you." She had her line in and squared around for another cast.

By the time the slant of the sun and my watch agreed that it was time to head for the marina, I had got all the questions in but had nothing to light a fire with. She doubted if Dennis Copes was involved because he was the hippie type and hippies aren't really headed anywhere, they just key up—according to her, not me. I know a hippie who tried—but he's not in this. She didn't know if Copes knew or thought he knew that Kenneth Meer inspected that drawer every day. She doubted if anybody inspected the drawer besides Browning himself, but if anyone did it was probably Helen Lugos; inspecting drawers is routine for secretaries. She had herself inspected it once, out of curiosity, about three years ago. Yes, it was twelve-year-old Ten-Mile Creek.

The Heron was in the parking lot at the marina and I drove Sylvia—sure, we had been Sylvia and Archie the last three hours—to a human hive in the East Seventies, only a block away from a spot where an FBI man had once insulted me because I was tailing a man he wanted to tail. She didn't invite me up. Wolfe was in the middle of dinner when I got home and he doesn't like to dawdle while I catch up, so I ate in the kitchen, with Fritz.

Later, in the office, when I asked him if he wanted Sylvia Venner verbatim he said yes, omitting only trivia, we had all evening. I asked, including the personal parts, and he said, enough of it to exhibit her. So I had a free hand. Omitting trivia, it took only ten minutes to get us on board the boat and under way, and another five to get us to the spot where we anchored and agreed that the air made us hungry. Of course I enjoyed my description of the picnic lunch in detail, but he didn't. He set his jaw and squinted at me, and did something he seldom does; he used profanity. "Good god," he growled. "Are you—how do you feel?"

"All right now. Of course it was tough, but what the hell, I was working. During the feast she said she supposed I knew what etymology is, and I said hah, I work for Nero Wolfe. She asked if that was relevant and said she didn't know much about him, that they tried to get him on her program but he wouldn't. You remember that."

"Yes."

"She said, quote, 'I think words are fascinating. Take words like "pecker" and "prick." In their vulgar sense, or maybe I should say their colloquial sense.' "

"Me: 'You mean "prick" as a noun, not as a verb.' "

"She: 'Yes, a noun. It means "a pointed instrument." "Pecker" just means "an instrument for pecking," and "peck" means "to strike repeatedly and often with a pointed instrument." So the definition of "pecker" and "prick" is identical.' "

"Me: 'Sure. I've never looked them up, but evidently—' "

His grunt stopped me. He growled, "I said omit trivia."

"This is not trivia. She was leading up to a point, and she made it. The point was that men make women say 'piss' and 'pee'—*p* -double-*e*—when they urinate because 'penis' begins with *p,* and what if *they* made *them* say 'viss' and 'vee'? Vagina. And she said it's male chauvinism. Doesn't that exhibit her?"

And once again I got a completely different reaction from the one I expected. I suppose I will never know him as well as I think I do. I did know where he stood on the question of male chauvinism, but I should have considered how he felt about words.

He said, "Indeed."

I said, "Yes indeed. Women's Lib."

He flipped a hand. "That's merely the herd syndrome. Fad. The issue is the influence of male dominance on language. Has that woman made a contribution to the study of linguistics? If so, there should be some indication in the record of matriarchy, but there is no adequate . . . "

Letting it hang, he pushed his chair back, rose, went straight to a spot in the shelves, got a book, and returned. As he sat, my good eyes told me it was *History of Human Marriage* by Westermarck. I had given it a ten-minute try one empty day long ago and decided I could get along without it. As he opened it, I asked, "Shall I tell the squad not to come in the morning because the issue now is a matter of linguistics, or will you need them for research?"

He glared at me, transferred it to the book, tossed it on the desk, and said, "Very well, proceed, but only what is material. No flummery."

So I no longer had a free hand. I reported. When I finished and he asked for comments, as usual, I said, "Nothing to raise my pay. One, I doubt if she is saving anything that would open a crack. Two, it would suit her fine if Browning dropped dead, but if she planted the bomb she wouldn't have risked a whole afternoon with me. She's not that kind. Three, at least we know that Meer had blood on his hands that other people could see, so maybe that helps to explain *him.*"

"Not enough to justify that outrageous meal," he said, and reached for the book.

Fritz had left to spend a night and a day and another night as he saw fit, so before I went upstairs to dress properly for joining Lily Rowan's party at the Flamingo, I brought a bottle of beer to help with the language problem.

11

SINCE Wolfe's nine-to-eleven session in the plant rooms doesn't apply on Sundays, he was in the office when the help came at ten o'clock. That was about the most useless two hours we ever spent with them. Wolfe's idea was to have them talk about everyone they had seen, in the slim hope of our getting at least a glimmer of some kind of a hint.

No. Nothing.

If you are inclined to quit because I seem to be getting nowhere, no wonder. I'm sorry, but in these reports I don't put in stunts to jazz it up, I just report. Of course I can leave things out, and I do. I'll skip that two-hour Sunday conference, except for one little item. Orrie said that Dennis Copes didn't have a secretary, and the girl in the stenographer pool who often took stuff for him was a stuck-up bitch, and he added, "Of course Archie would have had her holding hands." He can't quite ditch the idea that he should have my job. I admit there is one little detail of detective work that he can do better than I can, but he doesn't know what it is so I won't name it. They were told to go back in the morning and try some more. The theory was that somebody there must know *something,* which seemed reasonable.

The only thing that happened that day worth reporting was that Lily Rowan and I, at Shea Stadium, watched the Mets take the Cardinals, 7 to 3.

At ten o'clock Monday morning I sent a messenger to the CAN building with a white cardboard box addressed to Miss Helen

Lugos. The box contained a cluster of Broughtonia sanguinea. They had been picked by Wolfe, who won't let even me cut his orchids, but the card in the box had my name. At 11:30 I decided that she must have opened it, phoned, and got a female who said that Miss Lugos was engaged and did I wish to leave a message. When you get up to vice-president, especially one who will soon be president because the other candidate was murdered, even secretaries are often hard to get. I decided that she might not have seen the box yet and postponed it to after lunch.

It was after four o'clock and Wolfe was up in the plant rooms when I finally got her. She said right off, "Thank you for the beautiful flowers." Neither warm nor cool, just polite.

"You're welcome. I suggested them, Mr. Wolfe picked them, and we both packed them. It's a bribe. Mr. Wolfe thinks I understand women better than he does and wants me to have a talk with you. I don't think this office is the best place for it because that's too much like telling you to come to a—oh, the District Attorney's office. I can come to your place, or we can meet anywhere you say, or we can share a meal in the little pink room at Rusterman's. Perhaps dinner this evening? Women are supposed to like pink rooms, as of course you know. I'm going on talking to give you time to consider it; I didn't suppose you'd have a yes right at the tip of your tongue."

"I haven't got one anywhere. Thank you, but no."

"Then the pink room is out. Have you a suggestion?"

"I have a question. Has Mrs. Odell asked *you* to talk with me?"

"Mrs. Odell hasn't asked *me* anything. She has hired Nero Wolfe to do a job, and she has asked people at CAN to cooperate, from Mr. Abbott down, as you know. We would like to suit their convenience. In this case, *your* convenience."

"Mrs. Odell didn't hire you, she hired Nero Wolfe."

"I work for him."

"I know you do. And I work for Mr. Browning. When he wants to talk with someone, he doesn't expect them to be willing to talk with me instead. If Mr. Wolfe wants to talk with me, all right, I suppose I'll have to. At his office, of course. When does he want me to come?"

There was no point in prolonging it. I said distinctly, "At six o'clock today. An hour and a half from now."

She said distinctly, "Very well, I'll be there," and hung up.

I went to the kitchen, poured myself a glass of milk, and told Fritz, "I'm done. Washed up. I've lost my touch. I'm a has-been. You knew me when."

He was at the big table doing something to a duckling. "Now, Archie," he said. "He told me about that woman's diet when I took his breakfast up this morning, but you ate a good lunch. What else has happened?"

"Another woman. She spit at me just now. Spat. On the phone."

"Then *she* is washed up, not you. You are looking at the wrong side. Just turn it over, that's all you ever have to do, just turn it over."

"I'll be damned." I stared at him. "You sound like a guru."

There was no telling what would happen if Wolfe came down at six o'clock and found an unexpected female sitting in the red leather chair—or rather, there *was*—so when the glass of milk was down I went up three flights, entered, walked down the aisles between the rainbow benches of the three rooms—cool, medium, and warm—and opened the door of the potting room. He and Theodore were at the long bench, making labels. I stopped halfway across and said, "I'm not breaking a rule. Emergency. We have wasted forty dollars' worth of orchids."

He waited until I stopped to turn his head. "She's not available?"

"Oh, she's available, but not for menials. When she dies—the sooner, the better—and ascends, she won't waste her breath on Saint Peter, she'll speak only to Him, with a capital H. She'll be here at six o'clock to speak to You, with a capital Y. I apologize and will expect a pay cut."

"Pfui. I agree that you have not broken a rule." He made a face. "I'll be prompt."

On the way out I stopped to apologize to the two pots of Broughtonia sanguinea. On the way down, I decided that the milk needed help and went to the kitchen for a tall glass of gin and tonic with a sprig of mint and a dash of lime juice. Also for Fritz. I needed friendly companionship.

I was supposing she would be strictly punctual, maybe even a couple of minutes early, but no. She *was* female. She came at 6:18, in a peach-colored blouse with long sleeves and a brownish skirt, narrow, down to a couple of inches below her knees, and she talked to me. She said, "I'm sorry I'm a little late." Not being in a mood to meet her halfway, I said, "So am I."

Wolfe had not told me how he intended to proceed, though he had come down from the plant rooms on the dot at six o'clock, and though he often asks my advice on how to handle a woman and sometimes even follows it. He soon showed me, and her, that this time he needed no help with his game plan. As she got to the red leather chair, he said, "Good afternoon, Miss Lugos. Thank you for coming," and when she was seated and had her ankles crossed and her skirt tugged, he rose, crossed almost to the door, turned, and said, "I have an errand to do in the kitchen. My agent, Mr. Goodwin, will ask you some questions on behalf of Mrs. Odell."

He went.

"I'm as surprised as you are," I told her, "but it's just like him. No consideration for other people. I think I told you that he thinks I understand women better than he does. He actually believes that. So here we are, in a private detective's office which could be bugged, instead of the pink room at Rusterman's. If you like something wet after a day's work, name it and we may have it."

Her lips were twitching a little. "I ought to get up and go," she said. "But I suppose—that would only—"

"Yes," I agreed, "it would only. Anyway, you've flubbed it. On the phone you stiff-armed me. You put me in my place. But if you really meant it, you would have sent the orchids back, or even brought them. Unless you dropped them in the wastebasket?"

She flushed and her lips tightened. I believe I have mentioned that her face was different from any two angles, and it was different flushed. With most faces that you enjoy looking at, you know exactly why, but not with her kind. Flushed, it was again quite different, and I approved of that too. Then suddenly it became another face entirely. She laughed, with her mouth open and her head back, and I think I grinned with pleasure. I really did.

"All right, Mr. Goodwin," she said, "you win. I *didn't* drop them in the wastebasket. They're in a vase. I almost wish we were at Rusterman's. But as you said, here we are. So ask your questions."

I had erased the grin. "Would you like a drink?"

"No, thank you."

"Then let's see. First, I guess, that evening you heard what those people said, six of them, when Mr. Wolfe asked them where they were that weekend. Were they all telling the truth?"

"I don't know. How could I?"

"You might. Maybe you have heard Browning say something that shows he wasn't on a boat from Friday afternoon to Sunday afternoon, or maybe Kenneth Meer has said something that shows he wasn't hiking in Vermont. From your look I think you think I'm a damn fool to suppose you would tell me things like that. But I'm not. In an investigation like this only a damn fool would expect a full and honest answer to any question he asks anybody, but he asks them. For instance, the question I ask you now. This: Did Dennis Copes know that Kenneth Meer looked in that drawer every day to check on the whisky supply?"

"That's a trick question. It assumes that Kenneth Meer did look in the drawer every day."

"So it does. All right, did he?"

"No. As far as I know, he didn't. Mr. Browning checked on the whisky supply himself."

"Did he buy it himself?"

"He buys it by the case. It's sent to his home and he brings it, two bottles at a time."

"Does Kenneth Meer drink bourbon?"

"I don't think so. He drinks vodka."

"Do you drink bourbon?"

"Very seldom. I don't drink much of anything."

"Did *you* look in the drawer every day to check on the whisky supply?"

"No. Mr. Browning did the looking himself."

"I thought secretaries checked everything."

"Well—that's what you thought."

"You know Dennis Copes."

"Certainly."

"Two people think he might have planted the bomb to get Meer because he wants Meer's job. If so, he might have thought Meer looked in the drawer every day. Have you any idea why he might think that?"

"No. I have no idea why he thinks anything."

"One person thinks that Kenneth Meer planted the bomb to get Browning because you go to bed with him. Have you any idea about that?"

"Yes, I have. It's absurd."

"A newspaperman I know doesn't think it's absurd. Of course it's really three ideas. One, that you are intimate with Browning, two, that Meer knows it and can't stand it, and three, that he planted the bomb. Are they all absurd?"

She wasn't visibly reacting. No flush on her skin, no flash in her eyes. She said, with no change in pitch, "The police have asked me about this. My relations with Mr. Browning are my business and his. Certainly not yours. Women do go to bed with men, so it may not be absurd for people to think I am intimate with Amory Browning, but the idea that Kenneth Meer tried to kill him, *that's* absurd. Kenneth Meer has big ideas about his future. He thinks he's headed for the top, and he's counting on Amory Browning to help him along."

"But you're there. What if he wants you more than anything else? This *is* my business, Miss Lugos. The police think it's theirs, too, you just said so. It's not absurd to think a man's desire for a woman can be so hot that no other desire counts. There have been cases."

"Kenneth Meer isn't one of them. You don't know him, but I do. How much longer is this going to take?"

"I don't know. It depends. Not as long as it would with Mr. Wolfe. He likes to ask questions that seem to be just to pass the time, but I try to stick to the point. For instance, when Mr. Wolfe asked you that evening if you thought the person who put the bomb in the drawer was here in the room, you said you had no idea, but naturally you would say that, with them here. What would you say now, not for quotation?"

"I would say exactly the same, I have no idea. Mr. Goodwin, I—I'm tired. I'd like some—some whisky?"

"Sure. Scotch, bourbon, rye, Irish. Water, soda, ice."

"Just whisky. Any kind—bourbon. It doesn't matter."

She wasn't tired. The fingers of both hands, in her lap, had been curling and uncurling. She was tight. I mean tense, taut. As I went to the kitchen and put a bottle of bourbon—not Ten-Mile Creek—and a glass and a pitcher of water on a tray, I was trying to decide if it was just the strain of discussing her personal affairs with a mere agent, or something even touchier. I still hadn't decided when I had put the tray on the little table by her chair and was back at my desk. She poured about two fingers, downed it with three swallows, made a face and swallowed nothing a couple of times, poured half a glass of water, and swallowed that.

"I told you—" she began, didn't like how it sounded or felt, and started over. "I told you I don't drink much."

I nodded. "I can bring some milk, but it's an antidote for whisky."

"No, thank you." She swallowed nothing again.

"Okay. You said you have no idea who put the bomb in the drawer."

"Yes, I haven't."

I got my notebook and pen. "For this, since this room is *not* bugged, I'll have to make notes. I have to know where you were every minute of that day, that Tuesday, May 20. It was four weeks ago, four weeks tomorrow, but it shouldn't strain your memory, since the police of course asked you that day or the day after. Anyone going to Browning's room went through your room, so we'll have to do the whole day, from the time you arrived. Around ten o'clock?"

"There was another door to his room."

"But not often used except by him?"

"Not often, but sometimes it was. I'm not going to do this. I don't think you have a right to expect me to."

"I have no *right* to expect anything. But Mr. Wolfe can't do the job Mrs. Odell hired him to do unless he can get answers to the essential questions, and this is certainly one of them. One reason I say that is that Kenneth Meer told a newspaperman that anyone who wanted to know how it happened should concentrate on Helen Lugos. Why did Meer say that?"

"I don't believe it." She was staring at me, which made her face different again. "I don't believe he said that."

"But he did. It's a fact, Miss Lugos."

"To a newspaperman?"

"Yes. I won't tell you his name, but if I have to, I can produce him and he can tell you. He wasn't a stranger to Meer. They were choir boys together at St. Andrew's. When he tried to get Meer to go on, Meer clammed. I'm not assuming that when you tell me how and where you spent that day, I'll know why Meer said that, since you'll tell me exactly what you told the police and evidently it didn't help them any, but I must have it because that's how a detective is supposed to detect. You got to work at ten o'clock?"

She said no, nine-thirty.

Even with my personal and private shorthand it filled more than four pages of my notebook. The timing was perfect. It was exactly 7:30 when we had her in the file room and the sound and shake of the explosion came, and Fritz stepped in to reach for the doorknob. So it was time to eat. If I am in the office with company, and

Wolfe isn't, when dinner's ready, Fritz comes and shuts the office door. That notifies me that food is ready to serve, and also it keeps the sound of voices from annoying Wolfe in the dining room across the hall, if I have to continue the conversation.

That time I didn't have to, and I didn't want to. I wanted to consider a couple of the things she had said without her sitting there with her face, and I wanted my share of the ducklings with mushrooms and wild rice and wine while it was hot from the oven. It's one of the dishes Wolfe and Fritz have made up together, and they call it American duckling on account of the wild rice, and I'm for it.

So I said she was tired, and she said yes, she was, and got up, and I thanked her, and thanked her again as I opened the front door to let her out.

Of course I didn't mention her as I joined Wolfe at the dining table. He had one of the ducklings carved, so that would have been talking business during a meal, which is not done. But when we had finished and moved to the office and Fritz had brought coffee, he showed that the week of marking time was getting on his nerves by demanding, "Well?" before I had lifted my cup.

"No," I said.

"Nothing at all?"

"Nothing for me. For you, I can't say. I never can. You want it verbatim, of course."

"Yes."

I gave it to him, complete, up to the details of her day on Tuesday, May 20. For that I used the notebook. As usual, he just listened; no interruptions, no questions. He is the best listener I know. When I finished, the coffee pot and our cups were empty and Fritz had come for them.

I put the notebook in the drawer. "So for me, nothing. Of course she didn't open the bag and shake it, who does? She knows or suspects something that may or may not be true and might or might not help, and to guess what it is needs a better guesser than me. I don't think she planted the bomb. She wasn't there at her desk in the next room when it went off, which was lucky for her, but she says she often went to the file room for something, nearly always when Browning wasn't in his room. Of course the cops have checked that. Also of course it was a waste of time to have her name the seventeen people she saw go into Browning's room. The bomb wasn't put in the drawer while Browning was there unless he did it himself, and there's another door to his room. As for who entered his room when he wasn't there, there was a total of nearly two hours when *she* wasn't there, according to her. As for her reason that Kenneth Meer wouldn't want to kill Browning, toss a coin. You'd have to use a lie detector on Meer himself."

He grunted. "Miss Venner, and now Miss Lugos."

"Meaning I should have seduced at least one of them. Fire me."

"Pfui. I complain of your conduct only directly, never by innuendo. You offend only deliberately, never by shortcoming. Miss Lugos did not plant the bomb?"

"One will get you ten."

"Does she know who did?"

"No bet. She could think she knows. Or not."

"Confound it." He got up and went to the shelves for a book.

12

SIX DAYS later, at noon Sunday, June 22, the five of us sat in the office and looked at each other. Saul and Fred and Orrie and I looked at Wolfe, and he looked back, his eyes moving, not his head, from me past Orrie and Fred to Saul in the red leather chair.

"No," he said. "This is preposterous. Amphigoric. And insupportable." He looked at me. "How much altogether, including you?"

I shut my eyes and in less than half a minute opened them. "Say three thousand dollars. A little more."

"It will be a deduction on my tax return. Call Mrs. Odell and tell her I am quitting. Draw a check to her for the full amount of the retainer."

Fred and Orrie had to turn their heads to look at me. Saul, in the red leather chair, didn't have to turn his head. I looked at Wolfe, especially the left corner of his mouth, to see how bad it was.

Plenty of things had happened. There had been three thunderstorms in a row Wednesday afternoon. Jill Cather, Orrie's wife, had threatened to walk out on him because he didn't get home until five in the morning Tuesday after taking a CAN female researcher to dinner and a show, though he explained that the meal and the tickets had been paid for by the client. The West Side Highway, northbound, had been closed for repairs all day Friday. Fred Durkin, tailing a CAN male employee Thursday evening, had lost him, and he hates to lose a tail; and on Friday, Elaine, his oldest daughter, had admitted she was smoking grass. Saul Panzer had spent two days and a night at Montauk Point trying to find a bomb maker, and drawn a blank. On Friday the Labor Department announced that the Consumer Price Index had gone up .3 of one percent in May. A busy week.

Personally I had done wonders. I had answered at least a hundred phone calls, including dozens from the three helpers. They were *trying* to help. Also including three from Mrs. Odell. I had discussed the situation for about an hour with a member of the CAN news staff, brought by Orrie. His real reason for coming had been to have a chat with Nero Wolfe. I had spent an evening with Sylvia Venner and a male chauvinist friend of hers, also a CAN employee, at her apartment. I had washed my hands and face every day. I could go on, but that's enough to show you that I was fully occupied.

Wolfe hadn't been idle either. When Inspector Cramer had rung the doorbell at eleven-thirty Friday morning, he had told me to admit him, and he had held up his end of a twenty-minute conversation. Cramer had no chips on his shoulder. What brought him was the fact that Cass R. Abbott, the president of CAN, had come to see Wolfe the day before, a little after six o'clock, and stayed a full hour. Evidently Cramer had the old brownstone under surveillance, and if so, he positively was desperate in spite of his healthy ego. He probably thought that Abbott's coming indicated that Wolfe had a fire lit, and if so, he wanted to warm his hands. I think when he left, he was satisfied that we were as empty as he was, but with those two you never know.

What Abbott's coming actually indicated was that the strain was getting on his nerves, and for a man so high up that would not do. When he got parked in the red leather chair, he told Wolfe he would like to speak with him confidentially, and when Wolfe said he could, there would be no recording, Abbott looked at me, then back to Wolfe, and said, "Privately."

Wolfe shook his head. "Professionally nothing is reserved between Mr. Goodwin and me. If he leaves the room and you tell me anything relevant to the job we are doing—trying to do—I would tell him, withholding nothing."

"Well." Abbott ran his fingers through his mop of fine, white hair. "I have had a check on you but not on Goodwin. You hold up, but does he?"

"If he doesn't, I don't. What good is a chain with a bad link?"

Abbott nodded. "A good line. Who said it?"

"I did. The thought is not new, no thought is, but said better."

"You use words, don't you?"

"Yes. On occasion, in six languages, which is a mere smattering. I would like to be able to communicate with any man alive. As it is, even you and I find it difficult. Are you sure you can prevent my getting more or less than you want me to from what you tell me or ask me?"

Abbott's raised eyebrows made his long, pale face look even longer. "By god, I can try."

"Go ahead."

"When I say 'confidential,' I mean you will not repeat to Mrs. Odell anything I say about her."

Wolfe nodded. "See? You don't mean that. Of course I would repeat it if it would serve my purpose or her interest to do so. She has hired me. If you mean I am not to tell her your name, I am to give her no hint of who said it, yes. —Archie?"

"Right," I said. "Noted and filed."

"Then that's understood," Abbott said. He slid further back in the chair, which is deep. "I have known Mrs. Odell twenty years. I suppose you know she is a large stockholder in the Continental Air Network. I know her very well, and I knew him well—her husband. That's one point. Another point is that I have been president of CAN for nine years, and I'm retiring in a few weeks, and I don't want to leave in an atmosphere of distrust and doubt and suspicion. Not distrust or suspicion of me, not of anyone in particular, it's just in the air. It pervades the whole damn place, the whole organization. To leave when it's like that—it would look like I'm getting out from under."

He hit the chair arm with a fist. *"This goddam murder has got to be cleared up!* You probably wondered why I let you turn those three men loose in my building to go anywhere and see anyone. I did it because the police and the District Attorney were completely stumped, they were getting absolutely nowhere, and I thought you might. One reason I thought you might was that there was a good chance that Mrs. Odell had told you things that she hadn't told them. But that was a week ago, a week yesterday, and where have *you* got to?"

"Here." Wolfe patted his desk blotter. "I'm always here."

"Hell, I know you are. Do you know who put that bomb in that drawer? Have you even got a good guess?"

"Yes. You did. You thought they were going to choose Mr. Browning, and you favored Mr. Odell."

"Sure. All you need is proof. As I thought, you have done no better than the police, and you have had ten days. Last evening I discussed the situation with three of my directors, and as a result I phoned this morning to make this appointment. I am prepared to make a proposal with the backing of my Board. I suppose Mrs. Odell has paid you a retainer. If you will withdraw and return her retainer, we will reimburse you for all expenses you have incurred, and we will engage you to investigate the death of Peter Odell on behalf of the corporation, with a retainer in the same amount as Mrs. Odell's. Or possibly more."

I had of course been looking at him. Now I looked at Wolfe. Since he was facing Abbott, he was in profile to me, but I had enough of his right eye to see what I call his slow-motion take. The eye closed, but so slow I couldn't see the motion of the lid. At least twenty seconds. He certainly wasn't giving Abbott a long wink, so the other eye was collaborating. They stayed shut about another twenty seconds, then opened in one, and he spoke. "It's obvious, of course. It's transparent."

"Transparent? It's direct."

"It is indeed. You have concluded that Mr. Odell himself supplied the bomb, intending it for Mr. Browning, and mishandled it.

And that Mrs. Odell hired me, not to discover and disclose the truth, but to impede its disclosure and prevent it if possible. You assume that either she is hoodwinking me or she has been candid with me. If the former, you decry my sagacity; if the latter, your proposal invites me to betray a trust. A waste of time, both yours and mine. I would have thought—"

"You're taking it wrong. It's not—you're twisting it. We merely think that if you were acting for the corpor—"

"Nonsense. Don't persist. I am neither a ninny nor a blackguard. Under a strain you and your colleagues have lost your wits. There is the possibility that you want to pay me to contrive some kind of skulduggery for you, but I doubt if you have misjudged me to that extreme. If you have, don't bother. Don't try floundering. Just go."

Abbott did not get up and go. He had to take it that he wasn't going to get what he had come for, but he stuck for another half an hour, trying to find out what we had done or hadn't done and what we expected to do. He found out exactly nothing, and so did Wolfe.

When I went back to the office after letting Abbott out, Wolfe glared at me and muttered, "Part of his proposal is worth considering. Returning the retainer."

He considered it for two days and three nights. In the office at noon Sunday, after another two-hour session with us—as I reported six pages back—he told me to call Mrs. Odell and tell her he was quitting and to draw a check to her for the full amount of the retainer; and Saul and Fred and Orrie looked at me and I looked at Wolfe, especially the left corner of his mouth, to see how bad it was.

It was bad all right, it was final, but I did not reach for the phone. "Okay," I said. "Since I started it, I admit I should be the one to finish it, but not with a phone call. I'd rather finish it the way I started it, face to face with her, and to do it right I should take the check and hand it to her instead of mailing it. No deduction for expenses?"

"No. The full amount. Very well, take it."

If we had been alone I might have tried discussing it, but with them there it was hopeless. Discussion would have to be with her, and then with him maybe. I went and got the checkbook from the safe, filled out the stub, tore the check out, and swung the typewriter around. I type all checks. That was the first one I had ever drawn for an even hundred grand, and with all the 0's it was a nice round figure. I took it to Wolfe and he signed it and handed it back. As I took it, Saul said, "I've asked so many people so many questions the last ten days, it's a habit, and I'd like to ask one more. How much is it?"

Even from Saul that was a mouthful, and my eyes opened at him. But Wolfe merely said, "Show it to him. Them."

I did so, and *their* eyes opened, and Saul said, "For her that's petty cash, she's really loaded. Sometimes you ask us for suggestions, and I'd like to make one. Or just another question. Instead of returning it to her, why not offer it to someone who needs it? A two-column ad in the *Times* and the *Gazette* with a heading like COULD YOU USE A HUNDRED THOUSAND DOLLARS? Then, 'I'll pay that amount in cash to the person who gives me information that will satisfactorily identify the person responsible for the death of Peter Odell by the explosion of a bomb on May twentieth.' Your name at the bottom. Of course the wording would—"

Wolfe's "No" stopped him. He repeated it. "No. I will not make a public appeal for someone to do my job for me."

"You have," Saul said. "You have advertised for help twice that I know of."

"For an answer to a particular question. Specific knowledge on a specified point. Not a frantic squawk to be pulled out of a mudhole. No."

So when they left a few minutes later, they weren't expected back. By noon Monday Fred and Orrie would be on chores for Bascom or some other outfit, and Saul too if he felt like it.

As for me, my chore wouldn't wait—or I didn't want it to. As someone said, probably Shakespeare, " 'twere better done," and so forth. Of course a person such as a Mrs. Peter Odell would ordinarily not be in town on a June Sunday, but she would be. She was ignoring weekends, and from a phone call by her Saturday morning she knew there would be a Sunday conference. So I rang her and asked if I could come at five o'clock, because earlier she would probably have the television on and I didn't want to share her attention with Cleon Jones at bat or Tom Seaver on the mound.

Wolfe had gone to the kitchen. For Sunday lunch with Fritz away he usually does something simple like eggs *au beurre noir* and a beet and watercress salad, but that time it was going to be larded shad roe casserole with anchovy butter and parsley and chervil and shallots and marjoram and black pepper and cream and bay leaf and onion and butter. It would take a lot of tasting, and he can taste. I went to the kitchen to tell him Mrs. Odell would see me at five o'clock, and he nodded, and I mounted the two flights to my room.

That was a busy four hours; shaving and changing from the skin out, going down for my third of the shad roe, which we ate in the kitchen, looking at the telecast from Montreal—where the Mets were playing the Expos—on the color set, which, like everything else in my room, was bought and paid for by me, and writing. Not on the typewriter, because when I'm being particular, I do better longhand, and that had to be done right. When I went downstairs a little before four-thirty, the third draft was in my pocket, with the check. Wolfe was up in the plant rooms and I buzzed him on the house phone to tell him I was leaving.

Since parking shouldn't be a problem Sunday afternoon, I went to the garage for the Heron, crossed town on Thirty-fourth, and turned uptown on Park. Driving in midtown Manhattan can still be a pleasure—from two to eight A.M. and a couple of hours on Sunday. There was actually a gap at the curb on Sixty-third Street between Fifth and Madison. The LPS man at the entrance to the stone mansion was not the same one, and this one had better manners; he said thank you when he returned my card case. Inside I was ushered to the elevator by the same woman in a neat gray uniform and was told to push the button with a 4. In the upper hall, the client's voice came through the open door to the big room, "In here!"

She was on the oversized couch, one leg on it straight and the other one dangling over the edge, with sections of the Sunday *Times* scattered around. The television was not on—but of course the game was over. As I crossed to her she said, "You'd better have something. You certainly don't on the telephone."

"We got careless once when our phone was tapped and we're leery. I don't suppose it's tapped now, but once was enough. Yes, I have something." I got the check from my pocket. "I thought I should bring it instead of mailing it."

She took it, frowned at it, frowned at me, again at the check, and back at me. "What's the idea?"

"Mr. Wolfe is bowing out. Quite a bow, since he has spent more than three thousand dollars. Three thousand dollars in twelve days and we haven't got a smell. One reason I'm bringing it instead of mailing it, I wanted to tell you that that's all there is to it, he's simply pulling out. He thinks it shows strength of character to admit he's licked. I can't see it and don't intend to, but I'm not a genius."

She surprised me. Up to that moment she had given me no reason to suppose that the arrangements inside her skull were any better than average, but she had reached a conclusion before I finished. Her eyes showed it, and she said it, with a question: "How much did Browning pay him?"

"Uh-huh," I said, and turned a chair to face her, and sat. "You would, naturally. If I talked for five hours, giving cases, I *might* be able to convince you that he couldn't possibly double-cross a client, on account of his opinion of himself, but I think there's a shorter way. I've told you on the phone about the three men we have called in to help. They were there this morning when he said it was hopeless and he was quitting. When he told me to draw a check to return the retainer, Saul Panzer suggested that instead of returning it, he might put an ad in the *Times* saying that he would pay it to anyone who would give him information that would identify the murderer, and Mr. Wolfe said no, he would not make a frantic squawk to be pulled out of a mudhole. That was—"

"Of course! He *would* say that!"

"Please hold it, I've just started. So I drew the check and he signed it, and I phoned you. But I think I can prove that he didn't sell out, and I want to try. I think I can get him to tear the check up and go on with the job, with your help. May I use your typewriter?"

"What for? I don't believe it."

"You will. You'll have to." I got up and crossed to a desk, the one with a typewriter on an extension. As I pulled the chair out and sat, I asked where I would find paper and she said, "The top drawer, but you're not fooling me," and I said, "Wait and see," and got out paper and a sheet of carbon.

She preferred not to wait. As I got the third draft from my pocket and spread it out on the desk, she kicked the sections of the *Times* aside, left the couch, and came and stood at my elbow, and I hit the keys. I didn't hurry because I wanted it clean. No exing. As I pulled it out, I said, "I had to type it here because he might recognize it from my machine, and this is going to be your idea." I handed her the original and gave the carbon a look:

NERO WOLFE HAS $50,000

in cash, given to him by me. He will pay it, on my behalf, to any person or persons who supply information to him that leads to the conclusive identification of the man or woman who placed a bomb in a drawer of the desk of Amory Browning on Tuesday, May 20th, resulting in the death of my husband.

The information is to be given directly to Nero Wolfe, who will use it on my behalf, and the person or persons supplying it will do so under these conditions:

1. All decisions regarding the significance and value of any item of information will be made solely by Nero Wolfe and will be final.

2. The total amount paid will be $50,000. If more than one person supplies useful information, the determination of their relative value and of the distribution of the $50,000 will be made solely by Nero Wolfe and will be final.

3. Any person who communicates with Nero Wolfe or his agent as a result of this advertisement thereby agrees to the above conditions.

"With your name at the bottom," I said. "A reproduction of your signature, Madeline Odell, like on your check, and below it 'Mrs. Peter J. Odell' in parenthesis, as usual, printed. Now hear this. Of course he'll know I wrote it, but if he thinks I wrote it at home and brought it, he'll balk. No go. As I said, that's why I didn't type it there. It has to be your idea, suggested by you after I told you about his reaction to Saul Panzer's suggestion. He may phone you. If he does, you'll have to do it right. Then of course the question will be, what will happen? I think it will work, and certainly it *may* work. It's ten to one that someone knows something that would crack it open, and fifty grand is a lot of bait."

I was on my feet. "So if you'll sign it, the original, and keep the carbon, and I'll need two samples of your signature on plain paper, one for the *Times* and one for the *Gazette,* to make cuts."

"You're pretty good," she said.

"I try hard. Whence all but me have fled."

"What?"

"The burning deck."

"What burning deck?"

"You don't read the right poems." I swiveled the chair. "Sit here? That pen is stingy, I tried it. Mine's better."

"So is the one on my desk." She moved, went to the other desk, which was bigger, and sat. "I'm not convinced, you know. This could be an act. You can phone to say it didn't work."

"If I do, it won't be an act, it will be because he is pigheaded. I mean strong-minded. It will depend on you if he phones."

"Well." She reached for the pen in an elegant jade stand. "*I* have a suggestion. It shouldn't be fifty thousand. Figures like that, fifty thousand or a hundred thousand, they don't hit. In-between figures are better, like sixty-five thousand or eighty-five."

"Right. Absolutely. Change it. Make it sixty-five. Just draw a line through the fifty thousand."

She tried the pen on a scratch pad. I always do.

13

IT WORKED.

Driving downtown and across to the garage on Tenth Avenue, I considered the approach. Over the years I suppose I have told Wolfe 10,000 bare-faced lies, or, if you prefer in-between figures, make it 8,392, either on personal matters that were none of his business or on business details that couldn't hurt and might help, but I have no desire to break a world record, and anyway the point was to make it stick if possible. I decided on a flank attack and then to play it by ear.

When I entered the office at 6:22, he was at his desk working on the Double-Crostic in the *Times,* and of course I didn't interrupt. I took my jacket off and draped it on the back of my chair, loosened my tie, went to the safe and got the checkbook and took it to my desk, and got interested in the stubs for the month of June. *That* was a flank attack all right. In a few minutes, maybe eight, he looked up and frowned at me and asked, "What's the balance now?"

"It depends," I said. I twisted around to get Exhibit A from my jacket pocket and rose and handed it across. He read it, taking his time, dropped it on the desk, narrowed his eyes at me, and said, "Grrr."

"She changed the fifty to sixty-five herself," I said. "That heading could have been Archie Goodwin has sixty-five thousand instead of Nero Wolfe. She didn't actually suggest it, but she thinks I'm pretty good. She said so. When I told her you were quitting and handed her the check, she said, 'How much did Browning pay him?' I told her that if I talked for five hours I might be able to convince her that you wouldn't double-cross a client, but actually I doubt it. You may not give a damn what she thinks of my employer, but I do. I brought her to you. She said things and I said things, and when it became evident that nothing else would convince her, I went to a typewriter and wrote that. I don't claim the wording is perfect. I am not Norman Mailer."

"Bah. That peacock? That blowhard?"

"All right, make it Hemingway."

"There was a typewriter there?"

"Sure. It was the big room on the fourth floor where apparently she does everything but eat and sleep. As you see, the paper is a twenty-pound bond at least half rag. Yours is only twenty percent rag."

He gave it a look, a good look, and I made a note to pat myself on the back for not doing it on my typewriter. "I admit," I said, "that I didn't try to talk her out of it. I certainly did not. In discussing it I told her that I thought it would work, that it's ten to one that someone knows something that would crack it open, and that fifty grand is a lot of bait. That was before she changed it to sixty-five. This is a long answer to your question, What's the balance? As I said, it depends. I brought the check back, but it would only cost eight cents to mail it. If we do, the balance will be a little under six thousand dollars. There was the June fifteenth income tax payment. I'm not badgering you, I'm just answering your question. But I'll permit myself to mention that this way it would not be a frantic squawk for someone to pull you out of a mudhole. I will also mention that if I phone her that the ad—correction, advertisement—has been placed, she will mail another check. For sixty-five thousand. She would make it a million if it would help. As of now nothing else on earth matters to her."

What he did was typical, absolutely him. He didn't say "Very well" or "Tear the check up" or even "Confound it." He picked the thing up, read it slowly, scowling at it, put it to one side under a paper weight, said "I'm doing some smoked sturgeon Muscovite. Please bring a bottle of Madeira from the cellar," and picked up the Double-Crostic.

14

THE AD WAS on page 6 of the *Times* Tuesday morning and page 9 of the *Gazette* that afternoon—two columns, bold face, with plenty of space all around—and two more conditions had been added:

1. *The $65,000 may all be paid to one person, or it may be divided among two or more people.*
2. *The $65,000 or any part of it will be paid only for information, not for a suggestion, conjecture, or theory.*

The other conditions, with only three words changed, followed.

We had discussed a certain probability and decided nothing could be done about it. Would Homicide South see the ad? Sure. Would they keep an eye, several eyes, on our front door to see who came? Sure again. Then what? They would horn in on our investigation of a murder. They would try to get for nothing what our client had offered $65,000 for. They would probably even put a tap on our phone, and the scientists have done such wonders for mankind that you can no longer tell whether your wire has been tapped or not. I admit science works both ways; we intended to record all conversations with callers, either in person or by phone. Also, with the bank balance fat again, we had reserves ready. Saul and Fred and Orrie were back, and at two P.M. Tuesday they were in the front room playing pinochle.

The very first one was wild. There had been four phone calls, but they had all been obvious screwballs. The first one in the flesh rang the doorbell a little before three o'clock. Through the one-way glass panel in the front door, he looked like a screwball too, but I opened the door and he handed me a card—a small blue card with a name on it in fancy dark blue letters: Nasir ibn Bekr. Okay, a foreign screwball, but I let him in. He was slim and wiry, he came about up to my chin, his hair and face and eyes were all very dark, and his nose would have gone with a man twice his size. On that warm June day his jacket was buttoned and the collar of his blue shirt was limp. When I turned after closing the door, he handed me a piece of paper, the ad clipped from the *Times,* and said, "I will see Mr. Nero Wolfe."

"Perhaps," I said. "He's busy. You have information?"

"I am not sure. I may have."

Not a screwball. Screwballs are sure. I asked him to wait, motioning to the bench, took the card to the office and handed it to Wolfe, and was told to bring him, but I didn't have to. He was there, right behind me. The big Keraghan in the office is thick, but there's no rug in the hall; he was the silent type. He should be closer to me than the red leather chair, so I blocked it off and motioned to the yellow one near the corner of my desk. Then I went and closed the door to the hall, for a reason. The arrangement was that when I admitted a visitor and intended to show him to the office, I would notify the trio by tapping on the door to the front room. When I had got the visitor to the office, I would close that door so that they would not be seen as they went down the hall to the alcove at the kitchen end, and they would take a look at the visitor through the peephole that was covered on the office side by a trick picture of a waterfall. They would also listen. As I crossed back to my desk, Nasir ibn Bekr said, "Of course this is being recorded," and I said, "Then I won't have to take notes."

Wolfe said, "The conditions in the advertisement are clear?"

He nodded. "Certainly. Perfectly clear. The information I have, it is my personal knowledge, but its worth is for you to determine.

I must ask a question. We find nothing in your record to indicate clearly your position regarding the situation in the Near East. Are you anti-Zionist?"

"No."

He turned to me. "Are you?"

"No. My only objection to Jews is that one of them is as good a poker player as I am. Sometimes a little better."

He nodded. "They have learned how to use guile. They have had to." To Wolfe: "Perhaps you know that there are Arab terrorists —mostly Palestinians—active in this country, mostly in Washington and New York."

"It is said that there are, yes."

"It is not just said. There *are*. I am one." He unbuttoned the top button of his jacket, slipped his hand in, and brought out a small brown envelope. From it he got a folded paper. He rose to hand it to Wolfe, but terrorists are in my department and I moved fast enough to get a hand to it first. As I unfolded it, he sat and said, "That is the names of five men, but I am not sure it is their real names. It is the only names I know for them. We meet every week, once a week, on Sunday afternoon, in an apartment in Jackson Heights. That is the address and telephone number. Armad Qarmat lives there. I do not have addresses for the others. As you see, my name is not there. I have printed them because with names like ours that is better than writing."

I had given it a look and handed it to Wolfe.

"I see you have television," Nasir ibn Bekr said. "Perhaps you saw a program on CAN in May, May seventh, 'Oil and Mecca.' "

Wolfe shook his head. "I turn on the television rarely, only to confirm my opinion of it." Not having been asked, I didn't say that I had seen the "Oil and Mecca" program at Lily Rowan's.

"It was a full hour," the terrorist said. "It was partly a documentary in pictures of the production of oil in Arab countries, but it was also a commentary. It did not say that the existence and welfare of Israel were of more importance to civilization, and of course to democracy, than the Arabian oil, but it strongly implied that. It was definitely anti-Arabian and pro-Israel. That was a Wednesday. The following Sunday we discussed it, and we wrote a letter to CAN demanding a retraction of the lies it told. The next Sunday Armad said there had been no answer to the letter, and he had learned that the man responsible for the program was a vice-president of CAN named Amory Browning. That was Sunday, May eighteenth. We decided that it was an opportunity to take action against the anti-Arabian propaganda in this country."

His head turned to me and back to Wolfe. "I should explain that I became a member of the group only a year ago, not quite a year, and I am not yet completely in their confidence. Especially Armad Qarmat has not fully decided about me, and that is why I said I am not sure, I *may* have information. I do know they had three bombs, I saw them one day. In April. That Sunday, May eighteenth, one of them suggested using one of the bombs at the CAN office, and if possible the office of Amory Browning. There was some discussion, and I saw that Armad Qarmat stopped it on account of me. As I said, he has not fully accepted me. The next Sunday, May twenty-fifth, one of them spoke of the explosion of a bomb in Amory Browning's office, killing Peter Odell, another vice-president, but Armad Qarmat said that should not be discussed. Since then there have been four meetings, four Sundays, and the bomb has not been mentioned."

He tilted his head back and took a couple of breaths, then looked at me and back at Wolfe. "There," he said, "I have told you. This morning I saw your advertisement. Sixty-five thousand dollars is a great deal of money. It will be better if I am frank. At first I thought I would give you more . . . more detail. More that was said, as I am sure it must have been said, when I was not present. But then I saw it would be better to tell you exactly how it was, and that is what I have done. The advertisement does not say you require proof."

He slipped his hand inside his jacket, again produced the brown envelope, and took something from it. "In my position," he said, "I have to consider the possibilities. This is a piece of a dollar bill that I tore in half. If you find that what I have told you is the information you ask for in your advertisement, and if I do not come to claim the sixty-five thousand dollars, it may be because I can't. If I am dead, I can't. In that case someone else will come, and if so he will have the other half of the dollar bill. Will that be satisfactory?" He put the piece of the bill on Wolfe's desk, and I went and got it. It was a ragged tear. I handed it to Wolfe.

He cocked his head at the terrorist. "I suppose," he said, "you speak Arabic."

"Of course."

"Arabic is spoken at your Sunday meetings?"

"Of course."

"Fortunately. For you. Your attempt at speaking English as it would be spoken by a cultured Palestinian is inept. You shouldn't try it. What is your real name?"

He didn't bat an eye. "That wouldn't help you," he said. Then he asked a question. To me the words he used were only sounds, but I knew it was a question by the inflection.

"I did," Wolfe said, "but long ago. Arabic is not one of my languages. I want your name because I may need to ask you something."

Nasir ibn Bekr shook his head. "I have told you all I know that could help. This is a big risk for me, coming to you at all, and I will not add to it. You are right, Arabic is not my native tongue. My native tongue is Spanish. But my Arabic is good; it must be. I will say this, if something happens, if one of them says something that you should know, I will telephone or come." He rose and buttoned the top button of his jacket, looked at me and back at Wolfe, and said, "I must thank you."

"A moment," Wolfe said. "This house is under surveillance. By the police. Mr. Goodwin will show you out—at the rear. There's a passage through to Thirty-fourth Street."

The terrorist shook his head. "That isn't necessary. Thank you again, but I can't be followed. No matter who tries, even in Baghdad or Cairo I can get loose."

He moved, and I went to open the door. It would have been mildly interesting to step out to the stoop and see who came out from where, to tail him, but I didn't want to give anyone the idea that we gave a damn. As I turned from shutting the front door, I called down the hall, "All clear!" and the trio appeared from the alcove and followed me into the office. They lined up at the end of Wolfe's desk.

"Comments," Wolfe said. "Fred?"

"I don't think so," Fred said. "How would he get in Browning's room when no one was there, and why would he pick the bottom drawer?"

"Orrie?"

"The League of Jewish Patriots," Orrie said.

"No," Saul said, "he's not the type. They're all athletes. Of course he's a Jew, but not that kind. I agree with Fred. His reasons, and also the timing. The bomb doesn't have to be connected with the fact that that was the day they were going to decide on the new president, but it's hard to believe that it wasn't."

"But it's only ten to one," I said. "Even if it's twenty to one we have to give it a look."

"Actually," Wolfe said, "he is taking no risk. Even if he knows there is only one chance in a thousand, he is giving himself that chance to fill a purse.—Archie. Type this list of names, adding his name, and the address, and give it to Fred. Fred, you will see if it is worth an effort. Enter that apartment only with all possible precaution; it isn't worth even the slightest hazard. Our usual understanding, of course. Further comments?"

There weren't any. I swung the typewriter around, Fred sat, and Saul and Orrie went to the front room.

That's a sample of what the ad brought us. I don't say typical; it wasn't. Of course if you advertised in those two papers that you had sixty-five grand to hand out, no matter what for, and your name and address were in the phone book, you would know you would get plenty of calls and callers, and the best we could expect was that just one of them would really have something. If what I was after was merely to fill pages, it would be easy to add a dozen or so with the next couple of days, up to 9:42 P.M. Thursday evening. Some of the items might even add to your knowledge of human nature—for instance, the middle-aged man in a spotless white suit and a bushy wig who had had a dream Tuesday night. He came Wednesday afternoon. In the dream a man had opened the bottom drawer of a desk and fastened, with tape, a small plastic box to the partition above the drawer, about nine inches back from the front. A thin copper wire about a foot long protruded from the end of the box. With the drawer open only a couple of inches he had taped the loose end of the wire to the inside of the front of the drawer, and closed it, and departed. If we would show him photographs of the men who had entered or might have entered Amory Browning's room that day, he would tell us which one had put the box in the drawer, and he would so testify under oath. That was what made it really good, that he would testify without even being subpoenaed. Or the female star buff who phoned for an appointment and came Thursday morning—a skinny specimen with hollow cheeks and big dreamy eyes. If we would give her the birth dates of all the suspects she would supply information that would almost certainly do the trick.

There were three or four that Saul and Orrie spent some time and effort on. Fred had made no headway with the Arab terrorists.

To show you how low I was by Thursday evening after dinner, I'll admit what I was doing. First, what I wasn't doing. I was not at the poker table at Saul's apartment. I was in no mood for being sociable, and I would probably have drawn to an inside straight. I was at my desk in the office, scowling at the entries in a little looseleaf book which I call The Nero Wolfe Backlog. It contained a list of certain items that were in his safe deposit box at the Continental Trust Company, and I was considering which one or ones should be disposed of at the current market price if I was asked for a suggestion, as I would be soon if we got nothing better than Arab terrorists and dreamers and star buffs. Wolfe was at his desk with a book of stories by Turgenev, and that was bad too.

When he's low he always picks something that he has already read more than once.

When the doorbell rang, I glanced at my wrist watch as I rose, as usual. Sometimes it's needed for the record. Eighteen minutes to ten. I went to the hall, flipped the switch of the stoop light, took a look, stepped back in the office, and said, "You'll have to mark your place. It's Dennis Copes."

"You haven't seen Dennis Copes."

"No, but Saul described him."

He shut the book without using the bookmark, and of course no dog ear, since it was Turgenev. I went and opened the front door, and the visitor said, "You're Archie Goodwin," and stepped right in as if I wasn't there.

"And you're—" I said.

"Copes. Dennis Copes. Not as famous as you, but I will be. Is your famous fat boss available?"

I was so damn glad to see him, to see someone who might actually have something to bite on, that I thought that on him the long hair and two-inch sideburns looked just fine. And when, in the office, he marched across and put out a hand, Wolfe took it. He seldom shakes hands with anybody, and never with strangers. He *was* low. As Copes sat he hitched his pants legs up—the nervous hands Saul had mentioned.

"That was a good ad," he said. " 'Any person who communicates as a result of this advertisement thereby agrees to the above conditions.' Very neat. What agency?"

Wolfe frowned. "Agency?"

"Who wrote it?"

"Mr. Goodwin."

"Oh." He looked at me: "Nice going Archie." Back to Wolfe: "That ad would have made a wonderful five-minute spot—you and Mrs. Odell, you right here at your desk and her standing with her hand on your shoulder. You would do most of the talking, with your voice. She would have been glad to pay for prime time—say ten o'clock. A much bigger audience than the ad. Didn't you consider it?

"No."

"Too bad. How many nibbles have you had?"

"None."

"None? Impossible. All right, you're not telling and why should you? But you can't say it's none of my damn business, because in a way it is. If someone else knows what I know, and if they've already told you, I've missed the bus. Have you—let's see, how shall I put it—has anyone told you anything that makes you want to have a talk with Kenneth Meer or Helen Lugos?"

Wolfe eyed him. "Mr. Copes. Mrs. Odell's advertisement asks for information *to* me, not *from* me. I'll say this: if I had received information that gave me reason to speak with Miss Lugos or Mr. Meer, I would have arranged to see them, and I haven't."

Copes nodded. "Fair enough. Now I have to admit something. I have to admit that I should have told the police what I'm going to tell you. I admit I'm not exactly proud of the reason *why* I didn't tell them. I admit it wasn't because of any love I have for Kenneth Meer or Helen Lugos; it was because it would have put me right in the thick of a damn nasty murder mess. All right, I admit that. With you it's different on two counts. One, you won't handle it like they would. You'll have more consideration for—well, for *me.* Two, if you get what I think you'll get, *I'll* get sixty-five thousand dollars and *can* I use it!"

The fingertips of his right hand were dancing a jig on the chair arm, and he turned the hand over and curled them. "Part of what I'm going to tell you probably won't be news to you. You probably know why Odell went to Browning's room and opened that drawer. Don't you?"

Wolfe grunted. "Do you?"

"Yes. He was going to put LSD in the whisky bottle so Browning would bobble it at the directors' meeting or not even be there. You probably know that, from Mrs. Odell. I'm going to tell you how

I know it. How I *knew* it. I knew it the day before, that he was going to. I knew it on Monday, May nineteenth."

"Indeed."

"Yes. Of course you know there were two doors to Browning's room—one from the anteroom, Helen Lugos's room, and one from the hall. And here's another thing I have to admit, another reason I haven't told the police: that Monday afternoon I entered Browning's room by the door from the hall when I knew he wasn't there. It was right after lunch, and I—"

"Wasn't that door locked?"

"Not always. When Browning left by that door to go down the hall to the rear, he usually pushed the button on the lock so he could go back in without using his key. I wanted to look at something I knew was on his desk, and I knew he wasn't there, so I tried that door and it opened. I didn't make any noise because I didn't want to be interrupted by Helen Lugos, and the door to her room was half open, and I could hear voices—hers and Kenneth Meer's. Mostly his. I suppose this is being recorded."

"Yes."

"Of course. What isn't?" He took a notebook from his pocket and opened it. "So I'd better read it. The first thing I heard him say—he said, 'No, I'm not going to tell you how I found out. That doesn't matter anyway, I *did* find out. Odell is going to dope that bottle of whisky with LSD tomorrow afternoon, or he thinks he is, and I want to be damn sure you don't open the drawer to take a look at the usual time. Don't open it any time after lunch. Don't open it at all, don't go near it, because—well, *don't.*' And she said, 'But Ken, you'll have to tell me—Wait. I'd better make sure—' And there was the sound of her pushing her chair back."

The fingertips were at it again, this time on his knee. "So I got out quick. She was probably going to come to make sure there was no one in Browning's room. I hadn't got to the desk, I was only a couple of steps from the door—I had left it open a crack—and I got out fast. I didn't go back to my room because there's another man in it with me and I wanted to be alone, so I went to the men's room and sat on the john to think it over. Of course what I wanted to do, I wanted to tell Browning. Maybe Meer was going to tell him but from what he said it didn't sound like it. But I didn't want to tell Browning I had entered his room by the hall door—of course I didn't. And I didn't know what Meer intended to do. I knew he intended to do something since he had told her not to go near the drawer, but what? What would *you* have thought he intended to do?"

Wolfe shook his head. "I don't know him. You did."

"Sure, I knew him, but not well enough for that. For instance, I thought he might wait until about four o'clock Tuesday and then take the bottle from the drawer and put another bottle in its place, and have the whisky analyzed and have the bottle checked for fingerprints. He knew Browning never took a drink until about half past four or a quarter to five, when the program scripts had all been okayed. I considered all the possibilities, what *I* could do, and the one thing I *had* to do was make sure that Browning didn't drink any doped whisky. So I decided to be there in the room with him Tuesday when he okayed the last script—I usually was—and when he got the bottle out, I would say that there was nothing Odell wouldn't do to get the president's job, and it might be a good idea to open the other bottle. There was always another bottle there, unopened, often two."

"You knew that," Wolfe said.

"Sure, several of us did. Often a couple of us were there when he opened the drawer. One thing I considered: tell Browning that I had heard Meer say that to Helen, but not that I had been in his room. But that would have been very tricky because where was I and where were they? You may know that a lot of people think I want Meer's job."

"That has been said, yes."

"Maybe I do and maybe I don't. I want to get on, sure, who doesn't, but it doesn't have to be *his* job. Anyway, I had to consider that too. Of course if I had known what Meer was going to do, if I had even suspected it, I would have gone straight to Browning and told him just like it was. I didn't and of course I regret it."

"You're assuming that Meer had decided to put a bomb in the drawer?"

"Certainly. My God, don't I have to? *Didn't* I have to?"

"You made that assumption that day—the next day? When you learned what had happened?

"I certainly did."

"Five weeks ago. Five weeks and two days. What have you done to verify it?"

Copes nodded. "It's easy to ask that. What *could* I have done? Could I ask people if they had seen Meer with a bomb? Could I ask them if they had seem him go into Browning's room? Could I ask Helen Lugos *anything?* Could I hire a detective? Naturally you're thinking I may have cooked this up. Of course you are. You'd be a damn fool if you didn't. But there's one detail, one fact, that you have to consider. As I said, you probably knew that Odell went there to put LSD in the whisky because Mrs. Odell probably told you, but how did I know? One thing, Odell must have had the LSD with him, but there has been no mention of it. It could be that the police are reserving it, or it could be that he had it in his hand when he opened the drawer and no traces of it have been found, but I doubt that because they are very thorough and very expert on that kind of thing. Probably they're keeping it back. Maybe you know?"

Wolfe skipped it. "That's a detail, yes. Not conclusive, but indicative. You're aware, Mr. Copes, that without support your information is worthless. If I challenge Mr. Meer or Miss Lugos by telling them what you have told me and they say you lie, what then? Have you a suggestion?"

"No. The ad didn't say I have to tell you how to *use* the information. You're Nero Wolfe, the great detective; I'm just a guy who happened to hear something. Of course I realize Browning will have to know I entered his room that way, that will have to come out, maybe even on the witness stand. You've got it now on tape. If it costs me my job I'll need that sixty-five thousand. Should I tell Browning myself? Now?"

"No." Wolfe made it positive. "Tell nobody anything. May I see that notebook?"

"Certainly." He took it from his pocket and got up to hand it over. It was loose-leaf with little rings. Wolfe gave several pages a look and stopped at one.

"Did you write this that day? Monday?"

"No. I wrote it the next day, Tuesday evening, after the—after what happened. But that's exactly what he said. I can swear to it."

"You may have to." Wolfe handed the notebook back to him. "I can't tell you how I'll proceed, Mr. Copes, because I don't know. If I need you, I'll know where to find you." He leaned back, his head against the chair back, and shut his eyes. I honestly don't know if he realizes that that's no way to end a conversation. I do.

15

SAUL AND Fred and Orrie and I are still discussing what Wolfe said that Friday morning—or rather, what we *didn't* say.

They came at ten o'clock and I played it back for them twice—the tape of the talk with Dennis Copes—and we considered two angles: one, Was it straight or had he hatched it to get Meer? and two, If it was straight, how were we going to wrap it up? By eleven o'clock, when Wolfe came down from the plant rooms, we hadn't got very far with either one. He told us good morning, put a raceme of Dendrobium chrysotoxum in the vase on his desk, sat and sent his eyes around, and asked, "Have you a program?"

"Sure," I said. "Just what you're expecting, ask you for instructions."

"One thing," Saul said. "He comes first. How good is it?"

"Obviously. On that he said one thing that was strikingly suggestive. Have you considered it?"

We looked at one another. "Well," Saul said, "that line about him being just a guy who happened to hear something. We agree that that sounds good. If he's faking it that's *very* good. A wonderful line."

Wolfe shook his head. "I mean something quite different. One specific thing he said that suggests a possible answer to all questions. You haven't considered it?"

"We considered everything." I said. "What specific thing?"

He shook his head again. "Not now. Even if it means what it *may* mean, we must first decide about him. The detail which—as he said—we have to consider: if he didn't learn about the LSD as he says he did, then how? Of course you have discussed that. And?"

"And nothing," Orrie said. "We've talked with a lot of people these two weeks, and not the slightest hint of the LSD angle from anyone. You told us to keep that good and tight and we did."

I said, "The only mention of it we have heard has been from Mrs. Odell and Falk, and he got it from her. Possibly he also got it from his cousin who is an assistant DA, but he didn't say so. Apparently it *is* tight. Abbott evidently thinks Odell had a bomb in his pocket, not LSD."

Wolfe nodded. "We'll have to explore the possibilities. Orrie. You will try again with the CAN personnel, this time on the one question, could his knowledge of the LSD have come through anyone there? He need not have learned it a month or even a week ago; even yesterday would do. Take care not to divulge it yourself. Fred. Forget the Palestinians. You are on speaking terms with members of the police force. A dozen?"

"Only two in Homicide," Fred said.

"That may be enough. Knowledge of the LSD may not be limited to the Homicide men. The first to arrive at the scene may have found it. You need not take pains to reserve our knowledge of it; Mr. Cramer knows that we know about it. Does one of them know Mr. Copes or anyone connected with him?—Saul. You will try the other possible source, Mrs. Odell and Miss Haber. I doubt if Mrs. Odell has mentioned it to anyone whatever, but Miss Haber procured the LSD for her, and Mr. Copes would have needed to know only that to make a plausible conjecture. Does Mr. Copes know anyone she knows and might have told? Probably you should try from his end, not hers, but that's for you to decide. Have enough cash with you. If there is any urgent need for help, Archie will be here."

Wolfe's eyes went to Fred, to Orrie, and back to Saul. "We want this, messieurs. If you find another probable source for Mr. Copes's knowledge of the LSD, it will be more than satisfactory. Ironically, it will probably get him sixty-five thousand dollars for supplying the required information. I wish you luck."

As Saul stood he said, "I have a question. Might it help if we knew what he said that was strikingly suggestive? Could it hurt?"

"Yes, it could hurt. It could divert your interest. I shouldn't have mentioned it. My tendency to strut. Display, like diffidence, is commendable only when it avails. Ignore it."

Just fine. What else could they do? Not to mention me. So when they were gone, I ignored it. I sat and ignored it while he glanced through the little stack of mail I had put on his desk, and when he looked up I asked, "Do I do anything while I am being here?"

"Yes," he said. "This is Friday."

"Right."

"I would like to see Miss Lugos and Mr. Meer, not together. And not today. It's possible that today or this evening we'll get something. Miss Lugos at eleven o'clock tomorrow and Mr. Meer at three?"

"It's a June weekend and it may take pressure. I'm not objecting, I'm just asking. I would enjoy pressing somebody. Anybody."

"So would I."

I got at the phone and dialed.

16

THAT AFTERNOON Orrie and I had a two-piece argument, first on the phone and then face-to-face. Around three o'clock he called to say he would be working the whole weekend because he was taking a female CAN researcher to Atlantic City. I asked if he wished to leave a message for Jill, his wife, in case she called, and he said she was in Tokyo, which was plausible since she was an airline hostess. I said he would be paid to six P.M. Friday, and he said he would come and discuss it. He came a little after four, knowing that Wolfe would be up in the plant rooms, and said it would be a working weekend and he should also get twenty cents a mile for the use of his car; he might get something useful from her and he was certainly going to try. I said okay, eight hours Saturday and eight Sunday, he couldn't expect to be paid for the time he spent in bed, and he said bed was the best place to get really confidential, and I had to agree. But not eight dollars an hour for fifty-two hours, and not the hotel bill. He said Mrs. Odell had a billion, and I said not more than a hundred million even with inflation, and we should leave her something for groceries. We finally settled on a lump sum to cover everything, $364.00, which was seven dollars an hour. I may as well mention now that the client got exactly nothing for that little expense item.

By eleven o'clock Saturday morning, when Helen Lugos came, Fred had also drawn a blank. He had talked with five city employes he knew, one of them a sergeant in Homicide, and none of them had had any contact with Dennis Copes or had any information about him. He doubted if any of them knew about the LSD, but of course they might be keeping the lid on. He was proceeding.

Saul had collected a bag of facts about Copes—where and how he lived, his habits, his friends, his background, his personal finances—but nothing that gave us any pointers, so they wouldn't give you any either, and I'll skip them. He had found no connection whatever with Mrs. Odell or Charlotte Haber, but was preparing an approach to Charlotte's kid brother, since there had been a hint that it was on account of him that she had known how to get the LSD.

Helen Lugos not only wasn't late this time, she was ten minutes early, so she was stuck with a mere agent again until Wolfe came down from the plant rooms. She wanted to know what was so urgent that she had to change her weekend plans, and I explained that I only obeyed orders.

Wolfe entered, told me good morning first and then her, put the flowers for the day in the vase and arranged them so he would have the best view, swiveled his chair to face her, and sat.

"I don't thank you for coming," he said. "I'm not disposed to thank you for anything. I have reason to believe that you are withholding information that would be of value. Indeed, I think you have lied. Don't bother to deny it. I tell you that only to establish the temper of the conversation. I'll be trying to find support for my opinion. What will you be doing?"

She would be staring. She *was* staring. "I know what I *ought* to be doing," she said. "Leaving. I ought to be on my way out."

"But you're not. You wouldn't, even if I'm wrong, because you want to know why. That's what makes us the unique animal, we want to know why and try to find out. We even try to discover why we want to know why, though of course we never will. It's possible that upon consideration you have concluded, or at least suspected, that you may have made a mistake or two. For instance, nineteen days ago, a Monday evening, I asked you if you thought it likely that the person who put the bomb in the drawer was present in this room and you said you had no idea. 'None at all,' you said. And twelve days ago, again a Monday, when you were alone with Mr. Goodwin and he asked what you would say if he asked that question, you replied that you would say exactly the same, you had no idea. I'll try once more. What would you say now?"

"My god," she said. "How many times . . ."

"What would you say now?"

"The same!"

Wolfe nodded. "You should know, Miss Lugos, that this is being recorded electronically. The recorder is on a closet shelf in the kitchen, so that a man there can change the tape if necessary. I now have a special reason for wanting to learn beyond question the nature of your relations with Kenneth Meer. What you tell me will be tested thoroughly by wide inquiry. So?"

"It has already been tested by the police." Her chin was up and a muscle in the side of her neck was twitching, barely perceptible even by good eyes. "We're not—we're associated in our work because we have to be. Personally we don't—we are not close."

"But he would like to be?"

"He thinks he—yes."

"Do you read books?"

She did what everybody does when asked an unexpected and irrelevant question. Her eyes widened and her lips parted. For two seconds exactly the same as if he had asked her if she ate cats. Then she said, "Why—yes. I read books."

"Do you read much fiction?"

"I read *some.*"

"Then you may be aware that most competent storytellers, even lesser ones, have an instinctive knowledge of the possibilities of human conduct. They often present two characters who have a strong mutual attachment in secret but who have other people believing that they are hostile. But not the reverse. Not two who have a mutual animus but have others believing that they like or love each other. Storytellers know it can't be done. So do I. I know I can't learn if you and Mr. Meer are in fact close by asking you questions and watching your face as you answer them, so I won't try. I know it's futile for me to ask you anything at all, but I wanted to see you again and hear you speak, and I would like to ask one specific question, more for what the question will tell you than for what the answer will tell me. Mr. Goodwin got your detailed account of your movements on that Tuesday, May twentieth. I would like one detail of the preceding day, Monday, May nineteenth. In the early afternoon, shortly after lunch, Mr. Meer was with you in your room. Tête-à-tête. What did you talk about? What was said?"

I won't say I actually enjoyed what happened next, but I appreciated being there to see it. Having seen him walk out on people I don't know how many times, say a hundred, it kind of evened up to see him once as the walkee instead of the walker. She didn't glare or clamp her jaw or spit, she just got up and went. I admit he didn't glare or spit either; he just sat and watched her go. I did too until she was out; then I stepped to the hall to see that she shut the front door. When I stepped back in, he was opening the drawer to get the bottle opener—so he had rung for beer.

"Tell me once more," I said, "that I understand women better than you do. It gives me confidence. But don't ask me to prove it. I said two weeks ago that she didn't open the bag and shake it. I also said she didn't plant the bomb, but now I don't know. Did Copes strikingly suggest that she did?"

"Confound Copes," he growled. "And nothing can be expected from Saul or Fred during the weekend."

He picked up the top item on the stack of the morning mail. It was a check from Mrs. Odell for $65,000.

17

KENNETH MEER was early too. When I answered the doorbell a little before three, I saw his car down at the curb, a dark green Jaguar. He had an oversized brief case, brown leather, under his arm, presumably to save the trouble of locking the car, and when I asked if he wanted to leave it on the hall bench, he said no and took it along to the office. I said before, when I first saw him, that his poorly designed face was tired too young, and now, as he sat in the red leather chair and blinked at Wolfe, his long, pointed nose above his wide square chin looked like a exclamation point with a long line crossing at the bottom instead of a dot.

He kept the brief case on his lap. "I resent this," he said. He sounded as peevish as he looked. "Why couldn't I come yesterday —last evening? Why today?"

Wolfe nodded. "I owe you an apology, Mr. Meer. You have it. I hoped to have by now definite information on a point I wanted to discuss with you, but it hasn't come. However, since you're here, we may as well consider another point. Your bloody hands. A week after the explosion of that bomb you were in distress, severe enough to take you to that clinic and then to me. Later, when I became professionally involved, the nature of your distress was of course of interest. There were various possibilities: You had yourself put the bomb in the drawer and the burden of guilt was too heavy for you. Or you hadn't, but you knew or suspected who had, and your conscience was galling you; your imagined bloody hands were insisting, *please pass the guilt.* Or merely the event itself had hit you too hard; the sight of the havoc and the actual blood on your hands had put you in shock. Those were all valid guesses, but Mr. Goodwin and I didn't bother to discuss them; we rarely waste time discussing guesses."

"I like that, *please pass the guilt,*" Meer said. "I like that."

"So do I. Mr. Goodwin will too. He once said that I ride words bareback. But the devil of it is that after more than three weeks the guesses are still guesses, and it may possibly help to mention them to you. Have you a comment?"

"No."

"None at all?"

"No."

"Does the distress persist? Do you still get up in the middle of the night to wash your hands?"

"No."

"Then something that has been done or said must have removed the pressure, or at least eased it. What? Do you know?

"No."

Wolfe shook his head. "I can't accept that. This morning I was blunt with Miss Lugos and told her I thought she was lying. Now I think you are. There is another point concerning you that I haven't broached that I'll mention now. Why did you tell a man that anyone who wanted to know how it happened should concentrate on Helen Lugos?"

Meer didn't frown or cock his head or even blink. He merely said, "I didn't."

Wolfe's head turned. "Archie?"

"You said it," I told Meer, "to Pete Damiano. I can't name the day, but it was soon after it happened. About a month ago."

"Oh, him." He grinned, or make it that he probably thought he grinned. "Pete would say anything."

"That's witless," Wolfe said. "You knew it was likely, at least possible, that that would be remembered and you would be asked about it, and you should have had a plausible reply ready. Merely to deny it won't do. It's obvious that you're implicated, either by something you know or something you did, and you should be prepared to deal with contingencies. I am, and I believe one is imminent. I ask you the same question I asked Miss Lugos this morning, in the same terms: In the early afternoon of Monday, May nineteenth, shortly after lunch, you were with Miss Lugos in her room, tête-à-tête. What did you talk about? What was said?"

That got a frown. "You asked her that? What did she say?"

"What did *you* say?"

"Nothing. I don't remember."

"Pfui. I've asked you seven questions and got only no's and nothings. I've apologized to you; now I apologize to myself. Another time, Mr. Meer. Mr. Goodwin will show you out."

I rose, but stood, because Meer thought he was going to say something. His lips parted twice but closed again. He looked up at me, saw only an impassive mug, got up, tucked the brief case under his arm, and moved. I followed him, but got ahead in the hall, opened the front door, and waited until he was down and at the door of the Jaguar to close it. Back in the office, I asked, "Do we need to discuss any guesses?"

Wolfe grunted. "You might as well have gone before lunch. Shall I apologize to you?"

"No, thanks. The phone number is on your pad, as usual." I went and got my bag from the hall and let myself out, on my way to the garage for the Heron and then to the West Side Highway, headed for Lily Rowan's glade in Westchester. That's what she calls it, The Glade.

18

AMORY BROWNING did something Monday morning that had never been done before. He walked down the aisles of the three plant rooms, clear to the potting room, without seeing an orchid. I didn't actually see him, since he was behind me, but I'm sure he did. With that blaze of color, right and left and overhead, you'd think he would have to be blind. In a way he was.

It was twenty past ten and I had just returned from a walk crosstown to the bank and back, to deposit the check from the client, when the ring of the doorbell took me to the hall, and there was the next president of CAN. When I went and opened the door, he crossed the sill and went on by and headed for the office, and when I got there he was standing at the end of Wolfe's desk.

"Where is he?" he demanded.

"Where he always is at this hour, up on the roof. He'll be down at eleven. You can wait, or maybe I can help."

"Get him down here. Now."

The man at the top speaking, but he didn't look it. I had formerly estimated that he had been pudgy for about five years, but now I would have made it ten.

"It can't be done," I said. "With him a rule is a rule. He's part mule. If it's really urgent he might talk on the phone."

"Get him."

"I'll try." I went to the kitchen, sat at the little table where I eat breakfast, reached for the house phone, and pushed the "P" button.

After a two-minute wait, about par, the usual "Yes?"

"Me in the kitchen. Amory Browning is in the office. I once saw a picture somewhere of a dragon snorting fire. That's him. He ordered me to get you down here now. I told him you might talk on the phone."

Silence for eight seconds, then: "Bring him."

"Okay, but have something ready to throw."

The elevator will take up to 600 pounds, but I thought a little deep breathing would be good for him, so I took him to the stairs, and he surprised me by not stopping to catch up on oxygen at the landings. He wasn't panting even at the top. As I said, he was behind me down the aisles, but when I opened the door to the potting room I let him by. Wolfe, in his long-sleeved, yellow smock, was at the side bench opening a bale of tree fern. He turned part way and said, "You don't like to be interrupted at work. Neither do I."

Browning was standing with his feet apart. "You goddam cheap bully!"

"Not 'cheap.' I haven't earned that reproach. What do you want?"

"Nothing. Calling my secretary a liar. Getting her here on a Saturday morning just to butter your ego by insulting her. I came to tell you that you can tell Mrs. Odell that there will be no more cooperation from anyone at CAN. Tell her if she wants to know why, to call me. Is that plain enough?"

"Yes indeed. Is that what you came for, to tell me that?"

"Yes!"

"Very well, you've told me." Wolfe turned back to the bale of tree fern.

Browning was stuck. Of course with the "Is that plain enough?" he should have whirled and headed for the door. Now what could he do for an exit? He could only just go, and I admit he had sense enough to realize it. He just went, and I followed, and again he didn't see an orchid. I supposed that on the way down the three flights he would decide on an exit line to use on me, but evidently he was too mad to bother, though I passed him down in the hall and opened the door for him. Not a word. I went to the office and sat to ask myself why I had bothered to deposit the check.

And in three minutes the doorbell rang and I went to the hall and there was Saul Panzer.

It's moments like that that make life worth living, seeing Saul there on the stoop. If he had just wanted to make a routine report or ask a question or ask for help, he would have phoned. If he had wanted to consult Wolfe, he would have waited until eleven o'clock. And if he had bad news, he would have let his face show it as I came down the hall. So he had something good. I opened the door wide and said, "My god, are you welcome. How good is it?"

"I guess I'm awful obvious," he said, and stepped in. "I *think* it's satisfactory."

I slammed the door shut. "For a nickel I'd kiss you." I looked at my wrist: 10:47. "You'd rather tell him, but I don't want to wait thirteen minutes. Neither do you or you wouldn't be here yet. We'll go up."

It took us about half as long as it had taken Browning and me. I won't say that we didn't see an orchid as we passed through the rooms, but we didn't stop to admire one. Wolfe, still in the yellow smock, was at the sink washing his hands, and Theodore stood there with a paper towel ready for him. Theodore babies him, which is one of the reasons he is not my favorite fellow being.

Wolfe, turning and seeing Saul, was on as quick as I had been. He said, "Indeed," and ignored the dripping water from his hands. "What?"

"Yes, sir," Saul said. "Once in a while I do something exactly right and am lucky along with it, and that's a pleasure. I would enjoy leading up to it, but it's been a long time since we've brought you anything. Dennis Copes's twin sister, Diana, is the wife of Lieutenant J. M. Rowcliff. They have two children, a boy and a girl. Dennis and Diana see each other quite often—as I said, twins."

Wolfe took the towel from Theodore, patted with it, dropped it in the bin, took another, rubbed with it, missed the bin. It fluttered to the floor and Theodore picked it up. Wolfe flattened his right palm against his left and made slow circles.

"Are Mr. Rowcliff and Mr. Copes on good terms?"

"No. They see each other very seldom. Apparently never would suit them fine."

"Mr. Rowcliff and his wife?"

"Three people say they're happy. I know it's hard to believe that anybody could stand Rowcliff, but off duty he may be different."

"Have you caused a stir?"

"No."

That was Saul. Not "I hope not" or "I don't think so." Just "No."

"More than satisfactory." Wolfe took the smock off and hung it on a wall hook, got his vest and jacket from a hanger, and put them on. He looked at the clock on the bench: two minutes to eleven. "I want a word with Theodore and I'll consider this on the way down. Put a bottle of champagne in the refrigerator, Archie —and Saul, we'll probably need you."

Saul and I went.

I suppose I shouldn't include what happened next; it's just too pat. Who will believe it? But Fred deserves to have it in, and it happened. Saul and I had just got to the office, having stopped at the kitchen on the way, and were discussing how it should be handled, when the doorbell rang and I went. It was Fred. I opened the door, and as he entered he blurted, "Is he down yet?" I said he was on the way and he said, "If I hold it in any longer I'll bust. Copes's twin sister is married to that sonofabitch Rowcliff."

All right, it happened. In nineteen days they had got exactly nothing, and here came two of them, practically simultaneous, with the same beautiful slab of bacon. Saul, who had come to the hall and heard him, said, "So we need *two* bottles of champagne," and went to the kitchen. I was telling Fred that Saul had beat him by just sixteen minutes, when the elevator door opened and Wolfe was there, and when he saw the look on Fred's face, he knew what had happened, so I didn't have to tell him, but I did. He led the way to the office, and Saul came and he and Fred moved yellow chairs up.

Wolfe sat and said, "Get Mr. Cramer."

He has been known to rush it, and it had been a long dry spell. "You once made a remark," I said, "about impetuosity. I could quote it verbatim."

"So could I. If we discussed it all day there would still be only one way to learn if we have it or not. Get him."

"If he's not there do you want Rowcliff?"

"No. Only Mr. Cramer."

I pulled the phone around and dialed, and got first the switchboard, then a sergeant I knew only by name, Molloy, and then Inspector Cramer, and Wolfe took his phone. I stayed on.

Wolfe: "Good morning."

"Is it?"

"I think so. I have a problem. I must discuss a matter with Mr. Rowcliff as soon as possible, and it will go better if you are present. It relates to the death of Peter Odell. Could you come now?"

"No. I'll get Rowcliff on another phone."

"That wouldn't do. I have a tape recording both of you should hear."

"A recording of what?"

"You'll know when you hear it. You won't like it, but it may give you a useful hint. It has given me one."

"I can't—wait. Maybe I can. Hold it."

We held it for about two minutes, and then: "Does it have to be Rowcliff?"

"Yes. That's requisite."

"I never expected to hear this, you wanting to see Rowcliff. We'll leave in about ten minutes."

Click.

We hung up. I asked Wolfe, "The Copes tape?"

He said yes, and I went to the safe for the key to the locked cabinet where we keep various items that would be in the safe if there was room. Wolfe started in on Saul and Fred, asking questions that I thought should have been asked before calling Cramer, but he got nothing that tangled it. Fred had nothing but the bare fact that Copes's sister was Rowcliff's wife. Saul, knowing we would need more, had proceeded to get it, but he hadn't seen Diana herself, only neighbors and a woman who cleaned the Rowcliff apartment once a week, and two men who knew Copes. Almost certainly nothing had got to Rowcliff. However, one problem arose that had to be dealt with; Wolfe rang for beer and had the cap off of the bottle before he remembered that we were probably going to open champagne. He called Fritz in for consultation, and they decided it would be interesting to try eel stewed in stale beer, and Fritz thought he knew where he could get eel the next day. Wolfe told him Saul and Fred would join us for lunch, and it should be a little early if possible—one o'clock.

Lieutenant Rowcliff has it in for all private detectives, but I admit he has a special reason for thinking the world would be better off without me. When he gets hot he stutters, and with me it must be catching, because when he's working on me and I see that he is getting close to that point, *I* start to stutter, especially on words that begin with *g* or *t.* It's a misdemeanor to interfere with a police officer in the performance of his duty, but how could he handle that? Wolfe knows about it, and when the doorbell rang at a quarter to twelve and he told Saul to get it, I believe he actually thought I might greet them with "Gu-gu-gu-good morning."

I was at my desk. Fred was in one of the three yellow chairs facing Wolfe's desk, the one nearest me. Cramer, leading the way, of course went to the red leather chair, and Rowcliff took the yellow one nearest him, which left the middle one for Saul. As Cramer sat, he said, "Make it snappy. Rowcliff has someone waiting. What's this about a recording?"

"I'll have to introduce it," Wolfe said. "You probably know the name, Dennis Copes."

"I've heard it. One of the CAN bunch."

"I know him," Rowcliff said. "He wants Meer's job."

Wolfe nodded. "So it is said. As you know, Mrs. Odell's advertisement appeared last Tuesday, six days ago. Mr. Copes came here Thursday evening and said he had to admit something and that he had information to give me under the conditions stated in the advertisement. He did so. The recording is that conversation. —Archie?"

All I had to do was reach to the far corner of my desk to flip a switch. The playback, which was a honey and had cost $922.50, was on the desk at the back. We knew it was a good tape, since we had listened to it three times.

Copes's voice came. "That was a good ad. 'Any person who communicates as a result of this advertisement thereby agrees to the above conditions.' Very neat. What agency?"

"Agency?"

"Who wrote it?"

"Mr. Goodwin."

Naturally I watched their faces. The first few minutes they looked at each other a couple of times, but then their eyes stayed mostly on Wolfe. Then Cramer set his jaw and his face got even redder than usual, and Rowcliff started to lick his lips. It has been said that Rowcliff is handsome, and I'll concede that his six feet of meat is distributed well enough, but his face reminds me of a camel with a built-in sneer. All right, I don't like him, so allow for it. Of course licking his lips didn't improve it any.

It got to the end. Wolfe: "You may have to. I can't tell you how I'll proceed, Mr. Copes, because I don't know. If I need you, I'll know where to find you." I reached to the switch and flipped it.

"By god," Cramer said. He was so mad his voice was weak. "Four days ago. Four whole days. And you even told him not to tell anybody anything. And *now* you get us here and— How in hell you expect—"

"Pfui," Wolfe said. "You're not a witling and you know I'm not. If I had believed he was telling the truth, I might or might not have informed you immediately, but I certainly would not have risked telling him not to. I had good reason to suspect that he wasn't.

How could Kenneth Meer possibly have known that Odell intended to put LSD in the whisky? I don't know how much of an effort you have made to learn if anyone knew, and if so who, but I know how much *I* have. I thought it extremely doubtful that Meer could have known. But if he didn't, if Copes was lying, how did Copes know even now? Apparently it had been kept an official secret; it had not been disclosed by you or the District Attorney. And I had to know. I had to know if Copes could possibly have learned about the LSD from any other source. Unless such a source could be found, it would be impossible to challenge his account, and I would have to advise him to tell you without further delay. At ten o'clock Friday morning, five of us gathered here to consider it, and Mr. Panzer, Mr. Durkin, and Mr. Cather were given instructions and proceeded to inquire. The obvious possibil—"

"Three days you kept it. By God, three days and three nights." Cramer's voice was not weak.

"The weekend intervened. Anyway I would have kept it as long as there was any hope of finding a probable source. Three weeks or three months. Fortunately a competent performance by Mr. Panzer—and Mr. Durkin—made it *only* three days. Mr. Panzer brought it a little more than an hour ago, and I telephoned you almost immediately. Copes lied. I know how he learned about the LSD."

Wolfe looked at Rowcliff and back at Cramer. "There are several ways I could do this, and I'm taking the quickest, which should also be the most effective. As you know, a friend of Mr. Goodwin's, Mr. Cohen, is in a position of authority and influence at the *Gazette.*" He turned. "Your notebook, Archie."

With no idea what was coming, I got it, and a pen, and crossed my legs.

"A suggested draft for an article in tomorrow's *Gazette.* 'In an interview yesterday afternoon Nero Wolfe, comma, the private investigator, comma, stated that an attempt has been made by Dennis Copes, comma, an employe of the Continental Air Network, comma, to get the sixty-five thousand dollars offered in a recent advertisement by Mrs. Peter Odell, comma, by fraud. Period.'—No. Instead of 'fraud' make it 'by subreption.' It's more precise and will add to vocabularies. 'Paragraph.'

" 'Mr. Wolfe said, comma, quote, "Dennis Copes came to my office last Thursday evening and disclosed that he had knowledge of a certain fact relevant to the explosion of a bomb in the office of a CAN executive on the twentieth of May that caused the death of Peter Odell. Period. It was a fact known to me and to the police but had never been divulged, comma, by them or by me. Period. It was a closely guarded secret. Period. Mr. Copes's explanation of how and where he had learned it made it highly probable that the bomb had been placed in the drawer by another employe of CAN, comma, named by him. Paragraph.

" 'Quote. "I had reason to suspect that Mr. Copes's account of how he had learned the fact was false, comma, and I undertook to discover if he might have learned it some other way. Period. This morning I learned that there was indeed another way. Period. Mr. Copes has a twin sister named Diana who is the wife of a police lieutenant named J. M. Rowcliff. Period. I think it highly probable, comma, in fact I am satisfied, comma, that Mr. Rowcliff—' "

"Why, goddam you—" Rowcliff was up and moving.

"Back up!" Cramer snapped.

"Let me finish," Wolfe said.

"I'll finish you! You—"

"Can it!" Cramer snapped. "Sit down. Sit down and shut your trap." To Wolfe: "You know damn well you can't do this. We'd tear your guts out. You'd be done."

"I doubt it," Wolfe said. "The spotlight of public interest. I would be a cynosure, a man of mark. And my client's resources are considerable. I would have handled this differently if it were not Mr. Rowcliff. If it were Mr. Stebbins, for instance, I would have asked him to come and I would have told him that I wanted merely his private acknowledgment that he had told his wife about the LSD. That would have satisfied *me* that Mr. Copes had learned of the LSD from his sister, and no further proof would have been required. It would not have been necessary even for you to be told, either by him or by me. But with Mr. Rowcliff that would not have been possible. Would it? You know him. You know his animus against me."

"You could have asked *me* to come. And discuss it."

"Certainly. I have. Here we are."

"Balls. Discuss, my ass. 'In an interview yesterday afternoon Nero Wolfe, the private investigator.' That crap. All right, I'll discuss it with Rowcliff and you'll hear from me later. Probably today."

"No." Emphatic. "That won't do. It's urgent. There's a certain step I intend to take without delay. I'll postpone it only if I must. If you and Mr. Rowcliff leave without satisfying me, Mr. Goodwin will leave ten minutes later with the suggested draft for that article. It may be possible to get it in the late edition of today's paper. And of course reporters will be wanting to see Mr. and Mrs. Rowcliff —and you, I suppose. This is probably a resort to coercion, but I make no apology; the fact that I have Mr. Rowcliff to deal with makes it imperative. Actually I don't ask much. I require only a statement by him, unequivocal, that he told his wife about the LSD found in Peter Odell's pocket. I don't need an admission by his wife that she told her brother. That is a plausible assumption that for me will suffice."

Wolfe turned to Rowcliff. "You may know—or you may not— that there is an understanding between Mr. Cramer and me which he knows I observe. No conversation in this office with him present is recorded without his express consent. This is not being recorded."

"You goddam ape," Rowcliff said.

Cramer asked him, "Did you hear me tell you to shut your trap?"

No reply.

"Say 'yes, sir,' " Cramer said.

Rowcliff licked his lips. "Yes, sir."

"You're a good cop," Cramer said. "I know what you're good

for and what you're not good for. I even agree with your opinion of Wolfe up to a point, but *only* up to a point. That understanding he mentioned, you wouldn't trust him to keep it, but I do. That's a flaw you've got. Anyway the point right now is not our opinion of Wolfe, it's what he wants from you. There are aspects of this that you and I can discuss privately, and we will, but if you *did* tell your wife about the LSD, and you can be damn sure I'm going to *know* if you did, the best thing you can do is to say so here and now. You don't have to tell Wolfe, tell me. Did you?"

"Goddam it, Inspector, I'm not—"

"Did you?"

"Yes. I'm not going—"

"Shut up." Cramer turned to Wolfe. "I call that unequivocal, damn you."

"So do I," Wolfe said. "Thank you for coming."

"You can shove your thanks." He stood up. "You said something on the phone about a useful hint. You can shove that too. You and your useful hints." He turned to Rowcliff. "You, move. Move!"

It was an order and Rowcliff obeyed it. Anyone else I could name, I would have felt sorry for him. I knew what he had coming and so did he. Saul followed them to the hall; he had let them in, so he would check them out.

As Saul came back in, Wolfe told me, "Get Mr. Browning."

He was certainly making up for lost time, but it had worked with Cramer and Rowcliff so it might work with the next president of CAN too, whatever it was. I pulled the phone around and dialed, and told the switchboard I wanted to speak to Mr. Browning's secretary. When you ask for secretaries usually you aren't asked who you are, and in a minute I had her.

"Mr. Browning's office."

"Miss Lugos, please."

"This is Miss Lugos."

"This is Archie Goodwin. Mr. Wolfe would like to speak to Mr. Browning."

"Nero Wolfe?"

"Yes."

"What about?"

"I don't know. It must be important, since Mr. Browning called him a cheap bully only a couple of hours ago."

"I'll see. Hold the wire."

Of course she would tell me either that Mr. Browning was not available or to put Mr. Wolfe on. But she didn't. After a wait of only a couple of minutes, his voice: "What do you want?"

I didn't have to answer because Wolfe was on.

"Mr. Browning?"

"Yes."

"Nero Wolfe. I have just spoken at some length with Inspector Cramer of the police. He left my office five minutes ago. This afternoon, not later than four o'clock, I am going to tell him who put a bomb in a drawer of your desk, and I think it fitting and desirable that I tell you first. I would also like to tell Miss Lugos why I told her that she lied. Will you come, with her, at half past two?"

Silence, a long minute, then, "I think *you're* lying."

"No. A lie that would be exposed in three hours? No."

"You know who did that? You know now?"

"Yes."

A shorter silence. "I'll call you back."

He hung up. Of course that meant yes. He wouldn't call Cramer, and even if he did, what would that get him? I looked at Wolfe. Sometimes you can tell pretty well how good his hand is by the way he holds his head, and his mouth. That time I couldn't. No sign. I asked him, "Must we leave the room while you're telling them? We're curious. We'd like to know too."

"You will." He looked at the wall clock. 12:25. "Now. Saul, ask Fritz to bring the champagne."

As Saul left, the doorbell rang, and I went. It was Orrie Cather. I opened the door and said, "Greetings. Go ahead and tell me you know who Dennis Copes's twin sister's husband is."

"Huh?" He stepped in. "I didn't know he had a sister. I got bounced from the CAN building."

"Sure. They knew you like champagne. Go right in."

So Orrie was there for the briefing too.

19

THE VICE-PRESIDENT and his secretary came on the dot at half past two. Precisely.

We were well-filled. Inside our bellies were three bottles of Dom Perignon champagne, braised sweetbreads with chicken quenelles (small portions because of the unexpected guests), crab meat omelets (added attraction), celery and mushroom salad, and four kinds of cheese. Inside our skulls were the details of where it stood according to Wolfe and the program for the next hour or two. For where it stood I would have given good odds, say ten to one, and so would the other three. For the program, no bet. It was a typical Wolfe concoction. It assumed—*he* assumed—that if an unexpected snag interfered, he would be able to handle it no matter what it was, and your ego has to be riding high to assume that.

To prepare for it only two props were needed. One was the Copes tape in the playback on my desk. For the other all four of us went to the basement. I could have done it alone, but they wanted to help. In a corner of the big storage room there were two thick, old mattresses, no springs in them, which I had used a few times for targets to get bullets for comparison purposes. We decided the best place for them was under the pool table in the adjoining room, where it had been installed when Wolfe had decided that he needed some violent exercise. Doubled, the mattresses were a tight fit under it.

The three were to be in the front room, but when the doorbell rang Saul went to receive the guests and show them in. They didn't have their war paint on. Browning was not a dragon snorting fire, and Helen Lugos was not set to use her claws on someone who had called her a liar. He sat in the red leather chair and said he had an appointment at a quarter past three, and she sat in a yellow one and said nothing.

"This will take a while," Wolfe told Browning. "Perhaps an hour."

"I can't stay an hour."

"We'll see. I'll make it as brief as possible. First you must hear a recording of a conversation I had recently with a member of your staff, Dennis Copes. Here. He came last Thursday evening. — Archie?"

I flipped the switch, and for the fifth time I heard Copes speak highly of that ad. Another time or two and I would begin to think I had picked the wrong line of work, that by now I could have been a vice-president myself, at one of the big agencies. As I had with Cramer and Rowcliff, I watched their faces. Their reaction was very different from the cops'. They looked at Wolfe hardly at all. Mostly they looked at each other, him with a frown that developed into what you might call a gawk, and her first with her eyes wide and then with her lips parted. Twice she started to say something but realized she had to hold it. When it came to the end and I turned it off, they both started to speak at once, he to her and she to him, but Wolfe stopped them. "Don't," he said, loud enough and decisive enough to stop anybody. "Don't waste your breath and your time and mine. I know he lied. It was all a fabrication. That has been established, with the help of Inspector Cramer. He heard the recording this morning. I should tell you, and I do, that this conversation is not being recorded. I give you that assurance on my word of honor, and those who know me would tell you that I would not tarnish that fine old pledge."

Browning demanded, "If you know he lied why bother us with it? Why do *you* waste our time?"

"I don't. You *had* to hear part of it, and to appreciate that part you needed to hear the whole. I have—"

"What part?"

"You said your time is limited."

"It is."

"Then don't interrupt. I have a good deal to say and I am not garrulous. The kernel of Mr. Copes's fabrication was of course the quotation—what he said he heard Kenneth Meer say." To Helen Lugos: "You say he didn't say that? That that conversation didn't occur?"

"I certainly do. It didn't."

"I believe you. But his invention of it told me something that he did not intend and was not aware of. It told me who put the bomb in the drawer, and I'm going to tell you how and why. As I said, I'll make it brief as possible, but you should know that Kenneth Meer is responsible for my concern in this affair. On May twenty-sixth, a Monday, he went to a clinic, gave a false name, and told a doctor that he needed help; that he got blood on his hands recurrently, frequently, not visible to anyone else. He refused—"

Browning demanded, "A clinic? What clinic?"

"Don't interrupt! To include all details would take all day. I assure you that anything I do include can be verified. He refused to give any information about himself. A friend of that doctor, another doctor, consulted me, and Kenneth Meer, still using an alias, came to see me. He still refused to supply any information about himself, but by a ruse, Mr. Goodwin and I learned who he was, and of course we had seen his name in the published reports of the death of Peter Odell. That led to my being consulted by Mrs. Odell and her hiring me. Naturally—"

"So that's how—"

"Don't interrupt! Naturally I considered the possibility that Meer had supplied the bomb and was racked by his sense of guilt. But surely not intending it for you, and information given me by Mrs. Odell made it extremely unlikely that he could have known that Peter Odell intended to go to your room and open that drawer. I will not elaborate on that. I have included that detail, how I first saw Kenneth Meer, only to explain why he has been of special interest throughout. There has always been for me that special reason to suspect him, but there was no plausible basis for a charge. Or rather, there was, but I hadn't the wit to see it. I admit I should have. Mr. Copes revealed it to me."

He turned a palm up. "If you undertake to invent something you heard another man say and you're not a fool, you make it conform to his character, his knowledge, and his style. And Copes had Kenneth Meer saying to Miss Lugos, 'I want to be damn sure you don't open the drawer to take a look at the usual time.' Would he have had him say that to her, especially the 'usual time,' unless he knew, or thought he knew, that Miss Lugos was in the habit of looking in the drawer every day, and that Meer knew it? When he wanted to make the invented quotation not only conceivable but as credible as possible? He would not. He would have included that 'usual' only if it conformed to his knowledge of the facts. Of course if he knew that Miss Lugos had told the police—and Mr. Goodwin—that she had *not* habitually opened the drawer every day, it was a blunder to include the 'usual.' It was a blunder even if he didn't know that, because it wasn't necessary, but he included it because he thought it increased the credibility of his lie."

Wolfe looked at Helen Lugos. "So when you told Mr. Goodwin that you did not look in the drawer every day, *you* lied. And you knew that the bomb, put in the drawer by Kenneth Meer, was intended for *you.* You had known that from the day it happened. You probably knew it, at least surmised it, the moment you entered the wrecked room."

Browning was on his feet. "Come, Helen," he said. "This is absurd. We're going."

"No," Wolfe said. He turned to me, lifted a hand, and wiggled a finger. I went and opened the connecting door to the front room and stuck my head in and said, "Help." Saul and Fred headed for the other door, to the hall, and Orrie came and joined me. Helen Lugos was up and moving, with Browning behind her, but before they reached the door to the hall Saul and Fred were there, and

Helen Lugos stopped. Saul swung the door around, closed it, and he and Fred stood with their backs to it.

"You are *not* going, Mr. Browning," Wolfe said. "Come and sit down."

Browning turned. "This *is* absurd. Absolutely ridiculous."

"It is not. I have more to say and I mean you to hear it. You might as well sit."

"No. You'll regret this."

"I doubt it." Wolfe turned. "Your notebook, Archie."

I went to my desk, sat, got notebook and pen, and crossed my legs. A replay, though not quite instant.

Wolfe leaned back. "A suggested draft for an article in tomorrow's *Gazette.* 'Yesterday afternoon Nero Wolfe, comma, the private investigator, comma, told a *Gazette* reporter that he has learned who was responsible for the death by violence of Peter Odell, comma, a vice-president of the Continental Air Network, comma, on May twentieth. Period. Mr. Odell was killed by the explosion of a bomb in the office of Amory Browning, comma, also a vice-president of the Continental Air Network. Paragraph.

" 'Mr. Wolfe said, comma, quote, "I have established to my satisfaction that the bomb was put in a drawer of Mr. Browning's desk by Kenneth Meer, comma, Mr. Browning's assistant, dash, the drawer in which Mr. Browning kept a supply of bourbon whisky. Period. Mr. Meer knew that Miss Helen Lugos, comma, Mr. Browning's secretary, comma, was in the habit of opening the drawer every afternoon to see that the whisky was there, comma, and he placed the bomb so it would explode when the drawer was opened. Period. However, comma, Mr. Odell entered the room shortly after three o'clock and opened the drawer, comma, it is not known why. Paragraph.

" 'Quote. "In these circumstances, comma, established to my satisfaction, comma, it is not only reasonable, comma, it is unavoidable, comma, to suppose that Miss Lugos has been aware that the bomb must have been put in the drawer by Mr. Meer, comma, and the supposition is supported by the fact that she has consistently denied that she habitually opened the drawer every day to check on the whisky. Period. Also it is reasonable to suppose that Mr. Browning was aware of that too, comma, or at least suspected it. Period. Kenneth Meer knew of the intimate personal relationship that existed between Mr. Browning and Miss Lugos, comma, and was tormented by the knowledge. Period. He was torn by two intense and conflicting desires. Colon. His ardent wish to advance through his association with Mr. Browning, comma, and his concupiscence. Period. It may be assumed—" ' "

"This is worse than ridiculous." Browning was standing at the end of Wolfe's desk. "It's idiotic. No newspaper would print it. Any of it."

"Oh, yes. The *Gazette* would, with a guaranty from Mrs. Odell to cover all expenses. Yes, indeed. You're up a stump, Mr. Browning, and so is Miss Lugos. Not only the publicity; you would have to sue for libel, or persuade the District Attorney to charge us with criminal libel. That would be obligatory, and both of you would have to submit to questioning under oath. *That* would be idiotic, for a man in your position."

For the second time that day something happened that was hard to believe. Browning stood with his eyes glued to Wolfe, but probably not really seeing him, his shoulders set, and his chin back. Twenty seconds, half a minute, I don't know; and then he turned right around and looked at Helen Lugos, who had stayed over by the door, an arm's reach from Saul and Orrie. And she said, "Ask him what he wants." It was a suggestion, not a command, but even so, from a secretary to a vice-president soon to be a president? Women's Lib, or what?

Whatever it was, it worked fine. He turned back to Wolfe and asked, "What do you want?"

"I like eyes at a level," Wolfe said. "Please sit down."

Helen Lugos came back to the yellow chair, and sat. At least she left the red leather chair for him, and he took it, or some of it—about the front eight inches of the seat, barely enough to keep his rump on—and asked again, "What do you want?"

"From you, not much," Wolfe said. "I am not Jupiter Fidius. I want only to do the job I was hired to do. I think I know the present state of Kenneth Meer's mind. His mood, his spirit. I think he's pregnable. I want to get him on the telephone, tell him you and Miss Lugos are here, and ask him to join us for a discussion. If he refuses or demurs, I want you to speak to him and tell him to come. I don't know how things stand between you and him; of course during these six weeks you would have liked to turn him out, but didn't dare. Will he come if you tell him to?"

"Yes. Then what?"

"We'll see. One possibility, he may acknowledge that he put the bomb in the drawer, but claim that it was intended for Peter Odell —that he knew that Odell intended to come and open the drawer. There are other possibilities, and it may be that his real motive need not be divulged. That would please you and Miss Lugos, and I have no animus against you, but I make no commitment. This is your one chance to get out of it with minor bruises. I know too much now that the police *should* know."

Would he ask her for another suggestion? No. He looked at her, but only for a second, and then said, "All right. If you think—all right."

Wolfe turned to me: "Get him."

That was one of the possible snags. What if he wasn't there? What if he had got a toothache or twisted an ankle and left for the day? But he hadn't. I got him and Wolfe got on. I stayed on.

"Good afternoon, Mr. Meer. I'm calling from my office, at the suggestion of Mr. Browning. He and Miss Lugos are here. We have talked at some length, and have come to a point where we need your help. Can you come at once?"

"Why—they're there?"

"Yes. Since half past two."

"Mr. Browning told you to call me?"

"Yes. He's right here. Do you want to speak to him?"

"I don't—no. No. All right. I'll leave in five minutes."

He hung up. Wolfe told Browning, "He'll leave in five minutes. You and Miss Lugos may wish to speak privately. This room is soundproofed." He stood. "Would you like something to drink?"

Browning looked at her and she shook her head, and he said, "No." Saul and Fred left by the hall door, closing it after them, and Wolfe and Orrie and I left by the door to the front room. In a moment Saul and Fred joined us. Wolfe said, "I'm going to the kitchen. I'm thirsty. Any questions? Any comments?"

Orrie said, "It's all set. It's up to him."

Wolfe went by the hall door. Fred said, "If anyone wants a bet, I'm giving two to one that he'll have it."

Saul said, "I'd rather have your end."

I said, "I don't want *either* end."

They debated it. At a time like that, it only makes it longer to keep looking at your watch, but that's what I did. 3:22, 3:24, 3:27. At that time of day there should be taxis headed downtown on Ninth Avenue in the Fifties, and it was only nineteen blocks. At half past three I went to the hall, leaving the door open, and stood with my nose against the one-way glass of the front door. Me and my watch. 3:32, 3:34, 3:36. He had been run over by a truck or something. He was on his way to the airport. At 3:37 a taxi rolled up in front and stopped alongside the parked cars, and the door opened, and he climbed out, and he had the brief case. I called through the open door to the front room, "Okay, he has it!" and they came. Orrie went down the hall to the door to the office and stood. Fred stood at my left by the rack; he would be behind the door when I opened it. Saul stood in the doorway to the front room. Kenneth Meer mounted the stoop with the brief case tucked under his left arm. He pushed the button, and I counted a slow ten and opened the door, and he stepped in. With the brief case under his arm, that hand was pressed against his left hip, and his right hand was hanging loose. I don't think I have ever made a faster or surer move. Facing him, I got his two wrists, and I got them good, and Saul, from behind him, got the brief case. His mouth popped open but no sound came, and he went stiff top to bottom, absolutely stiff. Then he tried to turn around, but I had his wrists, and only his head could turn. Saul had backed away, holding the brief case against his belly with both hands. I said, "Go ahead and don't drop it," and he started down the hall to the rear, where the stair to the basement was, and at the door to the office Orrie joined him. I let go of Meer's wrists, and he stood, still stiff, and stared down the hall at Saul going. He still hadn't made a sound. Then suddenly he started to slump. He made it over to the bench, flopped down on it, bent over with his face in his hands, and started to shake all over. Still no sound, absolutely none. I told Fred, "Keep him company," and headed for the kitchen.

Wolfe was on his stool at the center table with a beer glass in his hand. "You win," I said. "He had it and we got it."

"Where is he?"

"In the hall."

You wouldn't believe how easy and smooth he can remove his seventh of a ton off of a stool. I followed him down the hall. Meer was still huddled on the bench and still shaking. Wolfe stood and looked down at him for a good ten seconds, told Fred, "Stay here," went back down the hall and opened the office door and entered, and I followed. Browning, in the red leather chair, asked, "Did he come? The doorbell rang five min—"

"Shut up," Wolfe snapped, and crossed to his desk and sat and glared at them. "Yes," he said, "he came. When he came Saturday, day before yesterday, he was in his own car, but he didn't leave his brief case in it. He kept it with him, and he kept it in his lap as he sat where you are now. When I decided today to ask him to come, later, I thought it likely that he would bring the brief case, and if so there would be a bomb in it, since he would know you two were here. It was only a conjecture, but well-grounded, and it has been verified. He came, and he had the brief case, and it is now in my basement under a pile of mattresses. On your way out, you will pass him in the hall—prostrated, wretched, defeated. Pass him, just pass him. He is no longer yours. I am now—"

"But my god, what—"

"*Shut up!* I am now going to call Mr. Cramer and ask him to come and bring with him men who know how to deal with bombs. If you don't want to encounter him, leave at once. Go."

He turned to me. "Get him, Archie."

I swiveled and dialed.

James Printer

A Novel of Rebellion

by Paul Samuel Jacobs

AN
APPLE
PAPERBACK

SCHOLASTIC INC.
New York Toronto London Auckland Sydney
Mexico City New Delhi Hong Kong

ISBN 0-590-97541-2

12 11 10 9 8 7 6 5 4 3 2 1 0 1 2 3 4 5/0

Printed in the U.S.A. 40

First Scholastic Trade paperback printing, October 2000

Title page illustration by Mark Summers
Book design by Marijka Kostiw
Cover design by Elizabeth B. Parisi

To Nancy Marlene Jacobs

More than twenty-five years ago and newly married, we visited the Fruitlands Museum in Harvard, Massachusetts, where I taught school. That's when we first heard of James Printer and thought of writing a book about him. Without Nancy's research and patience, love and friendship, this work would not have been possible.

CHAPTER ONE

Awakening Day

I remember the day I first saw King Philip.

My half-brother, Sam, rousted me from bed long before the sun began its climb across the sky. "Make quick," he said in his usual morning voice, which was loud and grating. "Work's waiting to be done."

Still, on this day, I left my warm bed without either complaint or delay. I washed my face by the thin light of a sputtering candle and smiled to myself in the little mirror above the basin. There I was, the same Bartholomew Green I had been before. The same clump of hair stood up stubbornly on my head, refusing to bend before my brush. The same gray eyes, now cleared of sleep, blinked back at me. The same small ears stuck out from my head just a little too much.

Yet all was to be different this day. An awakening day, I call it, when everything had to be noticed.

I raced downstairs, skipping steps in my haste. My brother already sat in the kitchen glumly eating his breakfast. He was almost twenty years my senior, the hair upon his head already wispy, and his face grown tired, soft around the chin and puffy about the eyes.

"Never have I seen you move so quick," he said. "Going somewhere this day?"

"We're going to Boston," said my cousin Annie, who sat across the table. She squinted up at me from her bowl, her spoon gripped in her hand. "Aren't we, Bartholomew?"

Annie was as overjoyed as my older brother was gloomy. He after all was to stay behind in Cambridge, toiling with my father in our print shop. “There is work to be done in Boston, do not forget that,” Sam reminded her.

She ignored him, while eating hurriedly. I admired the way her hunger outraced even mine, as if no amount of mush mixed with goat's milk and dried currants could ever satisfy her. Her face was dusted with freckles from working with my mother in the garden, and there was a golden streak in her long brown hair.

“I wonder what ships will be in the harbor,” she said. “And what fine persons we shall see. I hear that the ladies wear lace in Boston, and all the men wear capes and collars of fur.”

My mother put my bowl before me, just as my father came to take his seat at the table. He seemed old to me this morning. I could see the gray in the stubble of his beard.

“Is it safe for the children to go,” my mother asked him, “at such a time as this?” Safe? I wondered what she meant. This was not a season of blizzards or hurricanoes, and the road to Boston was an easy one in all but the worst of weather.

My father waved away her fears. “Of course, Mistress Green, it is safe for them to go. All this talk of uprisings is foolish prattle. A little argument between a farmer and an Indian boy is not a call to arms."

I had not heard any talk of uprisings before this or of a quarrel between a farmer and an Indian. I looked to my mother and saw the shadows of worry about her deep-set eyes, but she said nothing.

I was eleven in that year of 1675, on a day when my eyes were truly open. An awakening day, as I have said. My cousin and I were to go to Boston with James, the apprentice printer in my father's shop.

You might have heard of my father, Master Samuel Green, the printer who ran the presses at Harvard College in Cambridge town. People said that he was the finest printer in the New England colonies and as good as any who worked in London. And I, a lump of clay barely formed into the shape of a man, was the devil in his shop. The printer's devil, I mean—the one expected to sweep and scrub, and run for this or bend for that, and set things right when type was spilled or bent or broken.

Oh, I hated the work, as all boys, before and since, do hate the little jobs that are theirs to do. But even so, I was proud to call myself a printer's devil and work alongside my father and my half-brother, Sam, and especially the apprentice James.

Maybe you have heard of James, too. He became famous in his time, before this tale of mine is done. He shared in King Philip's fame. But not just yet on that spring morning, when James walked into our kitchen before the sky gave up the last stars to a fiery dawn. You could tell right away that he was not like the others. He was taller by far than my father or brother. His hair and his eyes were black as charcoal. He was handsome, I thought, even though his face had been scarred by the smallpox.

He was an Indian, but I did not think of him so. If you closed your eyes and heard him speak, you would not have known it. He talked like any Englishman, but much faster. His words raced from him in a wild gallop, like a horse without a rider.

"I have the cart loaded, Master Green," he said, "all the books stacked as snugly as bricks in a wall. Such a pretty volume, the lines as true as a schoolmaster's ruler. The bookseller will not have them long, before they are sold."

How cheerful he was, so early in the morning. But was there ever a time when he was not cheerful? I knew him all of my life, but I had never seen him either sad or angry. Until this spring day he seemed to be a man without fears or worries.

"To Boston, we will journey," he said, as if we were traveling to a far-off land. In truth, it was a trip of just a few hours each way, across the river Charles. But for me and my cousin Annie Clark, it might have been a journey over the sea, to Spain or Africa, to the West Indies or the Virginia colony.

I sat high atop our wagon, between James and Annie. I was not a quiet boy. It only seemed so between the two of them. They both chattered as we moved along. No person or house, no flowering plant or grazing animal, could we pass without a comment.

Annie was the daughter of my mother's brother, Robert Clark, newly arrived from England with his small family. They were to stay by us only briefly before they moved to the town of Deerfield, far to the west. But one day over supper, my mother announced to all that my cousin Annie was to stay behind.

"My brother thinks that Deerfield is too new, just yet," my mother announced. "Robert does not believe it right for a young girl to live like a savage in the wilderness. So Annie must stay with us until a proper house is built. When all is settled he will come for her, and not before."

Sam laughed aloud at this. "To Robert, even Cambridge seems too wild a place for a daughter of his, I think. Yet we have our own college, which must be as fine as any in the world!"

I was glad that my cousin was left behind. Annie was just a year older than I was, even if she stood a full head taller at the time. And I loved the stories she told.

"Tell us about your sail from England," I begged of her as we rode that morning.

"Most everyone on the ship grew sick, even the captain and his crew," she began. Her voice was as loud as if she were trying to win the attention of the thick horse that pulled our wagon. "Two children and a man died before reaching Boston. It was most horrible. Their faces were blue and blown up like a pig's bladder. I saw them myself." To demonstrate, she pinched her nose and filled her cheeks. I laughed to see her bloated face. "You wouldn't laugh if you had seen them. And when the captain had their bodies put overboard, they did not sink into the ocean but floated there, bobbing in the waves. The captain said that this proved their souls were wicked, but my father said that this was foolish talk. Men cannot know why God chooses to take some men into heaven sooner than others. Or why a body floats or sinks. That's what my father said."

James grew solemn. What Annie had said touched something in him. "There is so much that men cannot know," he said. "My mother died when I was younger than Bartholomew. No kinder woman lived in all the world than she, but I do not know, even to this day, why she was taken while others who were wicked stayed behind."

"What did she die of?" I asked.

"The English pox," he said. "I suffered from it, too. I was very small, yet I remember lying too weak to move upon a bed of skins in our great house of birch bark and bent willow branches. But my mother was sicker than I. Touching her, I felt my fingers might burn, and later she turned cold. She died, along with half the people of our village. When she died and I did not, my father said that this was a sign of my good fortune, that something was expected of me. But I did not find any happiness in it. And soon after, I was taken away."

Never before had I heard him speak of his mother. I never even stopped to think that he must have a mother. Now, I had a host of questions for him, but Annie did not give me a chance to speak.

"Is your mother now in heaven?" she asked. This was a constant concern of all of us—who would go to heaven and who would not.

"I pray she is," he said. "But she was not baptized. No Indian could be in those days."

I was struck by his sudden sadness. It was as if his mother had died just yesterday and not twenty years before. And I began to think how terrible it would be never to see my own mother again, not in this life or even in the next.

Soon, however, our somber mood was broken as we reached the bridge that crossed the Charles. The sun was risen in the sky, just a few short steps above the earth. The river did not smell of terrible things, as it does now, and a breeze swept upon us, full of the scent of sweet blossoms as we rode high across the swollen waters. There were boats upon the river and waterfowl of all varieties, ducks and coots and tumbler birds.

Slowly we left the muddy riverbank behind us and turned toward Boston. How peaceful it was this day. And it was beginning to be warm in the dappled sunlight. We moved toward a farmhouse set off like a castle behind a low, uneven wall of rocks and boulders cleared from the fields. There were no signs of the farmer or his cattle. Ahead, off to the other side, we could see an orchard of apple and nut trees, still full of flowers and alive with all manner of insects.

And then I heard a rush of air and felt a sudden sting on my forehead. And then another whoosh and a sting upon my arm. These were not bees, but rocks and stones arching through the air, falling down upon us like hail from the heavens. Annie surprised me by turning toward me and covering me with her body, but not before I felt another hit and another and another. I felt a little river of blood flowing down my face, as if a dam were broken.

"Ooo," said my cousin when a rock struck

the back of her head. And the fusillade of rock, pebble, and stone kept falling.

James leaped from the wagon and rushed toward the wall, straight into the barrage. Suddenly the stones stopped, and a dozen figures stood and ran from him. It was as if he were a hunter and had flushed a covey of quail, so suddenly did they appear and race away.

I saw them scatter across an open field and head for the woods beyond. They were boys, all of them, some smaller than myself, dressed in tattered clothing of sad colors. James jumped over the wall and was catching up with the slowest of them, a small, capless boy. The child was just within James's reach when a door was flung open from the farmhouse, and an old man walked out. His white hair was only partly covered by his tall hat. The musket he carried so unsteadily in his hands was as long as he was.

"Leave the boy alone, heathen!" he shouted. His voice was pitched high as a flute. The gun he lifted to his eye so that he might aim it.

James stopped still in the middle of the field, but his quarry did not. The boy kept running for the woods where he soon vanished with the others.

James stood frozen, like a rabbit cornered by a dog. He dared not twitch as the farmer walked toward him.

Annie said to me, "Stay where you are! I must help him!" and she jumped down from the high wagon seat and ran for James. I followed close behind her, ignoring my injuries. I could feel the cool blood upon my forehead.

She was far faster than I was and quick over the wall and into the field. "Do him no harm!" she yelled again and again. "You must do him no harm!"

I could not believe what I saw because she ran straight for the man and, to his surprise, boldly grabbed on to his musket and pulled it from his hands the way a mother might take a pointed stick from her baby.

"I won't let you harm him!" she said.

The man was more startled than angry to be treated so by a young girl. "No Indian may lay his hand upon an English child while Goodman Harry Frost is able to stop him," he said. But his voice was now a broken note.

"He had good cause," my cousin said. And

she pointed to me as evidence. I stood breathless before them, the blood smeared and clotted about my face. "Look what these terrible children have done!" Annie said.

"And who are you," the man said, "to be riding with an Indian on a Saturday morn in times like these?"

"I am Annie Clark, and this man is James Printer, apprentice to my uncle, Samuel Green."

"Looks like no apprentice I have ever seen," Goodman Frost replied. "He's but an Indian sneaking about, dressed up in English clothes."

"You are partly right in that," James said, smiling now. "I *am* an Indian dressed in English clothes, but also an apprentice."

"And talks like an Englishman, too!" said Goodman Frost. This seemed to surprise him more than the clothing.

"I was reared in the house of Master Henry Dunster and his good wife, at Harvard College," James said. "And it was there that I began to learn the craft of printing. They kept the college presses in their house in those days and treated me as one of their own."

Goodman Frost was befuddled. "Well, well," he said. "I remember Master Dunster. Some thought him a fool, but he never harmed me."

Annie became impatient and turned the barrel of the gun toward its master. "You might have killed poor James!" she shouted. Old Harry Frost stood trembling.

"Now, now, Annie," said James. "Goodman Frost meant no harm to me."

"That's true," the man now said in his own defense. "I saw an Indian clothed like an Englishman, chasing a boy across my field, and what was I to think? My first thought was that he was an evil savage and wanted to scalp that little fellow."

"That boy and the others might have killed us with their stones!" Annie said, still holding the long gun. "Look at him," she said, pointing at me. "He is the one who is wounded."

"But you cannot blame the boys," Goodman Frost said. "There are so many stories about savages who steal and rob from us English and would gladly kill us in our sleep for a few shillings or a bottle of West Indies rum."

James took the musket gently from Annie's hands and returned it to the old man, who seemed surprised to have it back.

"In future, Goodman Frost, you will use this to guard the safety of innocent travelers along this road and not a mob of ruffian boys who attack them," he said.

James turned and walked away, with the two of us following behind him. We left the old man muttering to a flock of crows that had settled in the field.

Once back at our wagon, I said, "You have saved James, Annie. How brave you are!"

"There was nothing brave," she said. "I did not stop to think. Besides, old Harry Frost did tremble so, he could not have fired his musket straight."

"Goodman Frost did not mean to injure me," James said. But it was Annie he first helped up onto the wagon, though I was the injured one.

When all three of us were again seated upon our high perch, Annie carefully cleaned my face with a white handkerchief that turned red in her hands. My head was tender to the touch, but the sight of my own blood upon the white cloth hurt more than my wounds.

"Why did those boys throw stones at me?" I asked her.

"Why, Bartholomew, they were not throwing at you!" she said. "It's James they wanted to harm."

CHAPTER TWO

The Indian King

In silence at first, we rolled toward Boston. I could not keep my gaze from James. I saw him now with fresh eyes.

"How did you come to be English, James?" I asked.

Annie laughed at my question, but James did not. Instead, he lifted his head a little, as if he were looking for an answer in the distance before he finally replied.

"I was a boy younger than you, when my

mother died," he said. "It was then that the Reverend John Eliot rode into our camp upon a large gray horse that seemed to be breathing smoke and fire. Before that day, I was only a person in my mind, not English or Indian. My family is Nipmuck. It means people of the rivers, for my people lived upon the flowing water. They traveled in bark canoes so light that one man could carry upon his back a boat large enough for six.

"Today Master Eliot is an old man, bent and gray, but then he was straight and lean like a tall and slender alder. I can see him before me, with his neat-cut hair without a single strand of silver. His nose looked like a protruding beak, and he often made a joke of it. He'd say it was right that he looked like a hawk, because he was a bird of prey. And pray he did, so often that every other sentence was a prayer.

"But what I noticed first were his eyes. They were a clear blue like the waters of a deep pond. And when he looked down upon me from his horse, I felt his eyes did cut and peer inside. I knew from the first that he wanted to take something from me and put something else in its place.

"My father gathered everyone before Master Eliot and at a signal from him, my father and the rest fell to their knees. And then the preacher passed out gifts to everyone. There were clay pipes and tobacco for the adults, who began to smoke all at once. And for the children there were apples and honeycomb and little bits of ribbon and cloth, or beads strung together on a cut of leather.

"But I cared not for any of these things. I looked instead at a strange object that Master Eliot held in his hands. It was a thing covered in leather and divided into thin, white pieces like leaves. This was the Englishman's magic. A book, my father said it was. There was no word for it in Algonquian but 'book,' same as in English.

"Master Eliot stopped his speaking and showed me a leaf with its scratches, black upon white. And he said that these were words that told stories older than the father of his father and if I listened, I could hear them.

"To me this was magic, and I told him that I wanted nothing more in the world than to know how to hear those words for myself. And he promised that he would teach me.

"Now, my brothers were there, too, and they laughed at the way Master Eliot spoke our tongue. And my father said that they must show respect to this Englishman. But my brother Anaweakin rose to his feet and took out his knife and rushed at Master Eliot.

"With one hand, he held Master Eliot by the throat, with the other he pressed a long knife against the preacher's chest. And Anaweakin asked if Master Eliot's lord was powerful enough to keep him from cutting out his heart. But my father told my brother to put his knife away, because the English had many more muskets than we did and they surely would destroy us if any harm came to so great a man as Master Eliot.

"My brother did as he was told, saying 'It is *I,* not your lord, who has let you live,' but we were all impressed by Master Eliot's courage. And I thought how powerful was the English God to stop my brother from killing him.

"Later that day, my father told me that my orphaned cousin, Wampus, and I were to go with the preacher to live with the English.

And on the spot Master Eliot gave us both our Christian names. Wampus became John, and I, Wowaus, became James.

"Master Eliot took us by horseback to the home of Henry Dunster, who was the president of Harvard College in Cambridge. I remember seeing his house, one story stacked upon the other, with pointed roofs and windows of glass. And I thought surely the English king himself lives here.

"Mistress Dunster took us in. She was a small woman, pale and a little wrinkled, but with very strong hands that kept their grip on us. I had never seen the inside of such a house before. And I saw how the English set their fires upon stone hearths, and how they sat on chairs raised up above the ground. Most marvelous of all was a small mirror that hung upon a wall in the kitchen. In it I could see a dark face, streaked with dirt, the hair greased with bear fat and tied with bits of ribbon and cloth. John and I laughed at these sad, dirty boys. No one would think that they could be English.

"She made us stand still in the kitchen, while she walked around us, all the time wrinkling her nose at the look and smell of us. Next she had her servants strip away our deerskin clothing and lift us up into a large metal pot near the fireplace. They began to pour kettles of steaming water about us. And I wondered if we were being cooked up into a stew. But instead we were soaped and scrubbed with brushes, then dried off and dressed in cloth of black and gray and white. Finally she chopped off our hair and brushed it out.

"Then she held a mirror up to us and let us see that we were made over completely. With only a little more soap and hot water, I thought that even our skins would grow pale and we would be the same as any English boys.

"It is an odd thing, but when I saw myself scrubbed clean in English clothes, I knew for the first time that I was different from the English, that I was an Indian."

I could not wait for him to tell the rest of his story but had to ask him, "How did you learn to speak English just the way we do?"

"My cousin John and I were taken to the charity school, but I think I learned English sitting at Mistress Dunster's table," James said. "Her sons ate with us, and there were always two or three college students who came to join us. I listened closely, especially to the arguments among them. And it was not long before I spoke just the way the Dunsters did."

We were getting close to Boston now. Sitting high upon my father's cart, we began to see more people. But instead of greeting them with good cheer, I saw them with suspicion. Who among them wanted to harm James, I wondered, just because he was an Indian?

Finally, we left the rutted road and turned into city lanes paved in stone.

And I noticed how the clothing had changed. Here many men wore capes and caps of bright color, and puffed upon clay pipes as they walked through the streets. And the women were dressed as brightly, in dresses decorated with delicate lace and colored ribbon.

"How lovely they are," Annie said, "like so many flowers, no two of them alike. I told you it would be so, didn't I, Bartholomew?"

But my eyes were open now, and I noticed things that Annie did not. There were boys and girls in tattered clothing; and haggard men, several missing arms and one a leg; and many soldiers carrying long guns. Here, too, were frightful bearded men in deerskin costume, trappers come to exchange their goods. And there were foreigners speaking strange, burbling tongues.

James pulled up our cart before the shop of Master Hezekiah Usher, the bookseller, who greeted us as heartily as if we had come all the way from England itself.

"I hope your journey was a pleasant and comfortable one," he said. He spoke to me before saying a word to James, as if I were a man of great importance like my father.

"Yes, sir," I said, "except that we were attacked by ruffians along the way."

"It was James who was attacked," said my cousin, "because he is plainly Indian."

"But it was I who was injured!" I proclaimed.

Master Usher took careful notice of me, touching my forehead and examining my wound. For all the blood, the damage was small, a little nick no wider across than a farthing. Still, he shook his head and sucked several times on his lips, making a kissing sound that meant his disapproval. "Ruffians, they were," he said. "Many such ruffians have we here in Boston these days."

He turned to James to ask, "I trust no harm has come to you, Goodman Printer?"

"None at all, thank you, Master Usher," James said.

"Oh, but that old farmer might have shot you!" said Annie.

Again, Master Usher made that kissing sound in the air. "Great burning wars are made from such little sparks as these," he said. "Calamitous days in calamitous times. But we have work to do."

He pulled a single book from the cart and unwrapped it from its paper. He turned it over and over in his hands, looking at the leather cover and the careful stitching of the binding. "I see your handiwork in this, Goodman Printer. It is sewn together as tightly as a lady's skirt."

And then he gently opened the book, oohing and aahing as his fingers marked the straight lines of type. "This is good, this is good," he said. "A book that sings as sweetly as the songs within."

Soon we emptied the load of books into a small storeroom. The shelves were already nearly filled with many books that were printed in Cambridge in my father's shop and others shipped in from London at considerable expense. I recognized an almanac, and a story of a shipwreck, and a history of New England, and a volume about the London fire and plague—all printed by S. Green, my father, who set his own name into type upon each title page. There were sermons and hymnbooks, too.

We carefully stacked the newest volumes in the space that Master Usher had saved for them. When we were done, he gave me a pail and a handful of pennies and directed me to a nearby tavern. "A good morning's work leaves a body dry," he said. "Tell the mistress at the Three Boars to fill this with her best beer."

The way to the Three Boars was crooked, and I thought I might be lost more than once. People were everywhere, but all too busy with purposes of their own to help a boy find his way in their hectic city. But soon I found the sign of three beasts with hairy backs and sharp tusks that were meant to be wild boars.

Inside, I handed my pail to a large woman with stout, bare arms who wore upon her face a habitual smile. The air within was rich with smells, of cakes and breads and beers, of all things made with yeast. As I waited for the pail to be filled, I looked about and saw idle men sitting around long tables. Some had children with them. And I saw that a small boy pointed at me and that all the men at that table took notice. One was a man with a torn coat, who stared at me with a single eye, for there was a patch upon the other. The man's good eye ran up and down me, like a tailor sizing me for a new suit of clothes. A ragged scar divided his face, which drooped in a perpetual scowl, broken teeth showing between his gaping lips. "A boy that loves Indians, are you?" he shouted.

I was so afraid that I could not speak. The boy must have been one of the ruffians who threw stones upon us.

"Answer when you're spoken to, boy," the man said.

"Oh, leave the child alone, Lemuel Brown," the mistress of the tavern said as she handed me back the pail, brimming now with frothy beer.

"It was an Indian who gave me this," the man replied, pointing to the patch. "And so it is that I have no use for Indians or for those who travel with them." He rose to his feet. He was a tall man, even without his hat, and he walked toward me with a grimy hand outstretched.

"Go, boy," the woman said, grabbing my shoulders and steering me toward the door. But Lemuel Brown stood before me, his face in mine, and reached for the patch as if to lift it.

But before he could, the tavern mistress bowled him out of the way. Sprawled upon the floor, he seemed more comical than menacing, and I laughed at him.

"Laugh if you must at this torn remainder of a man, but I'll remember you and your Indian friend," he said.

I ran down the narrow streets back to Master Usher's shop, splashing beer upon my path. The pail was half foam by the time I set it down again.

Annie stood alone in the shop.

"Master Usher has asked me to mind things until he and James finish their work in back," she said cheerily. "And you can help." There was nothing Annie wanted as much as to be left in charge of things.

But we had little to do until a tall man walked in, carrying a long gun, which he put down by the door.

Annie curtsied.

The man before her was a person of dark mood and frozen expression, one of those people who might keep his head down as he walked in hope that no one could speak to him and demand that he be cheerful.

"I am come for a book," he said, not bothering with the usual greetings or politeness.

"Then you, sir, have come to the right place," Annie said, teasing him. She smiled so hugely that it might have brightened a dark room, but he took no notice of her.

"It's a book of hymns that I want," the man said.

"Oh, sir, we have just the book for you, newly printed in Cambridge," she said.

Just then, James walked in with an armload of those very books. Annie plucked one of them away and tried to hand it to the stranger.

The man did not reach for the book but looked instead at James. And his expression, so glum before, changed to agitation and alarm.

"You are not an Englishman," he declared.

"In that, you are correct, sir," James said, placing the remaining books on a convenient shelf.

"And you have touched these books, sir!" the man said.

"Yes, that is true," James said. He did not appear puzzled, but I was.

"You have touched a sacred book!" the man said, his anger growing. "It is a defilement!"

"A defilement it is not, as you should well know, Captain Samuel Moseley, sir," said Master Usher, entering now with an armload of books.

"Still," said the captain, "I will take one of these instead." And the soldier plucked a book from the bookseller's arms.

The captain seemed pleased as he turned the little volume in his hands. How fine such a book feels to the touch with its soft deerskin cover. "How much will that be, Master Usher?" he said.

"Eight shillings for you," the store owner said.

"That seems rather dear," said Captain Moseley, now opening the book and seeing the handiwork of my father's shop. He reached into his jacket, pulled out his purse, and stacked the full amount upon a counter. With the book clutched in one hand, he grabbed his musket with the other and left us.

Annie began laughing, and when she laughed, with her voice as rich and high as any singer's, everyone could not help but laugh with her. And so we all did, James and Master Usher with the two of us children, not giggling or tittering, but with much heaving and bending over. "Oh, James," she said. "He did not want you to touch the book. But did you not touch every page of it in the printing?"

"There is not a page that I did not feed into the press," he said.

"The captain does not know, and I will not tell," said Master Usher, who now helped himself to the beer, or what was left of it after my hurried run through the streets. He was flushed and giddy. "Oh, Captain Moseley is a fiercesome soldier, most brave and honorable," he said. "But I think he has but little wit. And for that reason did I charge him eight shillings for that pretty new book of songs instead of six, which is the price for other, gentler persons."

Our business in Boston was not finished when we left the bookseller. Our printing shop devoured paper, which had to be shipped from London, and we were to fetch one hundred reams newly arrived in the port. Flags of many nations flew from the ships anchored in the harbor and snapped in the wind. Along the wharves, brawny men lifted huge casks and crates with block and tackle and lowered them into wagons.

The paper came in large sheets, packed into crates for shipment. And our poor horse, who I thought the strongest in the world, strained against the load. The wharves of Boston were little compared to what they are today, but to me they seemed splendid enough. I had to lean back in my seat to see the mast tops of the ships, these no different from the ones that brought my father to this same place full forty years before.

As we slowly rolled through the streets of the port, I spotted an odd figure of a man, an Indian dressed in foolish finery of women's ribbons and bits of lace, of gold buttons and turkey feathers stitched upon a bright blue English coat. He carried a large, round sack over one shoulder. I pointed to him, and after one look, Annie and I could not help but laugh to see this dark-skinned, prancing dandy of a man. James preferred not to look at all, but to mind the horse and reins.

Annie and I were not the only ones to laugh. A mob of English children, idle boys, mostly, tagged after him. "Your Royal Highness!" they shouted, doffing their hats to him. "Your majesty!"

"And who is this majesty?" I asked. "James, do you know him?"

"No kin of any king I know," said Annie, laughing at the antics of this mock monarch, who carried himself proudly, smiling at the rabble that taunted him as if they were gathered to amuse him.

"Oh, he is a king and a king's son," James said, "as truly a monarch as our own King Charles, though of a smaller realm."

"Look at the wampum about his neck," Annie shouted, pointing to the Indian's enormous necklace of white and blue shells. These were the pounds and shillings of Indian currency, and could be exchanged for English money. Like some rich English merchant wearing necklaces of gold, he was wearing his fortune for all to see.

"Who is he, James?" I begged. "Please tell us who he is."

But before he could answer, the "Indian

majesty" took notice of us, sitting high upon our cart. Ignoring the mob that surrounded him, the man fixed his eyes upon James and walked directly toward him. The ruffian children followed after him.

He stood in the path of our wagon. The horse reared up and then stopped. The Indian walked to the side of the wagon, put his sack on the ground, and reached for James's arm as if he intended to pull him off the cart. He succeeded only in bringing their two faces close together.

"What is your name?" the Indian dandy asked in ordinary English.

"James."

"I know of you," he said. "You are James the printer. You are a Nipmuck. I know your father and your brothers well."

James said, "I am the one you speak of."

The Indian had the most terrible expression upon his face, a fiercesome look where moments before there had been a tight and idiotic grin.

"You know who I am?" the Indian asked.

"I know you," James said. "The English call you King Philip."

I should have known him all along. My father often complained of this Philip, the Indian sachem who wore women's ribbons and lace and claimed to be the equal of our own King Charles. He was given the English name in jest when but a boy, after a royal Greek, Philip, the king of Macedonia and father of the great Alexander. My father said that he ran up debts among the English merchants and then refused to pay them.

The Indian did not let go of James, who held tight to the cart to keep from tumbling down. The little mob of children kept shouting out advice. "He's a king, all right," one boy said. "King of the savages."

"It does not trouble me if the English laugh at me," King Philip said, tightening his hold on James as he spoke. "They look upon me and see what it is they wish, a wild heathen, a child in love with bits of lace and bright cloth. Let them think me a crazy fool; I want them to. But you will speak of me as Metacom, sachem of the Pokanokets. My father was Massasoit, who knew this land before the English. My brother was killed by them. The day will come when no one of us is safe in our own land. And whatever clothes we wear, we cannot hide, for they will know us by our skin." He placed a hand on top of James's hand, both the same shade of brown. "One day I will call for you, and you will come."

And then, as suddenly as he had grabbed him, Philip let James go. He stood for a minute looking at us. It was then I noticed the large tomahawk with rounded stone and the long knife he carried on his belt—one to bash the skull of an enemy, and the other to take his scalp.

He bent to pick up his sack. I could not help myself. I had to know what was in it. "What do you carry?" I asked him.

Philip smiled at me and at the band of ruffian children as he reached into his bag and pulled out what looked like a ball covered in fur. Then he reached in again and brought out a second. With his arms outstretched above his head, he turned so that everyone could see. In each hand, he held the severed head of a wolf. Whatever beauty there might have been in these animals was gone now. The hair was dirty and matted. They stared at us through dull and sunken eyes.

"Once each year, I must take five of these to Plymouth, to fulfill the pledge I made when I agreed to keep the peace with the English," he said to James.

"And what do the English do with them?" James asked.

"They mount them upon poles and make great ceremony and mock my people, the Pokanokets."

"So why do you continue?"

"Better a wolf's head upon a pole than mine." The sachem laughed heartily at his own joke. "Better a wolf's head than an old Indian's."

Quickly, he returned the heads to the bag, picked it up, and marched away, the mob of children following after him.

"He frightens me," said Annie.

I was frightened, too, but did my best not to show it. "Father says that he's a weakling and a fool," I said as confidently as I could.

James looked at me severely. "Philip is not a weakling or a fool," he said. "And we would be wise to treat him like the king he is and not make him angry."

He clucked to the horse, which strained against the load and took us home.

CHAPTER THREE

SOUNDS OF WAR

IT WAS THE JOB OF MY HALF-BROTHER, SAM, to make me a printer. Sam was a large man, grown powerfully strong from working the presses every day, with bulging arms and a chest like the trunk of a giant sycamore. There was no more kindly man in the world when the work of the day was done and he had time to talk and joke about. But he also had another side, as if two separate people lived inside the one body. This other Sam was quick to anger and had no patience for a mere printer's devil.

One late spring evening, some weeks after I first saw King Philip, Sam sent the letters flying at my head like bullets. If they could have spoken, they would have sounded out whole sentences of harsh warning and stern advice.

In the year since I began to work as a printer's devil, I had made a poor beginning.

"You have forgotten all I taught you," he said.

He was wrong about that. He had taught me to hide from him when he was angry, a lesson I never forgot. Now I dodged the tiny pieces of lead and did my best to hide behind a table full of printed pages neatly stacked.

"Shiftless boy!" he yelled. "Half a brother of mine, but all the wit and brains from that other half!"

Now that was more than I could bear. This insult was aimed not just at me but at my mother, Sarah Clark Green, who was my father's second wife. She was two years younger than Sam, but mistress of my father's house. He was bound to be obedient to her and even to call her Mother. Yet this did not sit well with Sam, who seemed to be always picking quarrels with her.

There was no gentler person in all the world than my mother. She could not lift a rod against me, her firstborn son. If that was a fault, then it suited me just fine.

Now Sam had insulted her and I could not let it pass. "Half-brother! Half-wit!" I said. "Whole villain! Full knave! And fool complete!"

No boy of that time could say such a thing to an elder and not expect to be punished.

Sam reached for a willow switch. There was a good supply of them in the print shop, for just such an occasion as this.

What a sight we must have been, in the glow of burning candles, among the presses and tables in the printing room of the old Indian school at Harvard College. Here a stout man advanced toward a slight boy who stood as still as he could, flinching before the punishment that was due him.

Just then the far door opened and James walked in.

He wore no hat over hair as straight and gleaming black as if he had combed it with bear grease. I was glad to see him.

"What's this I hear, Bartholomew?" he asked in the pleasant voice of an English gentleman. "I could hear your voice all the way to your father's house. If your gentle mother were in her bed, your quarrel has surely wakened her."

The shop was next to Harvard College, in a two-story building called the Indian college, although Indians studied there no longer. Now the brick edifice was home to a few English students, who slept upstairs, and to my brother, Sam, who had a small room above our shop. As an apprentice, James slept in the shop itself, between the press and the hearth, the better to start work early and stay on late.

My father and mother's house, as James did know, was in the town, a full half-mile away near the creek road. My voice could not have carried so far, even on a calm, spring night.

But James's words shamed me.

As for Sam, he laughed as if the whip of willow in his hand were nothing more than a jest and put the branch away.

"It was but a friendly debate between loving brothers," he said.

"Enemies do not always cut so deep," James said. "What was the cause of your quarrel?"

"He has confused his 'p's' and 'q's' again," Sam said, sure that James would know just how terrible such mistakes could be in a printing shop. "And his 'b's' and 'd's,' and has them so often turned about that two cases of letters need re-sorting. I wonder that he will ever become a printer."

This hurt me as much as any piece of type thrown by my brother. There was nothing on earth I wanted more than to be a printer, like my half-brother and my father. Like James. My mother wanted me to sit all day in school, to become a minister as my Uncle Robert had. But I could not sit still for school and I fidgeted in churches. My dream was to rise in the printer's craft from devil to apprentice to journeyman and to master. I wanted to see my own name upon a title page, "printed by Bartholomew Green." But the lead letters used in the press were all reversed, as if they had been copied from a looking glass, and even after a year I did not know how anyone could read them.

"He will learn to sort type soon enough, if guided by a strong but kindly hand," James said.

"I have no patience for him, I'm afraid," Sam said. "James, won't you take over his instruction? For you can calmly see his faults when I cannot. Let us see what *you* can make of this bent piece of a boy."

"There is no better time to begin than now," James replied. "Before the candles are snuffed out for the night, he will make both these cases right."

"And pick each piece of type off the floor," Sam added. "For he is the cause of the rage that sent it there."

I was about to object, but James spoke first. "Of course, he will find every last piece. And once done, I will teach him the trick of reading type, how each letter is different from the other and how to know them all by touch as easily as sight."

Just then the door opened again, letting in a gust of springtime air along with my cousin Annie and an old woman.

"Good gentlemen!" the woman said. "I have a tasty cider for you tonight." It was Goodwife Gray, who each night at the same hour brought a bucket of ale or cider to the shop. Her nose and cheeks were covered in spidery red marks, the little signs, it was said, that she sipped too much of the drinks she brewed.

Sam took a full cup of cider, drank it down in a gulp, and then took another. He sat sprawled upon a chair near the fireplace, his day's work done. When Goody Gray offered a cup to James, he refused it as he always did. He drank only water, and took that plain, without sugar or spice, the way I learned to like it, too.

Now Goody sat down opposite Sam by the fireplace, with a large cup of her own brew in her hands, so the two of them could exchange gossip from around our town. Nothing happened that Goody did not know, it seemed.

James bustled around the shop, making it clean and ready for another day, as I crawled about looking for each missing letter. Then James stooped down with me, to begin going through the little compartments of type, as Annie watched over us.

"The little barbs and flourishes, the serifs, set

each letter apart," James explained. "Once you know them, there is no mistaking a 'b' for a 'd.' You can read them with your fingertips."

I began to study the two letters, taking my time and not rushing the way I always had before. "I see it," I said at last. "I can tell them apart."

James took one of each letter and put his hands behind his back. Then he held out a large, brown fist and opened it. This was a workman's hand, large-knuckled and callused. The little bit of lead seemed even smaller in his palm than mine.

"Which is it?" he asked. And I knew the piece of type was a "b"; there was no mistaking it. Soon he had scrambled all the difficult letters, and I found it easy to tell them apart.

"Now you will have no trouble setting all the type case right," he said.

I began doing so, pleased with myself for learning so quickly. But my cousin Annie, who had been watching the whole time of my lesson, had a different view.

"You are so slow," she said. She took the tray of type from my hands and quickly began to sort through it, picking out letters that were out of place.

She had learned by watching, and already was quicker than I.

James was delighted. "Soon enough the two of you will be as good as master printers, and I will be able to sit idle while you do the work of the day."

As the two of us sorted the type, James joined Goody and Sam by the fire.

"What news do you bring us, Goody?" James asked.

She sat in a wobbly chair, rocking back and forth, ready to ladle up the news she had gathered as she made her evening rounds through the college and the town. Before there were newspapers in New England, we relied on Goody for our news.

"Much news, this night," said Goody Gray. "Have you heard of the three Indians held at Plymouth for murdering John Sassamon, the Indian teacher?"

"I knew John Sassamon," Sam said. "He was a well-spoken man, and I was sorry to hear that he was killed last winter."

"I never did like him," Goody confessed. "He was such a sour-faced man, and liked to pretend to be better than he was born. He was always sneaking around the college as if he belonged here. And him a savage in English clothes."

I looked at James when she said this. Did she think our James was but a savage in English clothes? I could not tell if James paid her any attention, for at this moment he rose for a drink of water.

"They say these Indians killed this Sassamon because he was too friendly with the English. They say King Philip was behind it," Goody said, shaking her head as she spoke. "For you know that King Philip called him an English spy and wanted him killed."

"But what of the three murderers?" Sam asked. "They were the ones you were going to tell us about."

"Two of them are dead," said Goody, pleased that no one present had heard this news. "As for the third, when he was hanged, the rope broke neatly in two, and so he lived to be hanged another day."

"Then there will be a war," Sam said.

For weeks in my mother's house, there had been hushed talk of war, and King Philip was at the center of it. I dreamed of him, covered in ribbons and lace, the wampum belt about his neck, and holding the wolves' heads high above his own. I shivered at the thought of him.

"There will be a war," Goody agreed. "There are signs of it everywhere. Have you seen the comet in the sky? Now, I myself have not. My poor eyes fail me, but people with far better eyes tell me it's there, so it must be so. And in Boston, it is said, a baby was born with lizard skin and horns upon its back. I have not seen this child, you understand, but I heard it direct from someone who heard it from her cousin, who saw it herself. And you've heard what happened near Mendon. There was a chicken hatched that had two heads. These are omens of great events. War and rebellion are sure to be coming soon." She rocked back in her chair, pleased with herself for bringing us word of coming calamity.

"If there be a war, it will be a short one," Sam said. "The Indians are no match for the English. We will drive them from New England if they dare to take arms against us."

Annie spoke up. "My father says that the Indians have many just complaints against the English, who take their property and give them trinkets and ale in exchange. He says that those who have lost everything can be the most terrible foes."

"Not against our English muskets," Sam said.

James picked up a rag and wiped the printing press clean again, leaving it polished and gleaming. He took pride in his craft, in the printing of words upon paper. Surely, no one would want to drive him from New England, I thought.

"If there is a war, King Philip will not start it," James said. "He believes that whoever draws first blood must lose, and he will not strike first."

"Oh, he's a fool," said Goody.

"Do not be mistaken about him," James said. "He is no fool. He is wiser than he seems."

Goody Gray reddened, the color spreading across her cheeks as if ignited by her red nose. Custom did not allow an Indian man, no matter how well he had been taught in English ways, to speak like that to an English woman, even one who earned her living by the penny selling ale by the pint.

"Be careful how you speak," she warned him, "to old Goody Gray." To this, James again grew silent as he wiped the presses one more time.

After finishing a third cup of Goody's cider, my brother, Sam, was excited. "If there is to be fighting, then I will be the first to go," he said.

I could see him marching into battle with a musket upon his shoulder. And I said, "Oh, I wish I could go with you."

"Will many scalps be taken?" Annie asked. She and I had seen an old man who had lost his scalp in the war against the Pequots. He wore a funny patch of fur on top of his head. Sometimes, to entertain small children, he took it off to show an oblong spot that was covered with neither hair nor skin, but just plain bone.

"A good many scalps will be lost," answered Sam. "English and Indian alike, I am afraid."

Goody Gray touched her cap. "No one would want these old gray locks," she said. And then she laughed. I trembled to think that my own sandy hair could be hanging on an Indian belt or trophy stick.

"If there is a war," I said, "I shall ask Father for a musket of my own."

"And I will have one, too," said Annie.

Goody Gray drained another cup of her own cider and was feeling very jolly. "No Indian will be safe if you two are called to arms," she said, rocking with laughter.

Now the door opened, and my father, Master Samuel Green the senior, entered. Every night he came by to inspect the printing shop and see that all was in order.

"You burn my candles by the dozen," he said, and began snuffing half of them out one after another, pinching the flames with his fingers.

The evening air was cool, and my mother had seen that he wore a red cloth cap, and a scarf about his throat. He threw off the scarf and tossed the cap upon a writing table. His head shone as if it had been oiled and polished.

He was a hardy man of sixty, even stouter than my brother, Sam. He took a chair by his accounting desk and pulled out a ledger.

I ran up to him. "There's to be a war with the Indians, Father," I said. "Sam says so."

"Believe it not," he said. "For we taught

them a lesson in the Pequot war. No Indians want to risk the wrath of good, God-fearing Englishmen."

"But the two Indians were hanged," I said.

"Harsh justice will prevent a war," he said, "and not encourage it. And Master Eliot's Bible will not wait for a war. You know what that means to us? A new translation of Master Eliot's Indian Bible in the Algonquian tongue?"

"Endless trouble," said Sam, who had been a printer's devil years before when the first Indian Bible was put to press. He and James had both helped in the printing.

My father ignored Sam. "It means a great commission. Paper by the gross and ink by the barrel."

I had seen one of the old books, which was printed before I was born. How beautiful the words looked upon the page, so rich in "k's" and double "o's," the sounds that filled the Indian language.

Master John Eliot had translated it, and my father had set it into type. Now there was to be a new Indian Bible, as part of Master Eliot's plan to make Christians of all the savages.

Many believed that there would be no worry of war with the Indians if he succeeded.

"The Bible is such a fine book for a printer," my father said. "At eight pages to a sheet, one sheet per week, it's work for two and a half years. And to think, when I first came to Massachusetts Bay, I had so little to my name and no shelter from the elements. . . ."

"Except for an empty barrel," said Sam, supplying the end to the sentence. Whenever our father spoke of his progress in the world, which he did often, he began with that empty barrel. When he first came to Boston, he always told us, he had not a penny for lodging, and curled up each night in a large shipping cask and wondered whether he might freeze to death in the bitter cold of winter. We all smiled, even James.

"And now, here am I," my father said.

"A man of property," I said, knowing the speech by heart. "Printer of the laws. Clerk to the county of Middlesex. Deacon of the church. And an officer of the militia." I loved the sound of my father's many titles.

Sam laughed aloud now, his face red and grinning.

My father looked at him with a stare that might wither a prune. "You cannot know the hardship we Puritans suffered when we came new to this land. Scarce a dozen proper houses. Boston was an infant town, and Cambridge no more than a bog. Often I wondered that I might die here in the wilderness, so far from my home, as did so many others. But I put my shoulders to the work and my faith in God, and see how I have profited."

Once begun in this way, there was no stopping him until, like a clock, he had run all the way down. We all grew drowsy listening to the soothing rumble of his deep voice.

As soon as his history was done, he stood up, put on his scarf and cap, and was gone into the night. Goody Gray, walking wobbly, quickly followed. Sam left for his room, upstairs in the Indian school.

James patiently checked the type in the cases that Annie and I had sorted. He could find no mistakes. "I am impressed with your perfection," he said. "I will make printers of you both."

Annie laughed at the thought that a girl might become a craftsman. "If only I were a boy," she said. "Then I could become a printer, just like you, James."

I wished that she *could* become a boy, so that we would be printers together.

"James, when did you know you would be a printer?" I asked.

"When I lived at the Dunsters' house, they kept the college printing press in a room downstairs," James told me. "It was run in those times by the two Dayes, Stephen and Matthew, father and son. Master Dunster called them Night and Daye, because the son was so much sunnier a man than his father. It was Master Matthew who let me feed a piece of paper into the press and then helped me turn the handle. And when I pulled it out, I could see that it was full of letters and all manner of words. It was magic, surely. He said to me, 'You are a printer now.' And since that day that is all I wanted to be."

He sent my cousin and me home. The night was surprisingly cool, and the sky clear and moonless. I insisted that we stop and look for the comet that Goody told us about. We lay upon the damp ground, looking up and straining our eyes to pick out a single point from a haze of millions of stars. And to our amazement, we saw instead a shower of meteors, skimming across the sky like flat rocks bouncing upon still water. As soon as one was gone, another followed and another, hundreds of them splashing and skipping above us. And then, following the path of a shooting star, I noticed the comet, a tiny globe followed by a long tail of light—an exclamation point in the middle of the constellations.

"It is the comet, just as Goody says," I whispered, pointing to the place, hardly able to catch my breath.

"Then there will be war," Annie said softly.

We lay quietly for a while, expecting the comet to come crashing down to earth, but it did not seem to move at all. If this was a sign of horrible events to come, it should have been a larger spectacle. There should have been hot sparks and glowing lava like the volcano Vesuvius. There should be the smell of brimstone in the air. The air should roar, the earth tremble. But this was all there was, a little piece of punctuation in the sky, like the one I set at the end of this sentence! It was a disappointment. Then I heard an odd sound, a creature moving across the grass of the meadow, and then the high-pitched cry of an owl while on the hunt.

"Hear that?" I said most quietly.

"It's just an owl," Annie said, but she, too, spoke no louder than a whisper.

Gently, softly, I rolled around so that I lay flat on my belly. And so did Annie move as well. We looked in the direction of the screeching. There was something odd about the sound, like nothing any bird or animal might make. And it moved across the field, not with the quick speed of a bird in flight but with the easy amble of a man walking. And then we saw it by starlight, a dark figure gliding toward the Indian college and the printing shop, where lights still burned. It was calling out into the night, like a screech owl. I could feel a prickling in my scalp.

As it moved nearer, it took the form of a man wearing a great cape about his shoulders. Annie and I watched without speaking. I could hear my own breath now, which had become a rapid, raspy wheeze—a sound lost in the breeze that ruffled through the stiff grass of the meadow. The man—or what I now thought to be a man—moved past without noticing us, although just a few feet away. Soon he was at the door of the printing shop, which opened for him. James stood there with a candle in his hand, waiting as if he had expected this visitor. And when this stranger finally reached him, James stepped inside and closed the door behind them. All manner of trappers, traders, scholars, and ministers passed through our little town, but few at such a late hour, and fewer still signaling their arrival like a bird of prey.

"Who can it be?" I asked, finally able to breathe again.

"Let us go see," said my cousin. I wanted to do no such thing, but when she stood and walked to the printing shop, I could not help but follow her.

As quietly as we could, we tripped across the field. The two-story building had true glass windows, and those in the printing shop glowed from the candlelight within.

We looked through a window. James was speaking with a man who had his back to us. Across his broad shoulders was a great brown cloak. With an easy movement, he removed it and I could see that beneath it he wore an English jacket of bright blue, decorated all about with bits of ribbon and pieces of lace. Even from the back, I recognized him from our journey to Boston by the cut of his coat and its womanly decorations. Now he carried a musket in his hand and a powder horn at his waist along with the long knife and roundheaded tomahawk.

"King Philip!" I said, every breath now whistling through my throat.

"It is, certainly," Annie said. "What does he want of James?"

The two of them seemed to be arguing, but we could not hear about what.

All of a sudden King Philip turned around and glared toward the window. This was not the face I expected, the one I had seen by Boston harbor. It was now divided down the middle by a thick line of black paint that cut in two his forehead, nose, mouth, and chin. One side was red, the other blue. The colors made the face into a fearful mask, but it was the eyes that were most fiercesome, pitch-black circles upon a field of white.

I was sure he could see us through the glass. He was speaking loudly, spitting out his words like bitter seeds as if he were cursing every English boy who had ever taunted him.

Suddenly, he swung his body around, pulled on his cape, and bolted for the door, with James following behind as if to catch and stop him. Hardly breathing at all, I grabbed hold of Annie and the two of us hid behind a stack of firewood. James and the Indian king were outside, speaking loudly, sometimes in English and sometimes in Algonquian.

"Perhaps this war can be stopped before it has begun," James said.

"It is too late," Philip said. "The governor of Plymouth is set upon it, and will not stop until all of us are dead or sold into slavery. And I will not let happen to us what happened to the Pequots! We will not go so quietly. Wherever there are English, we will fight them. And we will take what matters most to them. It is by things that these English take their measure of a man. By houses, horses, cattle, and grain, by guns and candlesticks. All these things we will strip away until they cry out with pain. Then the time will come when a peace will be made, and that is why I need you. You can read and write the words of the English."

"I cannot go with you," James said at last. "My life is here, making words on paper for men to hear."

The other Indian laughed. "The time will come when you are as hated among them as I am hated. Then you will have no other place to go but to me. You will see. Fare thee well, James Printer. Fare thee well."

He left James standing there and marched straight in our direction. If he had found us, I don't know what he would have done. The great tomahawk that hung from his belt easily could have crushed my skull. And the long knife would have made quick work of my scalp. He walked by the woodpile, moving so swiftly that we could feel the breeze of his body as he raced by. He did not notice us at all.

When he was gone, James went inside. We waited for a few moments while he put out the candles. "We cannot say what we have seen," Annie said. "No one must know that King Philip was here."

"But why not?"

"James will be in trouble, don't you see?" Annie said.

And I did see that she was right. It was no fault of his that King Philip came to see him, but it might not be seen that way. And if there was to be a war against King Philip, James might take some blame for it. So, I did not tell my mother or my father what we had seen, although I knew it would be expected of any Puritan boy.

That night, safe in my bed, I could not seem to sleep. I could hear the breathing of my younger brothers, and felt the jostle of their every flop and turn. But later, the moon risen in the night, I dared to close my eyes. And soon I dreamed of an Indian with a face of red and blue, who grabbed me by the hair and pulled out a long, sharp knife to take my scalp. But it was not the terrible painted face of King Philip that I saw in my dream. No, the face in red and blue that I saw in my dream belonged to my friend, the printer James.

CHAPTER FOUR

FIRST FLIGHT

THE NEXT MORNING STARTED OUT ORDINARY enough. My brother Sam often said that my tongue was like a clapper on a bell, always ringing. But this day, the clapper did not ring at all, and I told neither Sam nor my father what had happened the night before. And Annie, too, was unduly quiet. The sun not yet fully up in the sky, I was already at the printing shop, where James taught me to fill a small wooden frame, called a composing stick, with type.

These blocks of letters would later be locked into a larger frame, called a chase, from which a page was printed.

James was no different than I had known him, but I looked upon him now in a new way. I saw in his face a little bit of King Philip's face, the color the same as King Philip's, the same dark hair and eyes. Yet I could say nothing about what I had seen.

I took comfort on this day in my work. There were sticks and chases to be filled or torn apart, and the letters sorted so that they could be used again. Several times I wanted to speak to James of King Philip, but I dared not, even to him.

My day proved long and I was weary. After I became a printer's devil, there was never enough time for sleep. At nightfall, I would fall into the bed I shared with my younger brothers and plunge into my dreams the way a pebble falls into a well and then sinks into dark water. Almost nothing could wake me.

But on this night I was awakened by the steady beat of a drum, *rat-a-tat-tat*. At the same time, the church bells began ringing. Every man, woman, and child in Massachusetts Bay knew what the bells and drumroll meant. It was the call to arms. Each man of the town was to bring his musket to the meetinghouse, close by the commons.

By the time I went downstairs, my father was already dressed. He was a captain in the militia. And he carried a long gun and a lantern.

"Go fetch James and your brother, Sam, double-quick," my father said to me. "Bring them to me at the meetinghouse." Then he added. "Do not forget James. Even more than Sam, he is the one I want to see this night."

As I raced down the street and across the field toward the college and the Indian school, I could see lanterns everywhere, floating through the night, joining together, flowing in one direction.

I was running, but someone overtook me when I was halfway there.

"It's me," said Annie. "I've come to help you." I needed no help, but was glad of her company.

First we went up the stairs to rouse Sam from his room, where we found him ready with his musket in hand.

"If war is to begin, let the enemy beware," he said. He charged down the stairs ahead of us, along with the young men of the college who carried no weapons but ran as fast as Sam did.

In the printing shop, James had already heard the drum and was preparing to join the others, although he had no musket.

"Father says you are to come to the meeting-house at once," I said.

"I am just leaving now," he said.

"Has the war begun?" Annie asked.

"It is my guess that it has," he said.

"Will you fight with us or with King Philip?" I asked him.

He looked at me with puzzlement. Did he suspect that I knew who had visited him just the night before? "How can you ask, Bartholomew? I am raised with the English. I work in your shop. I eat at your table. I read the same Bible. How could I take arms against you?"

I could keep back my secret no longer. "But we saw King Philip come for you, just yesterday night," I said.

"As you can see," he said, smiling now, "I chose to stay here and be with my English family." He did not seem surprised that I knew

King Philip had been to see him. He put his hand upon my bare head and then touched Annie's hair, too. "If I must fight, it will be to see that no harm can come to you."

Then he *is* English, I thought. More than he is Indian, he is English. But how, I wondered, could an Indian be English?

As he strode toward the meetinghouse, Annie and I had to run to keep up with him.

We joined a stream of men, and boys as young as twelve, with muskets, all marching to the meetinghouse. And they were joined by the women and children of Cambridge, by servants and slaves, too. All of the students at the college mingled among them, even though they alone of the young men would not be required to go into battle. If this was the beginning of war, everyone wanted to be there to see it.

Within a few minutes, a hundred men and boys with muskets were gathered before the meetinghouse, and there were many more without guns come to join them.

My father stood upon the meetinghouse steps with a lantern in his hand. On one side of him was Master Daniel Gookin, superintendent of Indians for the colony. On the other side was the same grim-faced man we had seen at Master Usher's bookshop in Boston, Captain Samuel Moseley.

My father quieted the crowd so that Captain Moseley could speak.

"There's been an attack at Swansea," the captain said. "A farmer boy rightfully killed an Indian, one of a band that slaughtered his cattle. That was what King Philip waited for. His followers have killed nine English, striking down six unarmed men as they returned home from church. Governor Leverett has promised to send our militia to join the troops from Plymouth. Our men will march to the south at first light to seek out King Philip's lair at Mount Hope and hunt him down. The war we have feared has now begun. Let us pray tonight that the war be brief and that God protect us from our enemies in this darkest hour."

With these words, the town of Cambridge entered what we called King Philip's War.

I expected the beginning of a war to be a sorrowful thing, a time of great fear and much weeping. But Captain Moseley's small speech touched off a celebration instead. The men and children of the town began building a huge bonfire upon the commons, throwing wood and even broken furniture into the pyre. Anything that could burn was used to feed the fire, which danced to the rhythm of drums and ringing bells and clanging pots and pans. Sparks rode up into the sky on clouds of smoke. And the crush of bodies moved around the fire, as wild as any forbidden dance about a maypole.

I saw my brother Sam by the fire in celebration. And Goody Gray. And even my mother who, unlike any of the others, looked forlorn as my younger brothers rushed around, more like savages than any Indian I had known. In the crush of bodies, Annie and I stayed by James, who climbed the steps to see my father.

"Master Green," James said, "I want to volunteer. I can fire a musket and be of use in putting down this rebellion."

"Of course you shall join us," my father said.

Captain Moseley stepped forward. "The governor has said that no Indians shall be armed," he said, "for we know not in which direction they might fire their muskets. And none will be allowed to come with us, because they might betray us to King Philip."

"But surely Governor Leverett was not

speaking of loyal, praying Indians like my apprentice James," my father said. "He will make a fine soldier and help bring this war to a speedy end."

"If I had *my* way," Captain Moseley said, "no Indian would ever more be allowed to carry a gun in any of the New England colonies."

"But many would starve without muskets for hunting," James said.

"I would let them starve before I would risk the life of one English man or woman," the captain said.

"You are a harsh and impractical man," said my father. "If Governor Leverett follows your advice, he will drive our friends among the Indians to the other side and double the numbers of our enemy. Tomorrow I will make my case to the governor himself, for we cannot allow such foolish policy."

Captain Moseley now seemed very angry. He said nothing, but even by lantern light I could see that his jaw tightened. My father took James aside and spoke to him outside of the captain's hearing. "Quickly get yourself to my house and out of sight. I worry now for your safety. And you children, go with him."

Annie and I followed James as he walked down the steps in the direction of the bonfire.

Just then a great black man came up to us. His name was Lazarus, a slave who lived nearby, on Marsh Lane. My father often said that it was wrong for a man to keep another as a slave, but many families in Massachusetts Bay had slaves and considered them property, to buy and sell as they wanted. Lazarus slept in a shed behind his master's house and tended fields and cattle.

"You'd better run," he said to James.

"And why should I run?"

"I heard my master and some others talk about taking their revenge upon the Indians."

"But surely he does not mean praying Indians like myself?" James said. "I've known your master since I was but a boy."

"That's why I am telling you to run," he said. "My master said it makes no difference whether an Indian pretends to pray or not. 'We must rid ourselves of all of them, or we'll be slaughtered in our beds.' That's what he said. And be sure he will spread that word, even if it is but a lie. I'm going to flee to the north to join with the French. I see no reason to fight a war for those who keep me a slave. You can come along if you like."

"Master Green will allow no harm to come to me," James said. "And he needs me in the shop to print the laws and proclamations."

"Please yourself," Lazarus said. "I have no time to waste arguing with you."

He turned and ran.

Just then, a man came up behind James and delivered a blow to his back with the butt of a musket. James fell to his knees, his breath taken away. Above him was the grim face of Captain Moseley. "I have my eye out for you," the soldier said. And now he swung his musket again, this time aiming it for James's head.

But James saw it coming and was able to grab it before it struck. He was a strong man, as anyone is who works a press for ten and twelve hours a day or longer, and he took the musket from him. Without the gun, the captain seemed to shrink before our eyes. "Be careful of that," he said, "for it is loaded and set to fire. And harm will come to you if you use it against me." James lifted the musket to his shoulder and pointed the weapon at the captain's head. He who was a bully large just a moment before now grew small and sniveling. With a yelp, he turned and ran away with notable speed. James followed his movement with the point of his gun. There was anger in his face, a hate as deep as any Moseley held for him.

How easy it would have been for him to put a lead ball in Captain Moseley's head. And then all James's life might have been different. But Annie cried out, "No, you must not!"

James did not lower the musket at first, but said, "Be you two witness at how easy it would be for me to strike down this Captain Moseley. But I did not. Tell your father and brother of what you have seen."

Saying this he threw down the musket and began running west toward the old Indian trail that followed the river Charles.

In the days that followed, Sam went off to war. He looked fine, I thought, with his long musket resting upon his shoulder and a bright blue cap upon his head. He and my mother had made a peace between them, and when he marched away, she wept for fear of his safety.

"Shed no tears, for he will return in glory," my father said. "There is nothing to fear, for the war will be quick and victory certain."

Yet we fretted over Sam and worried about James. There was no word from either for days. News of the war was slow to come to Cambridge.

Captain Moseley stopped by our printing shop one afternoon. "Any news of my Indian apprentice, sir?" my father asked him.

"The only good news would be word of his capture," said the captain, "and I have nothing joyful to report. It is said he has run off to join King Philip. And that would not surprise me."

"That would surprise *me* greatly," my father replied. "For he is a good man and a hard worker, who has only love for the English."

"A man does not run away unless he has treachery in his heart," said the captain.

"No, but a man does run if he has reason to be frightened, sir," my father said. "For you yourself know that a frightened man does run."

My father winked at me, because I had told him the story of how Captain Moseley had struck James with his musket and then run away himself.

"I will find this James of yours and bring him back myself so that he can be properly hanged upon the commons," the captain said before wheeling around and leaving the shop.

When the captain was out of hearing, my father said to me, "Better that James be gone for a time than to see his head upon a pole, looking out on the Boston Common."

That was the custom of that time, to hang criminals upon a scaffold and mount their heads on long staffs, which would be planted on the commons.

So I worried what might become of my friend James, as late spring turned into early summer. In Cambridge, the war seemed very distant at first. But then our Indian enemies went out on a cruel and daring raid, attacking the town of Mendon, which was close by. Eight English were killed there. And soon there was talk that Cambridge itself might be assaulted.

The summer grew terrible hot, and horrible vapors rose from the swamps and rivers and ponds. The thick air was ripe with mosquitoes and stinging flies. And in some places locusts came and attacked the crops. Ministers warned that these were signs that God was displeased with us and that we English might lose the war if we did not change our sinful ways.

The troops of Massachusetts Bay and Plymouth were said to have chased King Philip and his followers into swamplands. But the Indians knew their way and the English did not, and many English soldiers were lost. What was to be a quick war and a speedy return for my brother Sam and the other Cambridge men proved to be worrisome and slow.

Then late one afternoon in early August, the bells of every church and meetinghouse rang forth. Captain Moseley himself came riding in from Boston to say that there had been a great victory in the Pocasset Swamp, and that many of our troops would parade this day in Boston upon the commons.

My father wasted no time, but mounted up his favorite horse, a gentle, spotted mare. "Might I come, too?" I asked him. And he reached down a hand to me and lifted me up and seated me before him. Loping easily along, it seemed no time before we were again in Boston. Even with so many men away at war, it was a vast and teeming town. The dusty streets were full of all manner of persons as bells pealed and cannons fired in celebration.

On the commons, the governor and his council were gathered together. "Samuel Green," a voice cried out to my father. "Master Green." It was no less than Governor Leverett himself, dressed in black except for a crimson cape that hung from his shoulders. He grabbed my father by the hand and pumped his arm.

"We have a job for our distinguished printer. We have declared a day of thanksgiving for our victory in the Pocasset Swamp, and you must print the proclamation. The Almighty has rewarded his faithful people. The war will soon be over."

"Philip is dead, then?" my father asked.

"Not Philip," Governor Leverett said. "We will have him soon enough. But our men at arms have killed three of his closest followers, including a brother. And there they are."

He pointed toward a band of armored Englishmen, who were marching toward us in high spirits, as much from ale and hard cider as from the glow of victory.

In front of this company, three of the men carried long poles straight up over them, high above the crowd that teemed about them. And upon the end of each of the three poles was the head of an Indian. Each still wore black hair upon his crown, in death just as in life. I gazed at their lifeless eyes, wondering if I would know James if I were to see him thus, his head all by itself, cut away from the rest of him.

And as I stared at these three twisted faces, their mouths gaping, their skin blackened, I felt a chill start up at my feet and travel through my body. And when it reached my neck, the world turned black as a moonless sky. Next thing I knew, the governor of Massachusetts Bay himself was pinching my cheeks as I lay upon the ground. I had fainted.

But James's was not among the heads on the commons this afternoon.

Before the day was out, my father and I were back in our print shop, setting Governor Leverett's proclamation into type. Whatever joy we might have felt was dimmed by word that my brother Sam was not among the troops sent home in triumph. And just two days later, word reached us that there had been an ambush near Brookfield, far to the west.

It was there that young Captain Edward Hutchinson was killed. My family knew him well as a friend to Sam. It was a sad time for New England, for we knew then that we might lose this war.

So there was to be no thanksgiving. Instead, my father printed up another proclamation from the governor and his council. In place of feasting and thanksgiving, there were to be fasting and a day of mourning. Governor Leverett asked that churches everywhere in Massachusetts Bay begin collecting money for the many new widows and orphans, and for those that were to come.

It looked to be a long and ugly war.

One roasting August evening, when the trees did not sway to the slightest breeze, our neighbor and friend Master Daniel Gookin came to see us at my father's house. As superintendent of the Indians for Massachusetts Bay, he still made his round of friendly Indian villages, despite the dangers in this time of war.

My father wanted him to stay with us for supper, but Master Gookin had business in Boston and wanted to travel there that very night. "Then why have you come, if you cannot tarry awhile?" my father asked.

"I have been asked to deliver this to you," Master Gookin said. And with that he handed a folded letter to my father. "I think you will find some cheer in this," he said.

It had been creased tightly and was soiled, but my father shouted with joy when he saw its source. "It is from James," he said, and proceeded to read it aloud to us all.

"When last I saw you, on the night when this terrible war began, I was running for my life. And I did run the whole night through and into morning, until my lungs burned with every breath as if there were a fire blazing in my chest. I ran west along the Indian trails, far from any thickly settled place.

"Still, to be careful, I slept by day, hidden under thickets, sharing my bed with spiders and field mice. I had the clear water of the streams and ponds to drink, but no food at all to eat. I saw no one. Except one day, I crossed the path of a young Englishwoman, carrying a basket upon her shoulders. At first she saw me

from a distance in my English coat and was not alarmed. Yet as I approached, she let out a cry, 'Heaven help us, for the savages have come to kill us!' She dropped her basket and ran from me. It was then I knew that I was right to run from Cambridge. I stopped long enough to eat a few of the berries that spilled from the basket. Then I heard the first of the musket shots and I began running again, even more wildly this time.

"Now I stayed away from trails and roads and lost myself in deepest woods. I knew only the direction of the setting sun and I followed it until I dropped for need of sleep.

"On the fourth day, I was so tired that I could not continue any farther. I climbed a slow hill and thought of my mother, these many years dead. I wondered if I might soon see her.

"Below me, the woods opened up into a farmer's field. There were men and women working in it, dressed in somber blacks and grays. They must have seen me, for there was a great commotion among them. And a small group of them came toward me with long hoes in their hands, I thought, certainly to kill me.

"I dropped to my knees and prayed. The first

voice I heard did surely surprise me. 'He is not English,' the man did say in the Algonquian tongue. 'He is an Indian.'

"There were six men before me and all were Indians like myself. 'Where am I?' I asked.

" 'This is Okommakamesit,' one of them said.

"It was the praying village and plantation near the English town of Marlborough, just twelve miles from where my father and brothers lived. 'I know this place,' I said.

"And one of the men replied, 'And we know you, James the printer. Happy are we to see you.'

"Here I have stayed these many weeks and here I will remain, in safety and peace, until this war is done.

"Yet you should know that my thoughts are with you and your family, Master Green. Please send me news of your household, if you have any words to spare for me, but ask only Master Daniel Gookin to deliver them, for there are few other men who can be trusted.

"With greatest affection, I remain your obedient servant,

"JAMES PRINTER"

CHAPTER FIVE

Captured

I THOUGHT OFTEN OF JAMES AND WORRIED much about Sam. Yet I had no time for idleness. These were the busiest of days in my father's shop. So busy that my cousin Annie was given as much work to do as I. Just as James had become the first Indian printer in New England, my cousin, out of necessity, became the first girl to take up that trade. My father relied on the two of us to keep up with the heavy burden of business that a war leaves for those who stay behind. Without James and Sam, he had to work doubly hard to print all the proclamations and sermons, laws and almanacs, that were required of him. And no one could turn down any job, if he wanted to be sure he would be offered another.

Printing is a difficult craft, and for a while I was of little use to the main work of our shop. To set a straight line of type was no more natural than learning to read it. My lines sagged in the middle, or slanted off at the end. For a good appearance, it is often necessary to slip little slices of lead between the words and sometimes between the letters as well. Do it slipshod, and the spaces are uneven, and the sentences seem to stutter across a page. My father had spent a lifetime setting type, and seemed to give no thought to that task. I could have tied a kerchief over his eyes, as in the game of blindman's bluff, and with only his fingers to do his seeing, he still would have been able to set lines that were regular and pleasing to behold. For my part, the more I tried to make my lines right, the more they seemed to rise and fall like musical notes.

"It is a matter of knowing your craft by

heart," Father said, talking all the while his fingers were filling a stick of type. "What the heart knows, the mind does not need to remember."

I did the best that I could, and that was not very good. Yet, for Annie, the skills came easily. Quicker and surer than I, she soon was setting type almost as fast as my father. Taller and stronger than I, she could turn the handle of the press over and over as I stood by, feeding the sheets of paper into its jaws. When I grew weary of the work, she made a game of it. When my feet and arms grew sore, she spurred me on. She had that wonderful quality of being able to find happiness and purpose whatever her fortune.

We heard little from her parents. Trappers and traders, and sometimes settlers and ministers, would carry letters from us to Annie's father and mother in Deerfield. And from time to time one of these travelers would bring us a packet of letters from them in return. The war against King Philip, for all of its wild thrashings and cruel injuries, did not reach so far to the west as Deerfield. And my uncle wrote that he thought there was greater safety there than even in Cambridge itself. "In the vast emptiness of this wilderness, Indian and Englishman do not knock into one another as they might near a city, but have room enough to live at peace," he wrote. "May it be as peaceful with you as it has been for us here."

For Annie the work in the shop gave her little time to miss her parents, who were so very far away.

My father now worked harder than he had since he was a youth. Before James and my brother left, he minded the business of the shop but did little of its labor himself. Now, he stood beside Annie and me, sweating in the summer heat. He was already by this time an old man, and in that sweltering month of August, I worried for his health. His usually ruddy face was sometimes pale with exhaustion by the end of a day. But as the summer went on, the strenuous labor seemed to restore a measure of youthfulness to his body, and his bare arms bulged with strength as he took his turn at the press.

And all the time he worked, he talked cheerfully about the good fortune that was his from the time he first arrived in New England. "Blessed," he said, "I have been blessed in my trade. Even now with battles raging, I grow more wealthy by the day." My father could find blessing in anything that made a profit, even in this horrible time of King Philip's War.

Yet we did not escape the terrors and ugliness of wartime, even in our quiet village upon the Charles. Almost every day, men would return to us from their battles. They came home most often in groups of two or three, some with great wounds. And even those who came back with their bodies whole were changed in other ways. A neighbor of ours, the young Thomas Andrew, was home for weeks but sat silently all day before his house, unwilling to move from his chair. Sometimes as I ran by his house on some errand for my father, I would cry out to him heartily, "Good day to you, Thomas!" as if by shouting I could somehow rouse him from his wakeful slumber. But only his eyes moved in response, following me as I approached, passed, and left him behind.

Others returned home with tales of English triumph and their own valor. Jonathan Fisk showed anyone who listened how he had killed three Indians with his knife after his musket failed him. He acted out the drama with great enthusiasm. But showing us how he won this skirmish was not easy, because a bullet had wounded his right arm and now it dangled, shriveled and useless, by his side. Each of these men were heroes to those of us who were forced by our age or our sex to stay behind.

Yet when I heard of all the hundreds of Indian warriors who had been killed, I could not help but think of James. We had not received another letter from him and could not be sure he was still safe at Okommakamesit. Father often said he feared that all the Indians might soon be drawn into battle against us. And so I worried that James and Sam might one day aim their muskets against one another.

"Why so gloomy, Bartholomew?" my father asked as he took his turn at the press so that Annie might take a drink of sweetened cider. "This war will be over soon, and your brother home again."

"And what of James?" I asked.

My father now did not look so certain, but in the same cheerful way of his, he said, "James, too, will be back with us before long." The smile fled from his face, replaced by an angry determination. "I did not spend so much on his apprenticeship to lose the best printer in all of New England."

Yet I knew there was a greater cost to losing James than could be measured in pounds and shillings. My father missed his craftsmanship, his ability to set a straight line quickly, and sew a fine binding. But Annie and I missed his gentle nature and his good companionship.

One morning in late August, Sam came home, walking in the door of the printing shop as if he were returning from delivering books to Master Usher's shop across the river. Annie rushed up to him and threw her arms about his neck, grappling him so hard that he might have toppled to the earth if she did not release him. When I, more timidly, approached him, he surprised me by taking me up in his arms and spinning me about. He had never treated me before with such boisterous affection. I knew then that the war had changed him.

Father declared a day of thanksgiving. And for all the rest of that afternoon and into night, we did not one more jot of work, leaving the press just as it was, halfway through the printing of a proclamation. My mother roasted two fat geese and a dozen chickens, turning them upon spits set high in the fireplace so that their sweet aroma filled the house all the day. We celebrated into the evening, with neighbors joining in our festivities. There was plenty to eat, even for the children, and much cider and ale for all. It was a rowdy feast, and we only stopped for prayer three times, so large was our joy at Sam's homecoming.

My father was happier than Sam himself. "The work we'll do now that he's home!" Father said. "The commissions that he will bring us!"

But at first, Sam proved a disappointment. He was robust of body but not of mind, and given to idleness and ale. "What I have seen!" he told Goody Gray when she came by one evening with her buckets of cider. "I dare not tell you what I have seen!"

"Did you see any scalpings?" asked cousin Annie.

"Scalpings," Sam said, "and much worse. I cannot tell you all that I have seen." With our questions, Sam grew very serious.

"Were the Indians all terrible and frightening?" I asked him innocently.

He looked at me mournfully. "Yes, terrible. Yes, frightening," he said. "But ask me not about the Englishmen. About them, I will say nothing."

And for all those first weeks, as he sat idly in our printing shop as others worked about him, he was cheerful enough, but refused all talk about his many battles.

The month of August in the year 1675 ended with a terrible storm, which was called by some a furicane or a hurricano. Great winds came from the sea, pulling up whole trees as if they were but weeds plucked from a garden. The winds threw great ships up against the land and carried such a great downpouring of rain and hail that many crops were ruined and cattle swept away in sudden torrents.

At dinner, my mother complained that the vegetables she grew on a plot behind our house were destroyed. "I do not know how we will feed ourselves through the winter. These storms and the war, surely God has turned upon the people of New England," she said. "We have brought this upon ourselves with our wigs and fancy dresses."

"And the ribbons and the sweet scents and even dancing!" exploded my father. "Surely, the storm is punishment for our sins."

My brother Sam smiled at them. "Does not the same wind and the same rain strike our enemy?" he asked. "Perhaps the Almighty aimed His anger at them and missed His mark by a little."

Annie laughed and clapped her hands at this. Sam winked at her, as if there were a conspiracy between them.

Father looked at the two of them as he spoke to my mother. "Add to the errors of our day, that children no longer show their elders the respect that is due them."

But Sam spoke up. "If sins caused rain, then we would all be drowned," he said, "English and Indian alike."

I wanted to say that we should be happy that nearly all of us were safe and sound in a time of calamity. If only James were back with us! That night I prayed that he would return to us unharmed. Yet I did not expect my prayers to be quickly answered.

The next morning we were hard at work printing up a sermon for Annie's father, who was expected to visit us soon from Deerfield. Annie was not with us this day, but instead was helping my mother in the house. So it was that Sam helped my father and me and took his turn at the press. I marveled at how easily he was able to work the machine as we pressed out our pages one after the other, the ink black and gleaming upon the milky white of the paper.

It was not yet noon when we heard the steady booming of a drum. And then the church bell rang out, filling the town with its clangorous music. Sam rushed out of the shop and my father and I followed, racing to the beat of bell and drum.

Near the meetinghouse, we caught our first sight of them, a bedraggled little army of men walking in the heat upon the muddy road. Captain Moseley led the way, the only one riding upon a horse, which splashed mud upon all those who followed. Among them were twenty soldiers, a few in armored vests and helmets, and the rest in tattered clothing. Half carried muskets, the other half long pikes or swords, but all marched to the beat of the drummer, who followed behind them. Of all the soldiers, he was the best clad, his clothing somehow unsoiled. But under the summer's noon sun, he sweated as he banged out the rhythm on a huge kettle of an instrument that hung by a strap from his neck.

In the middle of this group were eight prisoners, a chain of men tethered by ropes that they wore about their necks. Their clothes were English, made of sad-colored cloth. But their heads were bare as were their feet. They were Indians in English clothes. And they, too, stepped to the clockwork beating of the drum. The street was lined with townspeople now, all watching this sorry parade of disheveled men. Yet there was great cheering. Men doffed their hats, and some threw them in the air. Young children squealed, while their elders shouted out huzzahs and hoorays. So must it have been when Julius Caesar returned to Rome with his captives in chains behind him. A crowd is thrilled at the sight of a conquering hero.

Yet there was nothing splendid in Captain Moseley's troop of men and nothing fearsome in his captives. When I reached the avenue I could see that their skin bled from the rubbing of the rough rope that tied them neck to neck, more like goats to market than men.

The prisoners walked with their heads down, from shame or the weight of the ropes that held them. One was much taller than the rest, a Goliath of a man, his legs like tree trunks. People shouted out that they knew him, that he was called Little John. Yet I did not stare at him for long because I thought I knew another one of them, walking at the end of the line. I ran along the side of the road to get a better look at him. Like the others, he was filthy, as if he had been made to roll about on the muddy earth. He was the sorriest of sights, but, yes, I knew him. His hair, which he had once worn neatly in the manner of a Puritan gentleman, had been cut down to an uneven stubble, like a field of hay that had been mowed with a scythe. Worse still was the sad look upon his muddy face, so forlorn that I thought at any moment he could burst into crying. My heart felt as if it had fallen in my chest, a heavy stone.

"James," I said, so softly that it is a wonder he did hear me, "can it be you, James?" This bent and muddy man turned his head and fixed his gaze upon me. In his eyes, I saw a spark, a flame, an anger. Yet I paid that no attention, for now I was sure that this was he, my friend and my teacher. "It's James!" I shouted, jubilant to know that he was here among us with his head still upon his neck and not mounted on a pole. I ran to him, ready to rescue and claim him back, for surely he did not belong here among these ugly and broken men.

Captain Moseley whirled his horse about and trotted toward me. He could have no choice now but to release him, and all would be as it had been before, with James working at the press.

James called out to me, his voice cracking like a crow's caw. "Back away," he said. "You do not know me."

I wondered if he meant to shun me. For, of course, I did know him, and I would not back away. I heard the heavy thwack of the blow across my shoulder before I felt the pain. I turned to see Captain Moseley still upon his horse, a cudgel in his hand, ready to strike again. His face was drawn tight in a toothy smile, his blue eyes wild with rage.

"You would strike a boy, Moseley?" It was my father stepping in the road in front of me, placing himself squarely between me and Captain Moseley's horse. My father, as I have said, was a man of stout and hearty build, but he looked small before the captain on horseback. "You ride through town, sir, like a victorious general. But who have you brought here but simple men, who mean us no harm. I know some of them and they are praying Indians, who would not strike a blow against the English. One of them is my own apprentice, a hard worker and as good and honorable a man as lives in New England." Captain Moseley did not lower his arm. "I have my rights in this," my father said. "He's been apprenticed to me these many years."

Moseley stared in wonder at my father. And then he looked at the crowd that lined the road. All movement was suspended. Children who had picked up pebbles and rocks to throw at the prisoners held back their hands. Jeering men and cheering women were suddenly silent. The drummer ceased his beating. The church bell did not stop, but continued in its joyful ringing. All watched my father, who stood firmly in the path of the cruel captain.

Moseley clucked his horse forward. The animal took two steps and balked at going farther, his warm breath in my father's face. "You will not obstruct me, sir!" Captain Moseley said. "These are my prisoners. They may wear English clothes and play at being Christians for their own cunning purposes, but they are enemies all the same. And I take them to the governor. You must stand away!"

"I will not move, Captain," my father said. "I know what awaits them in Boston and I cannot let you feed their innocent blood to satisfy the hunger of the mob."

"Then you be damned!" Moseley said. "Forward!" he shouted to his troops. He gave his horse a vicious kick and rode straight ahead, knocking my father to the muddy ground.

It was then that I understood what my father already knew. James might be hanged, even though he was guilty of no offense.

"Drummer!" the captain shouted. Suddenly, the drummer began rapping out his beat again, a fast cadence that made my heart rush to keep up with it.

I ran to my father to help him to his feet,

while the troops and their prisoners walked swiftly to the bridge that would take them to Boston.

Our good neighbor Master Daniel Gookin stood by us. Gookin looked my father over and checked his scrapes and bruises. He tested my father's limbs with his thick hands and fingers. "You are muddied, Master Green, but unbroken," he said. "At least we can be thankful for that. But we can all see what has come to pass. Many Indians who have stood by us in this terrible war will trust us no longer. If we treat our friends in this way, we will turn every one of them against us."

Clambering to his feet, my father agreed. "We must go to the governor and his council to see that Captain Moseley does no harm to these poor men," my father said. "They must know the value of my apprentice."

"I worry about the mob more than Moseley," said Gookin. "Our fellow Englishmen have developed a taste for revenge. And they have a weak eye and a poor memory for faces. All Indians have come to look alike to them. But our good governor, Master John Leverett, still has the sense to know one from the other. And he will listen to you and me."

I was told to help Sam ready our two horses, while my mother put together food for the journey. In the stable, my brother was even more outraged than my father by what he had seen. "Has it come to this, that honest men must be roped together and led through the streets like cattle?" he asked. Before I could answer, he said, "And then to see a respected tradesman like our father, knocked to the ground as if he were a felonious criminal! This vexes me greatly, and the governor will hear my opinion of it!"

He led the horses to the house. My father and Master Gookin mounted up and were soon nicely settled upon horseback. Sam jumped up behind my father on our poor old mare, who strained against the weight of them as they rode away. By the time the travelers turned upon Wood Street, the horses had reached a steady trot.

Now Annie came running from the house, followed by my mother.

I asked Annie, "Do you think they will be able to save our James?"

"We can only pray and hope," Annie said. Whatever she believed would happen, she did not cry, and I took heart in this.

My mother bid us both to go to the shop and to finish what work we could this day.

"If you keep busy, you will not worry so much as if you were idle," she said. But it was not so, even though there was much labor left undone. As we began sorting type, the work seemed more difficult than it had that morning. We toiled through much of the afternoon in silence. When we finally stopped to ready ourselves for supper, I thought I could hear distant bells pealing out their welcome to Captain Moseley and his men. Annie wiped away the ink from her face and hands. And suddenly she had an inspiration. For the first time, she broke into an enormous, crooked smile. "We must go to Boston, to help save James. If we leave now, we can be there not long after dark."

"Father will be angry," I said.

"Not if we save James," Annie said. "Then he will forgive us."

"It is true," I said. "But my mother will not allow it, and it would be a sin to disobey her."

"If we do not ask, we need not disobey," said my cousin. I looked at her now with a new appreciation. She seemed to have ideas that were all her own, as if she were a child no longer. We packed up what bread there was in the shop and a bit of cheese, wrapping them in spoiled paper from the press. And by foot, we set off for Boston, taking a roundabout way so that no one would see us. The only one who did was young Master Thomas Andrew, who followed us only with his eyes. "Wish us well, Thomas!" I shouted. "We are off to save James Printer!" But Thomas kept his silence.

CHAPTER SIX

The Noose

It was long dark by the time we reached Boston. Yet the streets were bright from a multitude of torches, and it seemed that few in the city were at home that night, long past the hour of curfew. There was a stream of them, men and women and children, all flowing in one direction with a single purpose.

"Hurrah for Captain Moseley!" said a little boy, a dark-haired urchin, grimy and with a terrible sore or growth upon one cheek. Small as he was, he held a smoking torch in a soot-blackened hand.

"Death to the savages!" answered another boy, this one taller and better cared for. "Death to the savages!"

The warm evening air was heavy with insects that circled about the flames the boys carried.

"Death to the savages!" the boys cried out together, and soon the crowd took up the cry.

"These foolish folks are the only savages I see," Annie said. "I worry that there is no kindness and courtesy left in this city."

She grabbed hold of my sleeve as we followed this meandering stream of people through the bent and winding streets. As the crowd grew thicker, she took my hand and I did cling to hers with all my might to keep from being separated. More than once, the moving mob congealed into a clot. Unable to stop, the people pressed ahead so hard that I easily could have been trampled, and Annie, too, if we were not careful to stay upon our feet. With all the smoke and flames, the jubilant anger of the crowd, I was glad to have Annie's hand in mine.

The moving crush stopped at the jailhouse, where the mob was chanting, "Death to the savages!" over and over to the beating of a military drum. A dark, heavyset man stood out front of the broad door. We soon learned that this was Captain James Oliver, the keeper of the jail. His face was strangely composed, one side of it drooping, his mouth in an odd half-smile. In one hand he held a cane, which he leaned upon.

Annie and I found a place to stand in a doorway at the top of a short run of stone steps, where we would not be squeezed by the crowd. We searched for my father, for Sam, for Master Gookin, but could not see them here.

Suddenly, someone shouted from the crowd, "Let us have them, Jimmy! Give us what is ours!" It was a man with an eye patch, the same Lemuel Brown I had seen in a tavern so many weeks before. I was not surprised to see him here, leading a mob. About him were men with ropes held in their hands or thrown over their shoulders.

I did not know from the look of Captain Oliver with his drooping half-face if he could change his expression if he wished, but he did not do so. "These men will have justice, Lemuel Brown," he said. His voice was not the loudest, but everyone could hear the force that was behind it. "They may be savages, but they have a right to English law."

"The outcome will be the same," replied Lemuel Brown. "Save yourself the trouble, Jimmy! Give them up." Others took up the cry. "Give them up! Give them up!"

Captain Oliver took one step into the crowd toward Lemuel Brown. He raised his cane and slapped it against his open hand. Snap. Snap. Snap. All other noise stopped, but for the insects singeing their wings in the torches.

"Most of you here know me. I am Captain James Oliver of the Boston militia, charged by Captain Samuel Moseley to keep these men in safety. What justice will finally bring to them, I cannot say. But keep them in safety is what I mean to do!"

"We'll give them justice ourselves upon the commons," said Lemuel Brown. I could see him clearly now in the light of the torches. His hair was dark and had been pulled out in odd places. There were sores on his cheeks, giving him a fearful look. Yet most frightening was not his appearance but that he now held in his hands a long coil of rope and had already fashioned a noose at its end.

"I can see what your verdict will be," Captain Oliver said. "Yet these men swear upon a Bible that they are God-fearing and never have made war upon the English."

"But I saw one of them myself at Brookfield, with my one good eye," said Lemuel Brown. "And it saw who killed our good Captain Hutchinson. It saw the one who struck him down without mercy."

Everyone in all of New England knew of the gallant Captain Hutchinson, who was killed at the battle of Brookfield a month before.

"And who is it you saw do the killing?" Captain Oliver asked.

"The enormous one, the one who is called 'Little John.' Let us have him tonight and we will trouble you no more, Captain."

The crowd was utterly silent as it waited for Captain Oliver's answer.

"Annie," I whispered, "he will not give him up, will he?"

But she did not reply.

Captain Oliver again raised his cane. Now

he shouted with a roar, "Go home! All of you, go home!"

But Lemuel Brown did not step back. And because he did not move, no one else moved, either.

And then with the suddenness of lightning, Captain Oliver struck Lemuel Brown across the face with the full force of his cane. Then wildly, he began turning in every direction, striking at the crowd over and over with all the fury of combat. It did not matter to him who was in his way, whether they be men or women or children. Because his anger was so much greater than all of the others' together, the mob moved back as if a whole battalion had attacked it.

And with some difficulty, because there was such a knot of humans assembled, the crowd turned in flight. Other soldiers now joined Captain Oliver, using clubs and muskets to push and jab the people of Boston away from the jail. Even Annie and I, who at first felt safe atop the little stairway, were routed out and forced to flee. How we escaped a beating I know not, but we ran as quickly as we could, following a trail of torches that set sparks flying like fireflies upon the air.

We ran far before we stopped, breathless, on a strange Boston street, unsure of where we were. It was then I caught sight of Lemuel Brown and some others, still carrying their ropes. They entered the tavern with the sign of the three boars. Master Usher's shop could not be far. And yet along the crooked paths and alleyways of Boston, we soon were lost.

"You be lost?" A boy of half my size came out of an alleyway, carrying a torch that filled the air with more soot than light. This was the same boy we had seen earlier, the one with a growth upon his cheek. Now that he stood still before us, I could see how poorly dressed he was, without a proper coat and hat.

"Lost we seem to be," Annie said.

"For a sixpence, I can help you find whoever it is you seek," the boy said.

"But we have not a penny with us," Annie said. "It would be a kindness if you could help us find my uncle and my cousin, who have come here to meet the governor."

"I know not who your uncle and cousin be, but as for the governor, he sits with the magistrates at the meetinghouse."

"Where is the meetinghouse?" I asked impatiently.

"You stand before it," the boy said. "But you won't get in unless you know a backward way. For the promise of a penny, I will show you."

"Then you have our promise," Annie said.

He led us down a dark alley that turned a sharp corner. Here he showed us where a window was left open in the summer's heat. "Through there and up the stairs," he said. "And for my penny, you can find me at the sign of the three boars."

He ran off in a shower of sparks from his torch. Now we stood in darkness. How still and warm was that night. Yet I shivered to think of that mob outside the jailhouse. Annie pulled herself up and through the window, and I was too frightened not to follow. Above us, up a flight of stairs, we could see the flickering glow of lamplight. And we were drawn to it the way the moths and insects fly into flame. We stepped slowly and carefully. But with each step, the boards of the stairway groaned with our weight. At the top was a brief corridor that quickly led to the open door of a large room, where men sat about a table in loud debate. No one noticed Annie and me, any more than if a pair of household cats had crept into the room and curled up in a corner.

I heard my father before I saw him.

"You, sir, know not the value of the man," he said. "You buy your rope by the shilling, but I measure this printer by the pound. If he is harmed, sir, there will be an accounting! An accounting! How many meals went into him, sir! Think of the flock of chickens, sir, devoured with a year's harvest of squash and beans and corn! Think only of the cheese, sir! A cartload of cheese has gone into him in all these years! And that is nothing to the expense of putting clothes upon his back! Harm him, and you will answer to me, sir!" He pounded the table. "You will answer to me!"

There was a mixed roar of anger and approval from the others. From where we stood, just outside the doorway, we could see my brother, his chair pushed out and his head tilted back as if there were a map upon the ceiling and he was studying it. Next to him sat good Master Gookin, his face flushed and puffed out with the words that he was ready to speak at any moment. And by his side was a man I had seen often in our village, Master John Eliot, the same man who removed James from his family and delivered him to the president of Harvard so many years before. Eliot was the author of the Indian Bible printed in my father's shop. His face was like no other I have ever seen, long and with a proud beak of a nose. There seemed to be no place for laughter in that face, and yet I saw that there was kindness in it. He was dressed all in black, as ministers always were in those days. His hair was long and white against the black cloth of his jacket. He looked down upon his hands now, as if he were in prayer or else half-asleep.

At the head of them all was Governor John Leverett himself. He was a handsome man, his hair still dark and straight. Like Eliot he dressed in black, with a white collar. There was no frill to his clothing this night, no splash of color like the red cape I once saw him wearing. Upon his head he wore a small skullcap. He thumped the table with a fist and asked for order. "Behave like the Englishmen you are and not the savages we fight!" he commanded. "Captain Moseley, what say you?"

Opposite my father, I saw the cruel figure of Captain Moseley. He rose to his feet. "Your honors, we came upon these men in an open field near the town of Marlborough, and they did turn and run. You know of the troubles that the English have there with these Indians. Thievery and worse. Storage sheds filled with grain that were burned to the ground. A cow cut loose from his owner's field and found some miles away, slaughtered. You talk of accounting. What price for this mischief? So when we saw these mischief makers run away, we did give chase for we knew we had found the guilty parties!"

Master Gookin now rose to his feet, much agitated, his hands in motion every way as he spoke. "I know them all, every one, and they are Christian men, all eight. And they no more deserve to be swung from the scaffold than any of us seated at this table."

"But they ran, sir," Moseley said. "Do you doubt that they ran?"

"And would you not run, Captain Moseley, if you were in their place, a company of men with muskets and pikes marching upon you?" Master Gookin said. "Tell me this, were you once fired upon? Did they show you even one sign of resistance? Your honor, Governor Leverett, these are praying Indians. They have no quarrel with us. They are friends to the English, our staunchest allies in this war against the truly savage tribes."

Moseley began to shout now. "Did you not hear yourself this night, the charges of Lemuel Brown, who saw one of these praying Indians of yours, one Little John, fire the musket that killed our own Captain Hutchinson? Your arguments fall to pieces against this cannon fire of evidence."

"I know not this Lemuel Brown or what he saw," said Master Gookin softly. "But the others among these Indians swear that John was at home near Marlborough at the time of the Brookfield battle."

"They swear it upon their Indian Bibles, I suppose," Captain Moseley said. "What they say cannot be trusted."

Now the Reverend Master Eliot seemed to awake, shaking his white mane as he spoke. "I, too, know these men, as you do not, Captain Moseley. There is Master Green's apprentice, the printer James. I have known him since he was a boy. No more devout soul exists among us. All of them have forsaken their savage ways. And if we turn against them now, if we take these eight men and march them to the commons, and hang them by their necks, we will have no Indian allies in this war. And who could blame every praying Indian for joining force against us?"

Governor Leverett now raised his hand, palm out, a sign that he had heard enough. "I see both sides to this quarrel," he said. "I understand the fears. Everywhere there are Indians still among us. They are servants in our homes. They work upon our wharves. If these, too, were to rise up in rebellion, who among us would be safe? In times such as these, we must take care. And it is also true that many of these so-called praying Indians are no more than heathens in English dress. They mouth the words, but their souls remain lost."

Master Eliot began to rise to his feet, but Governor Leverett raised his hand again. "Sir, hear me out," the governor said. "I know that there is truth in what you say as well. In the war against the Pequots, many of the Indian people were one with the English. And if we are to defeat King Philip, we will need our Indian alliances to hold, even if the governor of Plymouth colony is determined to drag every Indian into battle against us.

"So this is my decision. We will treat all eight of these Indians as required under the laws of Massachusetts Bay. If there be only suspicion of treachery and no evidence of it, then we must let them go."

Now it was Captain Moseley's turn to object. "But your honor . . ."

Again the governor raised his hand and with a wave of it brought back order.

"However, we cannot ignore the evidence brought forth by Goodman Lemuel Brown against the Indian known as Little John. I cannot say whether or not Goodman Brown is mistaken. That is for a court of law to decide. And so, tomorrow noon, this Little John is to be brought before the good magistrate, Master Edward Tyng, who will hear the evidence from all sides. And we must abide, Englishman and Indian alike, by the judgment of his court."

"And what of James?" my father said. "What of my apprentice?"

"We will hold him and the others for a time, and if there are charges against them, then a court of law must put them to rest."

With that, the governor rose. I raced to my father's side, troubled by what I had seen.

"Will he be hanged, Father?" I asked him. "Will James be hanged?"

Annie cried out, "You will stop them, won't you, Uncle?"

My father scowled. All thought of James seemed to be struck from his mind. "How did you come here? Have you disobeyed me?"

"We were afraid of what might become of James," I said.

"You should be worried more about the punishment due the souls of children who so freely disobey their parents," my father said, staring at me as if he were weighing the worth of my soul.

Annie came to our defense. "It is out of kindness we came," she said, "just as you have come."

My father paused. He rocked back and forth on his feet for several moments before he announced his conclusion. "You two shall stay the night with me at Master Eliot's house. And you will stand by me in court tomorrow to hear the arguments for Little John. I cannot say whether our James will be hanged or not, but you will know the outcome soon as I."

My father arranged to send a message home to my mother. "However good your intentions," he said to us, "you have brought great worry to that good lady. You will have to do much to earn her forgiveness."

We found our horses, which were stabled nearby. Master Gookin lifted Annie and me upon the back of one, and he led us down the Boston streets, which were quiet now except for the hollow beat of hoof on cobblestone. The old mare followed with Master Eliot upon her bowed back. My father and the others walked in silence all the way to Master Eliot's house in Roxbury. My brother and I were given a small bed to share, and all night long I did not sleep while Sam snored in my ears. Next morning, after a hasty breakfast, all of us walked back to the meetinghouse, where the trial was to take place. There was much talking now of who would speak first in defense of Little John.

Outside the meetinghouse, upon a post near the entrance where all were sure to see, someone had nailed a notice in an unpracticed hand. The writing said that "Guggins," meaning Master Gookin, was "a traitor to his king and country" and that this "Guggins" should "prepare for death."

Master Gookin tore down the sign, ripping it into fine pieces, which he cast into the street. "They who wrote this do not even have the courage to sign it! They sign themselves 'the New Society A.B.C.D.' When I know their names I will find them and thrash them just as I would a pack of pesky dogs."

"Take care," said Master Eliot. "Great fear brings even good men to do evil. Let us hope that this trial today can take that fear away."

But how gloomy all these wise old men looked to me that morning. And gloomy I must have looked as well, so fearful was I for James and the others. Only Annie smiled, taking pleasure in the sun of a new day. "Oh, I am not afraid," she said. "The truth is with us."

Already the meetinghouse was filling up. And as we walked in, many jeered at us, pointing and shouting out the names of us they knew. They singled out Master Gookin especially, calling him all manner of foul thing.

One tall boy in the crowd pointed at me and made frightful faces, putting his hands around his own neck as if he were choking me. I turned away, but he shouted, "Do not turn your head from me, for I know you, printer's brat!" he said. "The hangman waits for you, boy!"

"We've rope enough for all of them," said a man beside him in a raspy voice. "Indians and Indian lovers, all."

Annie took up my hand. "Do not fear these vile words, cousin, for they can do us no harm."

We found our seats near the front of the room, away from the angry rabble that filled the back. Still they shouted at us, and I turned to see the small boy who had guided us to Governor Leverett and my father the night before. He yawned now, after his late night. I thought that he must have earned the sixpence he was seeking, or even a shilling, by spreading word of the trial through the streets of Boston this morning.

Annie saw the boy, too.

"Have you the loan of a penny, cousin Sam?" she asked.

"What would you have with a penny?" my brother asked.

"Bartholomew and I have a debt to repay," she said.

Sam pulled out his money purse and found a full penny for her. When she stood up, all the jeering from the back of the meetinghouse was aimed at her, but it did not discourage her from her purpose. Slowly she made her way through the crowded aisles, with me following close behind, to the small, dirty boy. She handed him the penny.

"We make good our promises," she said.

"You are a kindly lady," said the boy, "and a brave one."

And as we walked back to the front, all the jeering stopped and a silence settled over the room.

When Captain Moseley entered, the crowd did rise all of a sudden to its feet to clap and cheer him. "Drunken babblers," I heard my father say. The captain did not wave or signal the mob, but upon hearing the roar of approval, he became ramrod straight, and I believe a small smile curled itself about his mouth. He pointed into the room and I followed the line of his finger to the place where I saw that Lemuel Brown now sat, his collar open, his face unshaven. Packed into a gallery of onlookers, Brown rose and slipped his body through the crowd. Captain Moseley bent down to speak to him, his mouth close by Brown's ear so that no one else would know what ideas he might be planting.

Just then Captain James Oliver hobbled in upon his cane. For a moment, the room was hushed and all could hear the rhythm of foot followed by cane, foot by cane. Then the gathering erupted into a volcano of jeering that was worse than was aimed at Master Gookin before. Still, Captain Oliver walked forward, his jaw set, his head as high as Captain Moseley's. When he reached the front of the room, he thumped his cane three times upon the wooden floor. "There will be order, or I will clear this court!" he said. And silence came upon the assembly with the suddenness of a summer rain. "Now bring in the prisoner!" he commanded.

Six men came in leading poor Little John. He had ropes about his neck and trunk, his hands were tied behind his back, and his feet were shackled together by chains so that he could only walk in small quick steps. To me, he seemed frightened, as if he had been crying.

And who could blame him? I knew in my heart that this large man, with a body like a bull's, was as meek in spirit as a lamb. The crowd soon began to shout terrible things at him. There were catcalls and much spitting. And some began throwing rotten fruit and worse. Little John was quickly covered and dripping with foul stuff, helpless to protect himself. Then Captain Oliver thumped his cane again, and all was still.

Now that Little John stood before us, I saw he had a large, misshapen jaw, and teeth that his lips could not keep covered. His arms were as large around as any blacksmith's. Yet, he was not much past being a boy, and was almost weeping.

Suddenly, a door was thrown open at the back of the room and a little, withered man walked briskly forward up an aisle that was partly blocked by onlookers. This was Master Tyng, the judge, and all rose to their feet and made way for him. When he reached the front, he wheeled quickly around and ordered us all, "Be seated!" And as if he were our schoolmaster, or the King of England himself, we all obeyed. He was old, even ancient, with hollow cheeks and a mouth so puckered, it looked like a piece of fruit, split open and dried in the sun. And he shook as he spoke, shivering as if it were not the hottest day of September but winter, and he had stayed out too long in the cold. But forget what a little man he was. Today he stood not alone, but as the entire colony of Massachusetts Bay. In a single sentence, written down on paper and signed in his own hand, he could set a man free or send him to the gallows.

"Where is the prisoner?" he asked. I thought the judge must be the only man in the room who did not know. Who else but this giant of a man, tethered by ropes, surrounded by guardians, could be the prisoner?

"He stands before you, here," said Captain Moseley.

"How is he charged?" asked the judge.

Captain Moseley read the charges from a piece of paper he held before him. The list was long. But the final one was the most important. "This Little John," Captain Moseley read, "did brutally and for no cause strike down Captain Edward Hutchinson."

The crowd murmured, but Captain James Oliver's cane brought quiet.

"How say you, the accused?" the judge asked the Indian.

"I have done nothing," the man said. "As Christ be my witness, I am an innocent man. I have no quarrel with you English and have never taken arms against you." I wondered how anyone could doubt this gentle man's honesty.

But the crowd stamped and clapped and whistled. "He lies!" shouted Lemuel Brown, who now rose from his seat and stepped up on a bench so that all could see and hear him. "I saw the deed myself. He brought up his musket and fired upon Captain Hutchinson. Shot him in the back of his head!" Now the others around him began screaming oaths so terrible that I cannot write them out.

The judge did his best to shout for order. But only Captain Oliver with his cane was able to silence this mob. This allowed Judge Tyng to bring out a jury, which had not one Indian upon it.

Seeing this, Master Gookin rose up to object. "Is it not the custom to have a jury of Indians of good repute to pass judgment on one of their own?" he asked.

"In this case," said Judge Tyng, "that will not be necessary." He called up Lemuel Brown to say what he had seen at Brookfield a month before. He spoke not to the judge but to the spectators in the room. And he appeared to enjoy every terrible detail. "Oh, I was there," he said, "and with my one good eye did I see this Little John shoot down the poor, young Captain Hutchinson."

The crowd moaned.

"And then with the same eye did I see this Little John cut off the head of Captain Hutchinson as the poor soldier lay bleeding in the field."

Master Gookin jumped to his feet. "This is a lie, sir! A lie! The late lamented captain's head never left his wounded body. It was buried with him. And it is well known that Captain Hutchinson did not die at once from his wounds but some days after the battle. This is a made-up tale."

"I may be wrong in some of the details," said Lemuel Brown, smiling now, "but I know that I saw this Indian before me fire his musket and bring down a fine young Englishman."

The crowd was impatient. "The verdict's plain!" one man shouted. "Hang the Indian!" yelled another.

But Master Gookin, still standing, turned around the room and addressed the crowd himself. "Does the truth not matter here? Does it not matter that others of his tribe say he never traveled to Brookfield at all, but was at Marlborough, a day's journey away?"

"You'd take a heathen's word over my own?" asked Lemuel Brown.

"No! No!" answered the spectators.

"This is for the jury to decide," said the judge.

The members of the jury left the room, but took little time in returning. The verdict was what I feared most. The jurors found Little John guilty. The crowd roared its pleasure. The judge calmed them so he could pronounce the sentence. The Indian known as Little John, he said, was to be hanged this very morning upon the commons.

Now the crowd did celebrate, dancing and clapping, shouting and singing. It was as if sending this sad giant to his death brought a victory over the dreaded King Philip.

"But, Father," I said. "This man did none of what he was accused. How can he be hanged?"

"I think you are right in that, Bartholomew," he said. "The Indian is innocent, but it is the jury's case to decide, not yours or mine."

"And now is James to die, too?" I asked.

"Master Gookin and I will work for his release. He is innocent of wrong, of that I am sure. But from what I see today, this mob is hungry and must be fed. How large an appetite it has, I know not."

I turned to see Annie, clinging to Master Eliot, crying.

We waited until the room emptied to push outside, where there was a huge crowd waiting, as large as the one outside the jail the night before. They followed Captain Oliver and the armed men who surrounded Little John. The air was full of wild taunts and ugly cries. It was strange that the sun shone down as on any summer's day, warm and bright, calling the children of Boston to play and swim in the long hours before night.

I saw Master Eliot push ahead through the crowd and reach the prisoner. He put a hand upon Captain Oliver's shoulder and spoke into the soldier's ear. I could not hear what was said, but afterward, Master Eliot was allowed to walk by Little John's side as we all marched toward the commons. There, I saw a high platform, so newly made that I could smell the sweetness of the raw wood even at some distance. The Indian named Little John walked up the steps with Master Eliot. The crowd was noisy all the time, even when Little John and Master Eliot kneeled together in prayer. "Before God, I am innocent," the Indian said, and with such force and honesty that the crowd grew still. For the first time this day, the mob had doubts. But then Captain Oliver stood beside the kneeling Little John and ordered him to his feet. He put a noose about the condemned man's neck, placing it there gently as if it were a necklace. "This is my sad duty, for I believe you are innocent," Captain Oliver said. "Please have no hatred for me."

"I hate you not," said Little John.

From the hushed crowd, Captain Moseley came forward and shouted, "Be done with it."

I saw that the slack rope ran over a high rounded beam and then down to three men of

Captain Oliver's company, who held the end in their hands.

My knees were weak and I thought I would crumple to the ground. My father seeing this said to me, "Be brave, Bartholomew. A man must know the world."

Pale as paper, Annie stood tall and tearless beside me. "You can look away," she whispered.

But I could not. My eyes were fixed on this gentle Indian who stood before us so alive.

Then James Oliver said, "Now! Be done quickly!" And the three men pulled upon the rope and hoisted Little John up into the air by his neck. But he was so heavy a burden that they could not hold him, and soon they let him fall to the ground. My stomach jumped up into my throat. And then they pulled again, and again he rose and fell to the platform with a heavy thump.

Once more Captain Oliver gave the order. But just then, an Indian in deerskin clothes leaped upon the platform and drew a knife. Before anyone could prevent it, he stabbed poor Little John in the chest. Blood burst from the wound like a fountain. And in no more than three heartbeats, the giant fell to the ground, dead.

I saw all this myself, as did many an English child on that afternoon upon the commons. And it was a terrible thing. I lost all that I had eaten. And I was not the only one who was made sick by what I saw.

We were to see many terrible events in the time of King Philip's war. But none was worse than this.

Later, there were many stories told about the strange Indian who took Little John's life. Some said that he did what he did because of the savage belief that if he drank the Indian's blood, the dead man's spirit and strength would enter his own body. But this is a false report. It did not happen. Instead, I think, this second Indian took pity on Little John and acted to shorten his suffering. Whatever his reason, he somehow vanished into the crowd and was never seen again.

Within minutes, Little John's head was mounted upon a pole. I stared at his bruised and lifeless face. "It is best not to look," said Annie, too late. "It is intended to put fear into the hearts of evil men. But it was not meant to torment goodly souls like yours." Yet how could I not look?

Master Gookin was angry. "That head of Little John's will frighten even innocent men," he said. And I knew that he was right.

Yet when I looked upon the head of Little John, I knew that what I saw was not the man but a discarded piece of him. It was no more Little John than his worn-out shirt or a lock of his hair.

My cousin Annie, she of the cheerful face and happy spirit, was now as glum as anyone. For once, I was the one to comfort her. "It will be all right," I said.

"If you think so, Bartholomew," she said. But still her smile was gone.

Instead of going home straight away, we stayed in Boston a while longer, and my father sent word to my mother that we would spend a few nights more with Master Eliot. The next day, Father and Master Gookin gathered all who knew of James, and we paid a visit to Governor Leverett. His house was three stories high and topped with many little peaks, the grandest home in all of Boston.

The governor greeted us himself but offered little comfort.

"Dear friends," he said, his eyes turned away, his face somber. "I will do what I can for the Indian printer. But you must be patient with me." We returned to Master Eliot's house and waited.

And all the while, I imagined James in a cramped jail cell, not knowing if this day would be his very last on this earth.

The next night Master Gookin woke us from our troubled sleep. Sam stopped snoring, and we quickly rose and dressed. Set upon a horse together, Annie and I rode through the darkened streets, not knowing where we were going. I was still only awake by half when we came to the jail. There was no mob, and only a single torch burned outside the door where a man with a musket stood guard. "We've come to see Captain Oliver," Master Gookin said.

"He has been expecting you," said the man. He knocked upon the door and it opened. We all crowded our way into a small, airless room—Master Gookin, my father and brother, Annie and I. The only furniture was a plank table and two chairs. At the far end was a heavy door with a small window in it. Captain Oliver took Master Gookin's hand in his. "I'll get him," the captain said.

He opened the thick wooden door and a foul smell swept into the room, the scent of sweat and sickness and fear. We watched as the captain walked down a dim corridor past another guard, with his cane in one hand and a ring of keys in the other. He unlocked a door and disappeared into a room.

When he came out again, he brought James with him. We surrounded our friend and greeted him with hearty handshakes and great embraces. I expected him to be glad and to smile, especially on Annie and me. But James said very little and seemed forlorn. He squinted in the lamplight. I saw that he was wearing clean English clothes and leather shoes upon his feet.

Captain Oliver said, "You may go now and wherever you please, James Printer. But I would not stay in Boston and I would chart my course clear of all cities and towns, for we have seen what my own countrymen can do when fright takes hold of them and throws out their better natures."

"I will stay far away," James said, and in his voice was more than sadness. "I have no longing to be in cities, no wish to be with people who hate and would harm me."

"Cannot James stay with us?" I asked. "We would let no harm come to him."

James turned to me and smiled kindly, just the way he would if I had set a crooked line of type or smeared the print upon a page. "There is no place I would rather be than in your shop, working upon your press, putting beautiful words on fine English paper. But the world has turned around, and it cannot be."

I was crying now, and Annie, too. He reached out to both of us and held us to him. And there we would have stood for hours, for days, if Captain Oliver did not open up the door and lead us into the night.

Outside the jail, my father gave James a sack of food to carry and a five-pound note. And Master Gookin gave him the hat from his head, a tall black hat that covered James's cropped hair and helped to hide his face.

"Go to Natick, James," said Master Gookin. "Or go to your father at Hassanamesitt. You will be safe in either place, at least for now."

"Will we see you again, James?" I asked.

James put his hand on my shoulder and squeezed it. "No man can know that, Bartholomew. For now, I must run to the west, as quickly and as far as I can go. There is safety nowhere else."

Annie leaned against him, and he gently stroked her hair. "When the war is over, we will look for you," she said.

"And if I am alive, you will find me," he said. But already he was looking to the west, probably trying to remember his way out of the city.

"You must fly, James," Master Gookin said. "Do not let the sun find you here."

James hesitated, looking at me among all the others, and said, "Do not believe all that you will hear of me."

He pulled the brim of his hat forward and walked quickly away, turning a corner and vanishing from our sight. For a moment, I wondered what horrors might be waiting him, and I could not bear the thought.

CHAPTER SEVEN

IN THE CAMP OF KING PHILIP

FOUR DAYS LATER, ANNIE'S FATHER CAME TO take her to Deerfield. "It will be as safe there as it is in Cambridge," he told my mother. "We have a fine new house, with wooden floors of solid planks, and my good wife, who is frail of health and needs the help of a daughter, will hear no argument against Annie's coming home."

And so, within a week, I had lost James again, and now Annie was leaving, too. She took with her a small parcel of clothing, no more than she had brought. "She is a good and obedient child," my mother told my uncle, "and we will miss her." Before he came, I had heard my mother say that Annie would be safer with us than in the woods of the west, where wolves ran in packs and bears burst into people's houses. And most worrisome of all, she said, there were reports of rebel Indian attacks upon little settlements in the wilderness, where there were no regiments to guard them. But my mother did not say this to my Uncle Robert. He had made up his mind, and it was said of the Clarks that they did not easily part with their opinions.

As for my father, a tear was rolling down one cheek but not the other. It was as if he had two minds: one sad that Annie was going, the other glad that she would no longer be an expense. But he said only, "I am losing the dearest printer in all New England." And I knew that my father had no kinder words to say of anyone. Annie gave my mother and father each a sweet embrace and then Sam lifted her from the ground in the heartiness of his farewell.

As for me, I suddenly grew shy of my tall

and freckled cousin. I knew not what to say to her, my dearest companion. She spoke before I could. "I will miss you most of all, Bartholomew," she said. And my throat would not let me speak. But I think she could see the words I wanted to say as plainly as if they were printed upon my face, like a page in a book. She touched my head with a gentle hand, then left us and mounted her father's horse, sitting close behind him. In the time it takes to turn a page, they were gone.

How saddened was I? It was as if a part of me had been taken away, a hand or a foot. There was no time when I did not miss her pleasant face and cheerful smile, and suffer for my loss. But in a time of war, there were many leavings and much sadness. The cure for the ailment, my father said, was to work all the harder. "A mind left idle will wander into swamps, and there stay mired, never returning to happiness or light," he liked to say. Over and over and over. For he also liked to say that a lesson worth knowing was worth repeating. And so, to keep me from wandering into a bog of loneliness and grief, he gave me work to do that filled every moment of my days and left me too tired at night even for dreaming. At the end of each long day, I tumbled into sleep as if I were falling into a dark and bottomless well.

No word of my uncle and cousin did we hear for many days.

One night after supper, Goody Gray came to our shop, but without her usual cakes and ale and cider. "Master Green," she said to my father, "there's terrible news. The soldiers were evacuating the town of Deerfield when they ran into an ambuscade at Muddy Brook. They are calling it Bloody Brook today. All have perished! And those who have not perished are enslaved by the savages! A disaster!"

"Deerfield, Goodwife Gray! An ambush! Is it Deerfield, you say?"

"Deerfield it is," said the old woman. "The same Deerfield where your little Annie and her papa are gone to. Forgive me, Master Green, but it is my unhappy duty to tell you this."

"But all cannot be dead," I said.

"Not Annie! Surely not!" said Sam.

"All of them. Perished or captured," said the old woman. "And captured is the worse of the two, from what I know of savages."

"Calm yourself, good woman," my father

said. "There have been so many false reports."

"And many that are true," she replied.

For my part, I simply could not believe what she had said. Was it not just days ago when Annie left us? And this was no time of plague, where hearty persons such as she are struck down dead. "Dead," I found myself saying. "They cannot all be dead."

Just then, Master Gookin rushed into the shop. He saw the dreadful looks upon all of our faces, and Goody Gray was sobbing now. "You've heard, then, of Muddy Brook," he said.

"It's true, then?" Sam asked him. "That all are dead or captured?"

"Not all," said Master Gookin. "Not everyone. A few escaped. But a very few. And one of them is your mother's brother, Robert Clark. He was wounded, but not killed. That's why I have called on you this night. He asked to be taken here, and will arrive by morning."

"How grave are his injuries, pray that you tell me?" my father said.

"Very grave," Master Gookin said.

"And what of Annie?" I asked.

"And her dear mother?" my father asked.

"We do not know for certain," Master Gookin said. "But Master Clark thinks they were taken by the Indians."

"My wife must know all this at once," my father said. We quickly closed up the shop and all went to our house. None of us slept before morning.

When I saw my uncle, I wondered if he was the same man who I had last seen leaving us for Deerfield. He came upon horseback, not riding upright, but slung over the animal's back like a sack of grain. My mother pronounced him pale, but he was not so much pale as gray, like a stone in a churchyard.

He could scarcely talk, and when he could, he would moan. "King Philip's camp," he said. "Both are taken to King Philip's camp."

My mother took command of him, and all in the household were her troops. Nothing he wanted was denied him. No need of his was too great for us to meet. She fed him with the frantic care a mother robin pays upon her fledglings. And to our happy surprise, she brought him slowly back to life.

One evening in October, Master Gookin came to call on us, only to find my Uncle

Robert sitting in a chair in the warmth of our parlor.

"Master Gookin," my uncle said, with a voice hardly louder than a whisper, "you seem surprised to see me sitting here. Well, I am surprised myself to be here, for I thought I would sit no more, but lie instead for all eternity."

Master Gookin took his hand. "Sir, I confess surprise at this, a miracle."

"You came at a good moment," my uncle said, "for I begin to tell the story of Bloody Brook, now that I have the strength to tell it."

And so he told us of the days that followed his leaving Cambridge.

"Annie was so happy on that last of summer days, singing and laughing as we rode along toward Deerfield, under swaying willow and rustling aspen. But soon we came to a cluster of burned-out cabins, the beams still standing but charcoal black. Each was no longer a house but the charred skeleton of one. Across a clearing, the contents of a household were tossed and scattered as if by a wild animal. A mattress ripped and shredded. A clothes chest split open, and the clothing torn and tossed. A mirror shattered. A dead ox lay in the middle of the road. The war had come here just days before.

"As we neared Deerfield, I rode all the faster. And there the village sat, a score of little houses, beyond the war, as safe as when we left it. Or so it seemed, off in the distance.

"But as we neared our house, I was puzzled to see men and women and children upon the green, whole families loading their belongings into ox-drawn carts. Large numbers of soldiers with muskets and pikes stood at the edge of the green and on the road, watching over them.

"My dear Elizabeth rushed out to greet us. She told us that a Captain Lathrop had come to warn of a pending Indian attack, and that all must pack up their possessions and leave this place. So my homecoming proved to be a leave-taking. We moved what belongings we could onto one of the carts and set off to the east. How proud I was of my Annie, who with her strength helped me pile our things upon a pyramid of furniture and crates and mattresses.

"The day was so hot, I pitied the oxen. Captain Lathrop would not let us rest. A few miles away we came to a little brook winding through trees and meadows. Now that it was summer, the water was low, but still it slowed the caravan as one ox-drawn cart after another dipped and tilted across its banks.

"Our company was only partly across when I heard the first arrow, heard it before I saw it, a feathered stick singing through the breathless air. This was followed by a rain of arrows, a storm showering upon livestock and villagers and soldiers alike. The sound was like a strong wind shaking boughs of poplars. They came in gusts, hundreds of arrows and then hundreds more.

"Then there was a brief moment of quiet, unbroken by wind or weapon, voice or breath. Finally, a wounded ox moaned and was answered by a wounded man, the two sounding alike. Annie and Elizabeth still stood. But I sat upon the ground. How I arrived in this position I did not know. A feathered arrow stood out from my chest, like a branch from a tree. Annie helped me to my feet so that we might run, but we did not know which direction to take.

"Captain Lathrop himself walked by, the shaft of a broken arrow protruding from his back. He did try to speak with us, but when he opened his mouth, no words came forth, only the dark eloquence of his spilling blood.

"Then we heard the cries of the Indian warriors and the slaughter began again. They hunt animals with greater mercy. And soon the stream ran red with English blood, and I thought that soon we all must die.

"I saw an Indian running toward us. He was half-dressed in deerskin leggings, a great tomahawk in one hand, a long knife tethered to his belt. His face was painted red, with black lines on forehead, cheeks, and chin. One of his eyes was clouded over with a gray cast. And about his neck he wore a necklace of fingers, and my terror grew so great that I could make no sound, but only wait. As he came closer, I could even smell the rancid bear grease he used to coat his hair. He raised his arm and in his hand, I saw the great rounded stone at the head of his tomahawk that would shatter our skulls. I thought how quick it would be. Our souls would fly up, fearless, free of the earth, lighter than any bird.

"Then I heard someone cry, 'Stop! Hold your weapon!' This was an English voice. I turned my head to see an Indian dressed in English clothes, a tall man made even taller by a high hat that seemed too large for him. He walked without hurrying, as if he moved in a calm in which there was no battle and no war.

"'James,' I heard my Annie say, 'he will save us.' But he paid her no attention and spoke instead to the warrior, calling him One-Eyed John. They argued for a time in a tongue I did not understand.

"This One-Eyed John pushed Annie and Elizabeth toward James. He then grabbed hold of my hair and was ready to take away my scalp, when this same James stopped him once again. Though James's manner was gentle, the wild warrior meekly obeyed him, as if the one had a magical power over the other. 'Have no worries,' James said to me. 'I will look after your wife and your daughter.'

"They were taken as captives, five women, three girls, and two young boys, altogether, Annie and Elizabeth among them. They left without time for good-byes. A trapper found me two terrible days later, still sitting in a field of carnage, the only one left alive."

My Uncle Robert, weary now, could speak no more that night. Still, his words gave me all the reason to believe that Annie was alive, and James with her. I thought of Goody Gray's terrible words, that it was better to perish than be captured. But I did not believe that, for my cousin had James to protect her.

My uncle's improvement continued as the fall air turned sharply cold, promising a snowy winter. It was Sam's belief that the war would ease with the first icy storm or blizzard, but it did not. The Indians persisted in their frightful attacks upon outlying towns and settlements. Some of these, the Indians burned to the ground, while the settlers stayed within their houses for fear of being massacred.

One evening, not long after my family had finished a meager supper and my uncle was gone to bed, we heard a fierce knocking upon our door. At my father's bidding, I ran to open it, and there before me stood a large, hardy man, as round as any well-fed Englishman and as tall as any Indian.

Under a cloak of bear fur, he was dressed in leather leggings and leather shirt, and he wore a cap of mismatched skins—of skunk and fox, beaver and wolf. I might have thought him an Indian, except for his beard, which was brown and silver as if it had been touched by frost. In one hand, he held a musket, in the other, a thin rectangular object wrapped in deerskin.

Even before he said one word, I knew him to be the trapper and trader John Hoar, although I had never seen him before. My father had known him since they were both penniless young men, first landed from England, and I had heard much of the trapper's adventures.

"John Hoar," my father bellowed, walking up behind me. "Good man, do not stand there letting in a draft on a cool night."

The trapper took two steps forward and put his gun to rest against a wall as my father slammed the door behind him. Father then grabbed hold of the big man's shoulders and embraced him like a lost cousin come home again.

"Still alive, I'm glad to see," said my father, who bid me pour out two cups of Goody Gray's cider as he led John Hoar into our kitchen. The trapper warmed his frosted limbs by the fire. I thought he smelled like a wet horse.

"Alive to the displeasure of many, for there's many an Englishman I know who would see me dead," said Master Hoar, gulping down the warm cider, then holding up his cup so that I would pour him another. "For I trade with the Indians. And I do agree that I trade with them, taking what furs they give me for pots and kettles and good English currency. That is what I do for my living. And I ask those who say I should give it up, how am I to eat and drink if I have no livelihood? And if I do sometimes exchange liquor for furs, what of it? Don't I give value for value? I am an honest tradesman like yourself, Samuel Green, and must make my living how I can." He finished his second cup of cider and all of a sudden sat down in a chair by the hearth, his long legs stretched out so far before him that I thought his leggings might be cooked by the fire. My father pulled up a chair beside him.

"No one questions your honesty here in this house," my father said, smiling.

"There are many elsewhere who do, Samuel Green, so I thank you for that," the trapper said.

"What brings you to Cambridge on a cold evening such as this?" my father asked.

"I have tidings," said the trapper, who picked up the rectangular object he had been carrying and unwrapped it. It was a book, nothing more or less. "You must see what is recorded here in this ledger."

With great care he opened up the book and turned one leaf after another. I moved close behind him, standing between the two chairs, so I could view what was on these pages, and what I saw looked ordinary enough. It was here that Master Hoar kept his accounts.

"William White of Natick," said one entry. "Fourteen beaver furs, finest. Five fox, two finest, three of middle grade. Eighteen rabbits, mixed. One pound and eight shillings. One bottle, canary wine."

He did not linger, but instead continued turning until he came to pages that were different from the others, written in a finer hand, in looping letters that grew thin and thick as they ran their course.

"Here they are," said Master Hoar. "These are what you will want to see." He pointed a thumb toward the middle of the page and then handed the book to my father, who sat next to the trader. Standing between them, I was able to look over my father's shoulder as he read.

"Annah Clark of Deerfield, late of Cambridge," it said, in a fine hand. "Daughter of the Reverend Master Robert Clark, Deerfield. Five pounds English, or two flintlock muskets, small keg powder.

"Elizabeth Clark of Deerfield," said the next entry. "Wife to the Reverend Master Robert Clark, Deerfield. Twelve pounds English, or five flintlock muskets, two kegs powder."

"You have seen them?" my father asked. "Annie and her mother?"

"Seen them?" said the trapper. "Why, my good friend, I have supped with them, conversed with them, laughed and cried with them."

"And are they well?"

"As well as they might be, living as they are, hostages in King Philip's camp!"

"The numbers there, five English pounds and twelve pounds more," my father asked, "these are the ransoms that King Philip asks for their release?"

"Indeed, they are, sir. I have gotten these from King Philip himself."

"Well, seventeen pounds, that is a princely sum," said my father with a sigh. "Yet, I will help to raise this and more, to win their release, if I am permitted. You see, Governor Leverett has vowed to send not one gun or ounce of powder or penny to the rebel Indians in exchange for captives. He says that to do this is to purchase the death or capture of many more good English people. He would starve these rebel Indians out this winter and then defeat them in the spring.

"But, tell me, John," my father continued, "how did they seem to you, my niece and her mother?"

"They are well, but not as well as I would like," answered Master Hoar. "Food is scanty among the Indians. All within the camp, captives and Indians alike, are given a fair share. But it is too little, I think, and soon there will be less. Why, Mistress Clark told me herself that most of the grain was gone and game scarce. When a sickly horse died, it was divided up, hooves, hide, and all. There were some among the English who would not eat of horse, and if they died by this choice, the Indians did not care. But Mistress Clark said that she and Annie ate their portion and thought little of it."

Now Master Hoar rapped a finger upon the open book and said, "But you have not read all upon this page."

"Why, certainly I have. There are only two entries here and I have read them both," my father said.

"Look further there," demanded Master Hoar. "Do you not recognize this hand?"

I blurted out the answer. "Why, it's James's writing, is it not, Master Hoar?"

"Indeed, you are a bright penny of a boy," said the trapper. "For James was in King Philip's camp and acted as my scribe, taking down in his well-schooled hand the names of captives and the ransoms wanted."

"He is a traitor, then," said my father sadly. "And I have lost the benefit of my investment."

"I do not call him traitor, Samuel," said the trapper. "For he is guardian angel to all the English captives. And it is James who urges Philip to release them. Why, it was James who told me that the Indian king has a fondness for canary wine and might give them all their freedom for a dozen bottles of that or any other liquor."

"I knew it!" my father said, more cheerfully. "He protects them all! And when this war is done, as it will be soon, I will have my apprentice back again!"

The next morning early, after showing his ledger book again and telling his tale for the benefit of my mother and my Uncle Robert, Master Hoar was off to see Governor Leverett. "I will urge him to make an offer to King Philip to release his prisoners," he explained. "The amounts are small weighed against the value of a life."

Soon we learned that the governor did not want to change his policy. "The winter is a cannon in our war against these Indians," he told Master Hoar. "It would be foolish to give King Philip a shield against our strongest weapon."

We saw no more of Master Hoar that winter, and there was not another word of poor Annie and her mother.

All was black outside in late February, the ground still frozen, the snow falling heavily, when we had a visitor to our printing shop. It was so dark, even in the middle of the day, that we had to burn a full regiment of candles to make our almanac ready before the first of spring.

Our visitor flung open the door. It was Captain Samuel Moseley, his scowling face as frozen as the river Charles in midwinter.

My father gave him every courtesy. "Captain, come warm yourself," he said, and ladled up a cup of mulled cider. This warmed his hands and thawed his belly, but did nothing to melt his frozen face.

"I have come to show you something, Master Green," Captain Moseley said. "It was found just four days ago, nailed upon the bridge at Medfield after the slaughter of most who lived there."

The soldier took a paper from his coat and unfolded it for us to see.

My father read the sentences aloud. "'Know by this paper, that the Indians you have provoked to wrath and anger will war this twenty-one years, if you will. There are yet many Indians. We come three hundred at a time. You must consider the Indians lose nothing but their life. You must lose your fair houses and your cattle.' This is a terrible note, Captain. A most troubling note. Whoever in New England hears of it will be stoked into a flaming rage against our enemy."

"I agree with you, Master Green," said Captain Moseley, who seemed satisfied with my father's response. "What if I told you that upon the word of an Indian spy, I believe this paper to be the scribbling of your apprentice, James the printer? Would your rage now be directed against him?"

"No, sir. It would be directed against your spy," said my father. "For I have only contempt for liars, Captain."

"And what if I were to tell you that I have reason to believe that this writing *is* by your James, and that he is well known to dwell in King Philip's camp."

My father sighed. "If I knew these to be James's thoughts, then I would be amazed, Captain. I do not believe he has changed as much as this."

"Then please have a second look at it, sir, and tell me if you know the writing to be his," said the captain.

Captain Moseley laid the paper upon a table before my father. I could see it plainly, although it was smudged with soot and grease from much handling. While my father studied the writing, so did I, following the lines as they curved upon the page, from thick to thin and thick again, in the pleasant sweep of a well-schooled hand. I knew I had seen the hand-writing before.

Yet my father puzzled over it, holding the note before him, first at some distance and then close to his nose as if he would know the author by its scent. "I know James's hand, certainly I do," said my father. "And whether this be his hand or not, I cannot say."

Captain Moseley, who had been sitting with a half cup of cider, now jumped to his feet, all politeness and patience vanished like melted snow. "*Cannot* say, sir, or *will* not?"

"I read the words and know they are not his," my father said. "He is not a man to be filled with wrath, who might threaten English homes. This is his home, here with us. And here he would be if he had not been driven away!"

"I ask not about the words expressed but about the hand that wrote them," Moseley said. "Did your printer James write them or did he not?"

My father shook his head as he looked upon the paper. "That is the problem I have. First, the words are not his. That to me is certain. Words are but thoughts upon paper, and these words are no thoughts that James might have set down. As for the lettering, sir, sometimes I think these letters are his and sometimes I think they are not."

The captain snatched the paper from my father's hand and put it before my face.

"What say you, boy? Do you know this hand or not? Remember, if you are not truthful, your soul must lie in Hell for all eternity."

I thought of Hell, full of sorrow that never ends, and I thought of my friend, of his kindly dark eyes and gentle manner. Then I said, oh so softly, "I do not believe these letters were made by James."

Angrily, Captain Moseley folded up the note and tucked it in his coat pocket.

"Your souls be damned, father and son!" he said, walking for the door. "As for the hand that wrote this note, it will be chopped from its arm and delivered to the governor before I am finished." He slammed shut the door and was gone with great haste.

"If anyone cuts off that printer's hand," my father said, with the captain gone, "he will have to answer to me!"

I could imagine before me an image of poor James's severed hand. Then my thoughts turned to what Captain Moseley had said.

"Do you believe in a Heaven and a Hell, Father?" I asked him.

"Well, of course, I do," he answered. "What Christian does not believe?"

"Will I go to Hell, Father?" I asked.

"Why so?"

"For lying to Captain Moseley," I said. "For it is a sin to lie, just as he said."

"Captain Moseley knows not whether you spoke the truth, my dear Bartholomew."

"But I know it, Father, and I worry that I will be cast into Hell," I said.

Now my father smiled upon me, his face as welcome as a glorious sunrise upon a fine spring morning.

"Hell is not for you, my good young man," he said quietly. "And when you in your time reach the Gates of Heaven, it is my fondest hope that I will be there to greet you."

"And James," I asked, "will he be there, too?"

"Whatever his sins, however terrible, I think that they will be forgiven," he said.

"And Captain Moseley, will he be in Heaven?" I asked, not at all sure I wanted to go if he would be there.

My father frowned and in his loudest voice declared, "Not if he does any harm to my Indian apprentice!"

CHAPTER EIGHT

WAR'S END

BECAUSE I WAS A PRINTER'S DEVIL IN MY father's shop in that year of 1676, I knew every tragedy and triumph of King Philip's war. For each joyous victory and every sad defeat, there was a proclamation or a sermon to be printed. In the spring there were new massacres of English troops. The towns of Groton and Marlborough were destroyed in Indian attacks. Part of the city of Providence in Rhode Island was burned to the ground. And news of these events I often set into type by myself, my fingers slapping the little pieces of lead into place, line by line with a click-click that was now faster than my father's.

It seemed there was no place that was safe, not even Cambridge, a quiet little town with half our men fighting the war and most of the other half preparing to do so when they were needed. Fear was everywhere, touching everyone. It was a kind of infection that spread like the pox among all who were English, and it made men rabid in their hate. No Indian was safe to walk alone upon our streets, and even one who traveled with an English friend or master might be beaten to death. The few Indians who were not sent away to misery upon Deer Island soon vanished from our sight.

And still, no one could rest easy. A gun discharged in the middle of the night could send the whole town scampering. And so a man of our town, named Thomas Taylor, was hired to sit all night in watch. He was a doubtful fellow. His tossed hair and uncombed beard were black as a young man's, but his mouth was as sunken and toothless as a great-grandfather's.

And his clothes! You would not want to smell his clothes! But if you saw him, even from a distance, you would surely smell them. Thomas Taylor lived by doing the odd work that no one else wanted, when he wanted. Now the town hired him to stay hidden through the night at the outside of our settlement and to fire his musket if he saw savages readying for attack.

Late one night, long after I had fallen into a deep and dreamless sleep between two of my younger, squirming brothers, I woke to hear the sound of Thomas Taylor's musket. How quick I jumped up to my feet, certain that the Indians were upon us, ready to slaughter us all in our sleep. I threw open the shutter to see a general panic through the town. Men raced about in their nightshirts in the cold, raising their muskets recklessly, ready to fire. Already the drums had sounded the call to arms, and soon the church bells rang as well.

By the time I was down the stairs, my father and Sam had bolted shut the doors and taken up their muskets, waiting by open windows for the first sight of the enemy.

My mother gathered me along with the

younger children, and took us back to our rooms and closed the shutters. I did not belong among them, I told her, for was I not a printer's devil and on the way to becoming a printer? "But you must take care of the others, Bartholomew," she told me. "Make sure that they be still," she said, "as still as the dead. Otherwise King Philip will come with his Indians and send all of you quick to Heaven."

Outside, the uproar grew. I confess I was as frightened as the small children. Who could sleep on such a night, wondering if his hair would still sit upon his head in the morning?

Finally there was quiet in the streets. And I heard from below Master Gookin singing out to the night, "All is clear! Rest peaceful tonight! All is clear! Rest peaceful tonight!" No nightingale sang as sweetly.

I fell into a doze and woke to crows upon our roof calling up the sun. I did not have to be roused from bed but raced down to the kitchen.

"Some excitement, eh?" said Sam, who was still unshaved and looked as if he had not slept one moment. "Well, it was all for nothing. Old Tom Taylor had too much of Goody Gray's ale and fired off his musket only imagining an attack. Would you like to come see him?"

I followed my brother to a place near the meetinghouse that was the town jail. Out front of it, shivering with the cold, was Thomas Taylor. He stood bent over like a tree bowed down by a heavy snow, his neck and wrists set in the stocks. "Look, boy, at this disgrace of a man," Sam said loudly. And the words seemed to hurt Thomas Taylor more than the carved planks of wood that locked his arms and head into place.

"Did you and I, Sam Green, not share many a glass together?" the prisoner asked, his face twisted, his hair unruly.

"And what if we have done that? Is your shame any less?" And my brother bent over to pick up a stone from the road. And he threw it with all his might at the man in the stocks. Thomas Taylor tried to pull away, but of course could not. The rock very nearly struck his head.

By now there were others about us, although the sun was not yet fully risen from a bed of clouds that lay upon the horizon. And these others, women and children mostly, but some young men as well, began to shower miserable old Tom with clods of dirt and spoiled vegetables. Dogs were set upon him. Even I took part with the others, rubbing his hair with rotten, battered fruit. I left to finish my morning meal and begin my work in the shop. When I returned to see Tom Taylor at noon, he was alone, a loathsome, foul, and bleeding sight.

After sundown, just before his release, the constable gave him a dozen lashes by lantern light in front of the whole town. And Goody Gray herself, who had sold him his ale, rubbed salt into his wounds for good measure.

I am sorry to say that all who watched this laughed and that I was among them. I have no doubt that old Tom deserved his punishment, but it now seems wrong to make mirth at any man's misery. Freed from the stocks at last, Tom sat upon the ground weeping from his injuries, just as the saddest child cries from a nosebleed. He was lucky not to be branded on his forehead with a "D" for drunkenness. Yet he was branded in another way. Forever after, the people of Cambridge, children and adults alike, called him "False Alarm Tom," a shame that burned deeper than any branding.

Tom's false alarm did not ease our worries, but seemed to increase them. Fear ran so wild among the people that some plotted to kill all the Indians sent away to Deer Island, most of them poor, praying Indians who my father said would never have harmed us.

That spring there were English victories at last. And every one brought with it a parade of soldiers, beating their drums as they walked through the streets. These came so often that I did not always stop my work to see the marching, smiling men who carried the heads of Indian sachems mounted upon their pikes.

I was tired of war. No, I was exhausted from it, from my fingers to my brain, for every triumph meant more work for us. Still, when the news came that a feared Indian sachem named Canonchet was captured and his head taken to Hartford, even I joined the dancing around the bonfire that evening.

All the while, my Uncle Robert was growing stronger. He spent long hours with the governor, trying to persuade him that the tide of the war was with us English and that it would harm nothing to pay King Philip a ransom for the release of Annie and the other captives. Governor Leverett took pity on my uncle and finally agreed. After much pleading from my mother, my father pledged a handsome twenty pounds, but my sweet mother thought he should give even more.

"More, madam?" he said to her. "Mistress Green, have I not already done enough for your family? Let me remind you that I have paid the expenses of your brother's recovery. At this rate, I will have nothing left for my old age. I will be a pauper, just as I was when I first got off the boat from London, so poor that I had not a penny for lodging and spent my nights sleeping in a barrel."

There it was, that ancient barrel again. I worried that he would not make good on his promise to win Annie's release. "Have no fear for your old age, Father," I said, "for I will support you."

"And how shall you do that, Master Bartholomew Green? How is it you will make your living?"

"I will be a printer like you, Father," I said, "with a shop of my own."

Now my father laughed. "There's little money in that, my son. I fear we shall all be sleeping in a barrel."

For all of his complaining, my father kept his promise and paid the needed ransom. We prayed that the money would be the key that freed them all from their captivity.

One night while we were at supper in early May, there was a great rapping upon our door. I opened it to discover again that large Englishman in Indian leather, the trapper John Hoar. He followed me into the kitchen where he and my father greeted one another, each in his turn shaking the other by the shoulders with teeth-rattling vigor.

"Is there news of the captives?" my father asked.

"Yes, there is news," Master Hoar said. "For I have delivered the ransom myself to King Philip and his followers. There are some who say I trade in captives, that I'm in the business of trading human souls," he said.

"I have not heard that said about you," my father said.

"It *is* said about me. I know this," said Master Hoar. "Some people compare me to a slave trader. Well, you know, Samuel, I have no use for slave traders. No use for them at all. I make no profit in arranging ransoms for the release of captives. Not a cent have I made. The good will of men is all I seek."

"And you have mine," my father said. "But what news have you, John?"

"Oh, I have more than news," the trapper said. "I have the captives themselves, and by this time, they should be outside your door."

My father and I rushed to the door and flung it open. My Uncle Robert and the others were close behind us. There, standing in front of our house, were three horses, their breath like smoke in the cool, damp night.

Holding their reins were two men dressed in leather with fur-skin caps upon their heads. They were Indians. But they did not carry either knives or muskets, and their faces were not painted.

Still sitting upon the horses were three haggard women, dressed in ragged dresses.

At first, I must admit, I recognized none of them. I looked at one of them, a girl with dark eyes and sunken cheeks. She was so thin that a breath of wind might have blown her from her horse's back. I was not sure I knew her.

"Why do you stare at me so, Bartholomew?" Annie said. "Have I changed so?"

Yes, she had changed, grown taller like a reed, but frail at the same time, like an old, sickly woman. Yet I did not say so. "I hoped it was you, Annie," I said.

She jumped down and grabbed me by my neck and pulled me toward her. "How can you not know me?" she cried. "Have I been gone so long that I am forgotten?"

"I could never forget you," I said.

Next she went to my uncle. "Oh, Father," Annie said. "I thought I might never see you again."

"Nor I you, when last I saw you. Never in this world," Uncle Robert said.

One of the women still on horseback began to cough and cry and carry on. And right away, I knew that this was my aunt, who looked very poorly. My Uncle Robert helped her down and to her feet. She was so slight a person that she seemed to disappear in his arms.

I did not recognize the third rider, even after

much staring. Master Hoar helped her dismount. She was uneasy on her feet.

"This, good friends, is Mistress Mary White Rowlandson, who asks if she may stay the night," said Master Hoar.

"Of course," my mother said. "You shall stay as long as you like."

"I know of this family, even if you do not know me," Mistress Rowlandson said. "The books you have printed were on the shelves of our house at Lancaster." Her voice was loud and sure, far stronger than her sad appearance.

My father bid them all join us at supper, the two Indian men included, for they, too, were tired and hungry from their journey. Inside, with food and warmth, the captives began to melt a little, to come again to life. All but my poor aunt, who was overcome with fits of coughing. My mother took her off to bed, treating her with tenderness as if she were a sick child.

The rest of us talked for a while. The hour grew late, but what work was still to be done that night in the printing shop could wait.

At first, it was Mary Rowlandson who did much of the talking in a lively voice in spite of her weariness. There was a madness about her appearance as she sat by the fire, with her gown torn and her fine hair, which was the color of straw, all in tangles.

"Master Green, were it not for your apprentice, we would have died in King Philip's camp," she said. "I was taken at Lancaster on the tenth of February, my beloved daughter dying in my arms. When I came to King Philip's camp after a journey of almost three weeks, I was near dead from my wounds.

"Of all the Indians in that camp, only James was of comfort to me. He bid me to be of good cheer and said that he would speak to King Philip about my release. And this he did along with other good deeds. He gave me tobacco, which I was able to exchange for food. He gave me bits of cloth, which I did sew into English aprons, which were greatly valued by the Indian women.

"When I would not eat, he told me that I must, even if the soup was made of horses' hooves and the smell most foul.

"He brought Annie to me, to nurse me when I was still sick. And he told Master John Hoar that for a jug of liquor, my master in King Philip's camp, the wicked sachem Quanopin, would agree to release me.

"It was King Philip himself who set my ransom at twenty pounds, and James who wrote the ransom note just as Philip told him. Good Master Green, if your apprentice requires a good word to win his pardon when this war is done, I am one who would gladly give it."

"Still it shames me that he has gone to the enemy's camp," my father said.

"Have no shame for him, Uncle Samuel," Annie said. She had been sitting quietly by herself. "Without him, I, too, would be lost. After we were captured, we were five days on the journey to King Philip's camp. We had to run to keep up with the others, for if we fell behind we were prodded with sticks and severely beaten.

"James watched over us to stop the beatings when he could and to see that we had enough food and water.

"When we came to King Philip's camp, James sent my mother and me to the wickiup of his friend Sagamore Tom, who was once a praying Indian. We were treated kindly by him, no different from the way he treated his own children. At the end of the day, he liked me to read to him from the Bible and I did so with great happiness. But I wondered if he prayed for a victory over the English just as I prayed that his people be defeated.

"One day, James took me to King Philip, who remembered me from the day we saw him in Boston, Bartholomew. He told me that I had grown and was not a child anymore but a woman, and would fetch a good price from the English.

"James told me, 'Be of good cheer, Annie. It will not be so long before you are ransomed and released.' So you see, Uncle, I have no kinder, dearer friend in all the world than James."

The next morning, my father declared that there would be no work in the printing shop. Sam and I caught two geese and five large hens. And we did slaughter and help to pluck them. Goody Gray, hobbling now with aching joints, came with buckets of ale and cider and breads and cakes. "We shall have a feast!" my father said as he counted out the coins for Goody Gray.

All the while, my mother helped Annie and the others with warm baths and found clothes for them.

By noon the whole town had heard news of the captives' release. And the church bells rang, and all our neighbors came by, and many stayed with us for a day of feasting. I know that some say today that the Puritans of my youth were a sad and brooding lot. But if only they could have seen us on this day of rejoicing, for our grins were large and our hearts full to bursting.

And yet the captives themselves were not as glad as those who received them. My aunt stayed in bed, too sick to raise her head. And my cousin spent much time beside her. Only Mary Rowlandson seemed merry. Yet even she acted strangely. Often I saw her seated away from the others, never letting go of her Bible, whispering its soothing words to herself. In the early evening, my father sent me to the brewer's shop for more ale, and Annie asked if she might come with me.

As we walked in the darkness, the moon not

yet high, she held me tightly. And when an owl sounded, she gripped my arm so fiercely that I was sure I would see marks upon it in the morning.

"What frightens you?" I asked her.

"Everything frightens me," she said. "I have seen things too horrible to tell. And with every bird cry or horse's whinny, I hear an Indian giving signal to a new attack."

We walked in silence all the rest of the way.

In the morning, Sam helped Mistress Rowlandson upon our wagon and took her in to Boston, to be reunited with her husband.

In the next days, as the flowers began to open in the joy of spring, Annie's mother grew ever more gravely ill, despite my mother's careful nursing. Even bleeding did nothing to restore her strength, but seemed to make her weaker. All day she coughed and gasped for breath. At night she thrashed about so violently that she could not be left alone. After many days of this, she seemed to tire of her struggle to stay on this earth.

My mother opened her shutters by day and filled her room with candles at night so that there was always light about her. She was never alone. My uncle stayed by her and Annie did, too, and they tried to help her rest when she was racked with coughing.

But she grew no better. And one night, she grew suddenly very quiet, shuddered, and slipped away. Many died in Cambridge during that winter and spring, of flux or croup or other disease, more than died at the hands of the savages. There was no one to accuse, but people still did blame the Indians, as they did for all their sorrows.

Annie and her father stayed on with us for a time, the two of them slowly regaining health, if not happiness. I did what I could to cheer my cousin, but my own days were spent in the printing shop, for there was much work to be done. Every victory meant another proclamation to be posted. So did every Indian raid and massacre. And who should print them, but Samuel Green and his sons?

Our house was so filled with visitors that I slept upon a pallet in the printing shop. Annie was no longer strong enough for the heavy labor there, but every night she came by with my father after supper to sort type. And Goody Gray would come by to bring us news of the war. It was as it had been before the war. But it was also very different.

"Where is James this night?" I wondered aloud.

"Hiding and skulking," said Goody Gray, rocking back and forth while drinking too much of her own ale.

"No, Goody," Annie said. "He is a kind and decent man."

"No kind and decent man would be party to King Philip and his savages."

"But if he was not there, I would have been killed, and so would my dear father."

"That's true," said Goody Gray. "It is providence that put him there, my dear girl, so that you could find your way home again."

My father was turning the pages of his account books. "I suppose it was providence that put me here so that I might spend a great many pounds to win the girl's release, eh, Goody Gray?" he said.

"So it was," the old woman said. "So it was."

Yet for all his spending to release my cousin and her mother, the war was good for my father's account books, with all the printing to be done. In June, Governor Leverett sent to us a special notice to be broadly circulated by Master Hoar and Master Gookin and many others who traveled among the Indians. The notice was short, and I said I could set it myself.

"What a printer's devil I have in you!" my father said. "I have never seen the like of it in someone of your tender years. You'll be apprenticed before you know it! Why, James will come back and find his job is taken!"

The proclamation said that in fourteen days, all Indians at large in Massachusetts Bay should surrender themselves to Governor Leverett. Those who did so would be forgiven their misdeeds during the war. But those who did not would be punished when the war was over.

My father held up the proof sheet and admired it. "Let us hope," he said, "that these words will be as good as bullets and put an end to the fighting."

The proclamation proved that there was magic in words. Soon Indians were coming into towns like ours to lay down their arms and give themselves up. One of the first who came into Cambridge was an old chief, or sachem, known as Captain William, who rode in upon a horse and gave himself up to Master Gookin.

Captain William was a praying Indian, a chief of the Nipmuck. And before the rebellion, he was an assistant to our friend and neighbor, Master Gookin. Together they held court to judge the misdeeds of Indians by the standards of English law. At first during the war, he stayed loyal to the English, but he refused to be taken to Deer Island with the others. Instead, he ran away to join the rebels.

How William was treated would show how the English could be merciful in victory. My father knew Captain William, and Master Gookin asked that he journey to Boston to speak for him. He drove our wagon so that Annie and I could go with him. "I want you to see," he said, "how we English can be as generous in victory as we were fierce in battle."

We sat upon the seat next to him. Master Gookin and Captain William sat behind us in the bed of the wagon. The way was slow, but it was a fine day and my father and Master Gookin talked happily. They said it was certain that there would be peace before summer.

Captain William was a large man. And his face was made fierce by black marks upon his nose and mouth that would not wash off no matter how strong the soap or stiff the brush. If these were the markings of war, then Captain William's face could be said to be always ready for battle. To soften his looks, Master Gookin had seen to it that his hair was cut in the English way. He was also given an English coat and hat to wear. But no jacket could be found large enough for his enormous body or cap big enough for his huge head. So he looked as if he were wearing another man's clothing, perhaps stolen from a fallen Englishman.

We drove to the house of Governor Leverett, who was expecting our arrival. Outside there was a restless crowd, which stopped our wagon a hundred feet from the governor's door. There was Lemuel Brown again, exciting the crowd, lifting his eye patch and blaming Captain William for the loss of his long-lost eye. The mob soon began throwing rocks and vegetables at the poor Indian. Master Gookin jumped to his feet in a fury. "Is this the way we English keep our promises? Be ashamed if we cannot keep our word, for we are worse than the savages." He pushed through the crowd, shouting as he moved with Captain William at his side, and we followed. I held tight to

Annie's hand until we were safely inside the governor's house, the door safely closed and bolted.

Governor Leverett came down to meet us. He wore clothing of black cloth, and his face was surrounded by a white, wimpled collar. He seemed startled to see the giant Indian with the painted face.

"Good heavens, Master Gookin," he said, "you bring him without shackles?"

"There was no need, your honor," Master Gookin said. "He comes willingly to claim his pardon."

My father said, "He has been of no trouble to us, your excellency. We know him to be a gentle man."

The governor looked Captain William over as if he were studying the poor fit of his clothes.

"Was this man an ordinary soldier or was he one of their chiefs?" he asked.

"He is a chief among the Nipmuck, Master Leverett," said Master Gookin. "And before these wars he was an assistant to me, a kind of clerk when I was judge of English law among the Indians."

"He is one of their sagamores, then," said the

governor, walking around Captain William as he spoke. "These were the mischief makers. Them we hold responsible. Not like the ordinary Indian who did what he was told."

Captain William spoke up for the first time. "I beg for your pardon, your excellency." And the large man dropped to his knees and bowed his head.

Governor Leverett whispered something to a servant. While Captain William still kneeled, the servant came back with two soldiers, one holding chains and the other armed with a gun that he aimed at the Indian's heart.

"Rise up, Captain William," the governor said. When the Indian obeyed the command, the chains were locked about his ankles. They hung loosely enough so that he could walk but not run. That done, Governor Leverett bid his soldiers, "Take this fellow to the jailhouse and commend him to Captain James Oliver's keeping."

Without thinking, Annie shouted out, "You cannot do that! He has come for the pardon you yourself offered to all! You must set him free!"

I knew she was right about what the governor promised, because I had set the type myself. Frail as she still was, Annie should have been severely punished for speaking so to his excellency, the governor of Massachusetts Bay, Master John Leverett. Or to any other adult. But Master Gookin stepped forward to take her part. "Sir, you cannot do this! He has surrendered on the promise of a pardon, and pardoned he must be."

Governor John Leverett was angry now. "Master Gookin, sir, how dare you interfere! I am the elected governor and do not act on my own behalf but for the safety of the people I serve. The ordinary Indian, whether or not he was a soldier against us, will be taken to Deer Island until the war is done. But the sagamores, the chiefs in this rebellion, they must answer to the General Court. The one called Captain William will have a chance to make his case before a magistrate tomorrow. If he was not one of the mischief makers, he has nothing to fear. But if he was one of them, leading others to burn towns and kill English men and women, then he must pay for these offenses."

Now my father spoke. "But, your honor, the council did not say this in its proclamation. I know the words well. This son of mine set them in type, and I printed them myself."

The governor was in a fury, his face red with rage. "How many of these villains will come to us freely, if they know they must answer for their foul offenses?"

"Then it is a dishonest trick," said Master Gookin, now swinging his hands wildly as he spoke. "And it will soon work against your intent. For who will come forward of his own accord if he knows he will be punished?"

"Master Gookin, sir, and you, my friend, Master Green," Governor Leverett began. His anger had vanished like a puff of smoke before the wind. "Please do not be unreasonable. If your friend is as you say, he will be fairly treated. We are English gentlemen and wish no harm to any but those who merit it."

And so, poor Captain William was taken away by the two soldiers. We watched as the three of them moved through the crowd. The Indian looked back upon us and shouted, "Pray for me, sirs. For I have never harmed the English. Before God, I am innocent." And I remembered the Indian called Little John, who said those same few words just before he was hoisted up by his neck upon the Boston Common.

Master Gookin stayed on in Boston, but my father sadly took my cousin and me home. "We have seen enough senseless slaughter," he said.

Captain William was hanged the next day.

But not all Indian sachems were treated in so terrible a fashion. The squaw sachem Awashonks promised to fight against King Philip and all Indians who stood by him. She and her warriors were to be spared all punishment for their many misdeeds. The end of the war was near. The night of her surrender, we had yet another bonfire upon the commons, and I saw that wars end as they begin, with great fires and celebration. And I frolicked with the rest. But Annie sat by her father through the night and prayed.

CHAPTER NINE

RETURN

THE WAR DID NOT END IN A SINGLE MOMENT; rather, each new day brought little victories. More and more rebel Indians came home to claim their pardons. Whole tribes came over to the English side.

Near the end of June, with the summer's heat full upon us, Governor Leverett declared a day of thanksgiving, and my brother Sam left me to set the type. Alone, I finished the job by candlelight. When the work was done and the last candle snuffed, I lay down upon my pallet by the printing press and fell at once to sleep.

Nothing, I thought, could wake me. If a fire ran through the print shop, it would have consumed me, so weary was I. And yet, a man's voice disturbed my sleep. It was soft and breathless. "Bartholomew!" it said with urgency. "Bartholomew, you must wake up and do me service." The words sent chills through me, as if they had been spoken by a dead man. I started to shout out his name, but his hand covered my mouth.

When he removed his hand, I spoke to him softly. "I knew you would come, James," I said. "How glad I am that you are still alive."

"I am glad of it, too," he said. "Just two days ago, an old English woman fired upon me from the window of her house, and I could hear the lead fly by my ear. And this morning I was almost shot by an old sagamore who wanted my horse. If he had not recognized me at the last, I would certainly be dead.

"This was my friend, Sagamore Tom, into whose care I trusted Annie and her mother.

And he did treat them like his own children. I felt such pity for him that I gave him the horse."

"How did you come to own a horse?" I asked.

"King Philip himself gave it to me when we parted. He made a joke of it, saying if the animal were not so thin, we would have eaten him long ago."

"Did you bring King Philip with you?" I asked, frightened now.

"No, Bartholomew. All the sagamores have scattered to the winds. When last I saw King Philip, he was heading home upon a better horse than mine."

"Will he ask to be pardoned?"

"He knows there can be no pardon for him, even if he begs for one. No more than there was for poor Captain William."

"What of you, James? Will you be pardoned?"

"I will need your help to remain among the living," he said.

He had me light a lamp for him and then he wrote out a note, while I studied his appearance. James looked different now. Perhaps it was the dancing flame, but he seemed thin, even gaunt. His cheeks were sunken, and his eyes seemed older and more weary. Even in an English hat and coat, he looked more Indian than I remembered, his skin weathered and dark.

"Take this note to your father and Master Gookin," he commanded me. "Show it to no others! My life depends upon it!"

I ran across the meadow and down the street to my family's house. I was able to rouse my father from his slumber without waking up my mother. He dressed hastily, adding a scarf and his red cap to protect his hairless head, even though the night was warm and balmy. The two of us were soon knocking upon Master Gookin's door most loudly, until he admitted us. With Master Gookin in the lead, we were not long arriving at the printer's shop, where James sat silently in the dark.

Gookin was the first to speak as I lighted a lamp. "I was not sure these blurry old eyes would ever see your face again," he said. "You are as welcome here as a returning son. Soon we will have you working at the press as before."

My father was equally happy. "Master Eliot still talks of a new Indian Bible. One without the mistakes of the old one, that the savages will not laugh at, and he says you are the one to help him with his translation. And you know what that means to an honest printer. Three years' work at a good wage paid in English coin. And you shall be entitled to your share, an apprentice no longer."

James smiled now. "I wish it to be so," he said.

"And why not?" my father said. "The governor will give you the pardon he has promised. Master Eliot will insist! *I* will insist upon it!"

"Just as he promised Captain William," James said without anger, but sadly. "I do not want to end my days hanging from a rope. If that is my fate, it would be better to be killed by an English musket."

"Trust in God," said Master Gookin.

"And did not Captain William trust in God? It is Governor Leverett I do not trust."

"You are right, there," Gookin said. "We cannot allow the governor and the General Court to repeat that terrible mistake. You must stay here, away from sight, while I talk to the governor and set the terms of your surrender."

For two whole days, James hid away in an empty room above the printing shop. He was to stay quiet all the day, while my brother Sam and I printed three hundred copies of the governor's thanksgiving declaration, to be taken to the farthest reaches of our colony. But all the while we worked, we waited for the news from Master Gookin.

Late on that second afternoon, Master Gookin returned with my father to the printing shop. Annie, dressed in dark clothes and looking a grown-up woman, came with them. I took all three to James's room, being careful not to be noticed by the college students.

James was too restless to be seated.

"Captain Moseley spoke against you, as you might have expected," Master Gookin said. "He called you demon and deceiver, and said your conduct during the war was proof that you were no praying Indian but a lying heathen. It was awful how he carried on against you. But there were others there.

"Mistress Rowlandson and her husband, the

good pastor, spoke in your defense. And when that gentlewoman spoke, it brought a quiet to all who came to talk against you. Even Lemuel Brown held his spiteful tongue after her account of your good deeds, for how could *he* deny them?

"And then, to drive the nail home, Mistress Annie Clark here rose to speak in your behalf. When she described how you had saved her and her father from certain scalping, the case was settled in your favor! Now the score is even, for you owe this young woman your life as she owes you hers."

Annie said to James, "Oh, I was not alone. Many in the room cried out in your behalf."

"Then I am pardoned?" James asked.

Annie and Master Gookin now fell silent, leaving it to my father to say the rest.

"Yes," he said, "you are pardoned. But with conditions."

"Conditions?" James asked. "What conditions?"

"These great and sober men who rule us worry about the opinion of the general rabble," my father said. "They worry that your kindness to the captives will be seen as but a sham to win your pardon. And so they ask for proof of your faithfulness to the laws of the English."

"I will give them whatever proof they ask of me," James said. "Tell me what it is I must do."

Annie, who had been sitting down, now rose up and ran from the room, crying, "It is too terrible for me to listen!"

Master Gookin walked up to James and put his hands upon his shoulders. I could see that he was in tears as he spoke. "Governor Leverett says that the General Court has agreed to forgive any and all of your misdeeds. But as a sign of your regard for English authority, you must bring them two heads."

"Heads?" James laughed. "Of wolves, or bears, or cows? For two heads I will bring them, if that is their only price."

Master Gookin shook his head. "Two heads of Indians," he said.

James sputtered his reply. "Two heads from me, who never has raised his hand in anger against Indian or English?"

"That is what the governor asks of you, my friend," Master Gookin said.

"Then I am doomed," James said. And now he wept as a child would, and I was glad that Annie was not there to see it.

That night, my father saw that James had a good supper and gave him a knife that was sharpened well. By the time I awoke the next morning, James was gone.

A week went by, and the business of the shop went on. But my heart was not in my work. I thought constantly of James. Where could he run to find a place outside the English law?

I was asleep by the press one night when I was awakened by the cry of an owl in its flight. The door to the printing shop opened and James walked in, carrying a round deerskin bag. I said nothing, acting as if I did not hear him enter. He curled up on the floor and went to sleep.

Next morning, I wanted to ask about the bag, but he stopped me, saying that I should fetch my father and Master Gookin. At my father's command, Sam drove our wagon by the printing shop and James slipped into the back, where he lay hidden under a cloth cover. My brother, my father, Master Gookin, and I took him straight away to Boston on that early summery afternoon, the second of July, 1676. Annie wanted to go, but her father would not allow it.

With James still in the wagon, my father knocked upon Governor Leverett's door. A servant let him in, and, after many minutes, my father came for the rest of us.

Governor Leverett stood before us without his coat on. While he stood, none of us could sit. Although it was a hot day, he offered us nothing to satisfy our thirst. We could say nothing until he did, and he was in no hurry.

Finally, he spoke directly to James. "You have been the cause of great mischief among us English. In another case, we would have seen you hanged upon the gallows here. But your friends say that you are a good and Christian man. For that reason, we agreed to pardon you, but only if you give us signs of your loyalty and good intent. Have you brought us the signs we asked for?"

James's face, usually so full of spirit, was blank as any piece of paper. Usually so talkative, he said nothing, but reached into his bag. One by one, he pulled out the remains of what had once been human heads, holding them by their long, black hair. He held them high above us, not just to show us but to horrify.

"These I have cut from the corpses of my fallen comrades," he said. "I have done as you have asked."

This brave governor, who had seen much combat, now gasped at the sight and the smell of these terrible trophies. For a while, I wondered if I would breathe again or would be struck down in fright.

My father stepped in front of me so that I might not see any longer and said, "It's enough. Put them away. This is too much for the boy." And James did as my father told him.

"Now you will release him?" my father asked Governor Leverett.

Master Leverett seemed surprised. "I cannot release him. He would not be safe upon the streets of either Boston or Cambridge, or anyplace where English men and women dwell. For his sake, I must keep him." And the governor ordered that James be taken at once to the jailhouse to wait for his passage to Deer Island.

James looked at me and cried out, "I am lost." He was shackled and taken away.

But the governor kept his word. There was no general announcement of James's imprisonment. No crowd gathered outside the jail to demand that he be taken to the gallows. Early the next morning, before Lemuel Brown or any of the others of his kind could learn of James's capture, he was put into a small boat and rowed to Deer Island, where his father and two of his brothers still dwelled.

As for the heads, Governor Leverett ordered that they be placed upon long poles and set upon the commons alongside the heads of Little John and Captain William and the many others. These most gruesome decorations were to be a warning to anyone who might dare rise against the English. But in time, nothing remained of them but barest skulls, bleached white by the weather, grinning at those who stared upon them. They were so changed by time that they might have been English skulls instead of Indian. And they took on a different meaning from the one intended, for they spoke of the cruelty of the English against their vanquished foe.

A few days later, my father and I rowed out to Deer Island to visit James under a soldier's watchful eye. We came with sacks of cornmeal and pickled meats and the fruits of our garden. What we saw there was as terrible as any battle scene. Disease had done the work of warfare. Only a few of these Indians slept in regular wigwams, sealed tight against the fog and foul weather that blew in across the bay. The rest slept under little sheds that provided little protection. We found James with his father, old Priambow. They said that they lived on clams and fish and what roots and nuts they could find upon this barren island.

But many of the others had lost heart or were sick, and had become skeletons even as they lived. Even the youngest seemed old and weary of living.

I said good-bye to James, unsure I would ever see him again. "Remember me, Bartholomew," he said as we departed the island. And how could I not remember him?

A few days later, Sagamore Tom was captured and put to death because the horse he rode was believed to belong to a man killed in the Hatfield massacre. He told the court that the horse was a gift. But the animal was easily recognized, for the owner had cut three notches in the horse's right ear.

And one by one, the sachems were put to death or died fleeing from the victorious English. Soon King Philip himself was found, sitting peacefully upon a log not far from his home. He was captured easily. He did not put up a fight. But he was shot through the heart by an Indian named Alderman, who wanted to show his devotion to the English. His body was cut into four pieces and left in the trees for crows. For his pains, Alderman was given King Philip's hand, which he carried with him for the rest of his life. An odd reward, I thought, for one man's treachery to his brother.

King Philip's head was taken to the governor of Plymouth, who placed it upon a pole for all to see. I know that it remains there still, for I saw it myself, a slack-jawed skull gazing out on the people of Plymouth and haunting their dreams. Gone were the gleaming dark eyes I remembered that could grapple with a man's soul. But even the bare bones of that large skull were frightening to behold, with its shadowy caves and long-toothed smile.

As for James, he and his family stayed on Deer Island until the following spring. They were among the few who survived that terrible winter of imprisonment. When the time came for their release, none was allowed to stay in Boston or Cambridge, not the kindest of workmen or the most devoted slave. Many returned to the praying villages, to Natick or Hassenamesitt, where they lived more or less like Englishmen, but separate. Others traveled farther away, to the French lands to the north or west over the mountains, beyond the reach of all but a few settlers and traders.

I did not see James in those first years. But I heard that he worked at his crops at Hassenamesitt until his hands grew coarse from the labor. He did marry a woman said to be half-Indian and half-English, and they had children, all called by the name of Printer, as if James had been born to it.

As for me, of course, I became an apprentice in my father's shop, a printer's devil no longer! My brother Sam, ever restless, left for Hartford to start his own press there. Halfway through my apprenticeship, Master Eliot, ancient and gnarled as an old apple tree, came into our shop with a commission for his new Indian Bible. He said that James would return to work with us, for we would need every hand that we could find now that Sam was away. Permission would be granted for him to live as he had done before, in the print shop of the Indian school at Harvard.

James, who once had been so full of talk, spoke little now as he worked. Yet often he would complain to me if a line of type was not perfectly straight or if I had dropped a needed letter from a word or inserted an unneeded one. "This book," he said, "will be remembered long after you and I have left this earth, and we must make it right."

I could see that he had changed. He was far too somber now. All the play had left him. And when at first I asked him about the war and especially about that great villain King Philip, with his war paint of red and blue, James would only say, "Those days are best forgotten. Do not speak of them."

How very old Master Eliot seemed when he came around with the latest revisions to the manuscript. He walked with a limp now, as if every bone of his body ached with every step.

His hands shook so that the papers shivered in his fingers as he handed them to James. But he did not complain, and his eyes were as bright and fearless as they had ever been.

James treated him with wonderful courtesy. It was in the spring in the year of 1679 when the work began. And James found again the rhythm of his work, as if he had never lost it, the click-click-click of lead letters slapped into place, for hours at a time. To my shame, he was still far faster than I.

Often we worked at the press, standing side by side, pulling around the lever that would imprint the Indian words onto paper. And when I complained that I could not read this text, written in his strange tongue and full of double "k's" and many "q's," he said, "A printer does not need to understand. The letters are what matter."

Yet, every printer I have ever known cares about the meaning of these ink spots upon a page. And I do believe that James did care, for when a word was wrong he would rip up the proof sheet and reset whole pages at a time. For it can be said that no one understood the strength, the magic, of words as much as he.

My father still bustled about the shop, but he left most of the work to James and me. He was forever calculating and recalculating his payments and expenses. But when the proof sheets were struck, no one had a better eye for a broken letter or a crooked line.

We worked at it six full days each week. In a little over a year, we had finished with the New Testament and bound some five hundred of these into a pretty little volume. Next we began setting the Old Testament, an even longer work that would take us years. We began each day before first light and scarcely stopped until long after the sun had set. By the end of each day my fingers ached to the touch of lead and fine paper. Other laborers might grow sick and be forced to stop their work, but we dared not.

"I must see this work done before I die," Master Eliot would say, if one of us grew sick for a time or begged for rest.

Yet sometimes, when Master Eliot was not to be seen, my father would take in other, much smaller, jobs as well.

Much to our surprise, into our shop one day came Mistress Mary Rowlandson. She greeted my father and me warmly. But she treated

James as if he were the governor or the king himself, taking his hand and curtsying before him. She was not so bone white now as when I saw her last, and her cheeks were flushed and healthy as if she had dabbed them with a rosy color, as some women do these days.

"Master Printer," she said to James, "I have a manuscript for you." She handed him a sheaf of papers. "It is the tale of my captivity. The bookseller, Master Usher, wants one thousand copies of this little book. He wanted it printed on the new press in Boston, but I said it was more fitting that your hand should set my words in type."

"That will not be possible, Mistress Rowlandson," my father said. "For all his time is promised to Master Eliot's Bible. But my son, Bartholomew, could turn his hand to this and do it as well as if I set the type myself."

"That will not do," Mistress Rowlandson said. "For I promised myself when I was freed from King Philip's camp that I would not forget James's kindness. This little book is his reward, and yours, too, Master Green, for you will find much profit in it."

The word "profit" never failed to bring my father to life, no matter how tired or occupied. It ignited him the way a match does light a fire.

He bowed to Mistress Rowlandson. "I think that our James can make quick work of this," he said. So it was that James set all the type. And he proofed each page himself so that he might read it. He was moved almost to tears, not just by the words themselves and the account of her suffering, but by memories of friends that the words revived. Philip was there. And Sagamore Tom. And Master Hoar. And to his own surprise, he found himself in the type that he set by his own hand, click-click-click. She wrote that her Indian master Quanopin, "went out of the wigwam and by and by sent in an Indian called James the Printer, who told Mr. Hoar that my master would let me go home tomorrow if he would let him have one pint of liquors."

James knew that was not everything. She told only the smallest part of the story and often left out the most important part. But still, there was James, a name whispered in black marks upon a page, to be heard one day by his own children and their children's children, long after he had left the earth.

When the printing of her book was done, we folded the pages together using sticks of antler bone. Then James, my father, and I bound them up between leather covers and shipped them off to Master Usher's shop. Never did a book sell so many copies so quickly. And it was not long before James and I had to set the type again for another edition. And another. All over New England, men knew the name of Mary Rowlandson and cried over her suffering as if it were fresh.

All the while, the work on Master Eliot's Indian Bible continued. Soon every storage bin was filled and all the tables. Finished sheets were stacked upon each other, squared off in rectangular blocks like houses, a little village of them rising up inside our printing shop.

"I will die before it's done, I know it," Master Eliot often said.

"It will be the death of me," said my father.

In 1685, fully six years after the work had begun, James and I began sewing whole books together, binding them in the best quality deerskin. How pleased we were when it was done.

And it did not matter to us that neither of our names appeared upon the title page. "Printed by Samuel Green," it said, in two different languages, English and Algonquian. But we knew the work was ours.

The next morning, my father handed that first finished copy to Master Eliot. He held it in his shaking hands as tenderly as a newborn child. He turned it over, examining every inch of the deer hide. Then he opened it and turned the pages, running his long fingers over the black letters as if he could feel the imprint upon the page and read it with a touch.

He said to James, "You remember the day when I first read to you from a book like this?"

"I cannot forget it," James said. "It was the first day of my life."

Now Master Eliot handed the book to James. "This book is properly yours, not mine. I am happy enough to live to see this day. This book, it is a little miracle."

James took the book, and he, too, turned it in his hands. "I, too, never thought that I would live to see this," he said.

Many months later, when all the books were bound, James moved away. My father gave him twenty pounds owed him at the end of his apprenticeship. And that allowed him to purchase some land for a house near Hassenamesitt, near the English town of Grafton.

I ended my apprenticeship just two years later. With the fifty pounds my father gave me, I moved to Boston, where the main printing work of all New England was being done. There were many printers in Boston and many presses and much competition among them. My brother Sam returned to Boston about this time, and he and my father and I sometimes were given work to do together. But then Sam died of the pox, and I spent much time at work with my grieving father.

The years flew by like the flocks of geese winging their way to the south every fall, quickly and with great majesty. I married, and my sweet wife, Mary, bore ten children, all but two of them now grown to adulthood. My cousin Annie married also, to a merchant who owned more than a dozen ships that brought thousands more Englishmen here to New England. I became the printer of a newspaper, the *Boston News-letter*. Many years later I was able to purchase it. Like my father before me, I became the printer of the laws of Massachusetts Bay, a handsome position that assured a profit and my prosperity.

Sometimes we heard of James Printer. Little things. There was a property dispute with some English near Grafton, which he and his cousin John Wampus were able to settle by trading some of their lands. He was a man of considerable property. And I heard that he devoted much time among the Indians, teaching them to read in English and in their native Algonquian.

I saw him once, at the funeral of Master John Eliot. More than a thousand people came to it, to pin a note of remembrance upon the old man's coffin as was the custom. Annie pointed James out to me. He stood beside Master Eliot's coffin, dressed like a prosperous merchant, wearing white gloves and a high hat. I could not shout out to him, but Annie and I pressed through the crowd to try to catch hold of him. But when I reached the spot where I had seen James, who should be standing there but Lemuel Brown, the same one who had accused Little John and Captain William. "How dare the likes of him, that printer, show up at a solemn occasion such as this," Brown was telling the crowd. "Some of us will not forget how he betrayed us during the war, sneaking away to be with that villain, King Philip himself. So I says to him, this printer James, I says, 'Even I who has but one eye can see you. How dare you show your face among good English folk like us.' And I would have beat him with my walking stick if he did not disappear in this crowd before I could land a single blow upon him."

But for the memory of good John Eliot I would have set upon this Lemuel Brown with *my* walking stick. Instead, I said, "That printer has more right to be here than you do, Lemuel Brown. Be gone with you before I have the sheriff send you on your way!"

And this maker of trouble between people did run away from me, because he knew I knew him.

It was many years later before I saw James again. In 1709, my wife died. My cousin Annie, by then a widow, kindly agreed to help run my household. As glum as I was, Annie tried all the harder to keep me of good cheer.

One day at dinner, a Master Experience Mayhew came to call. He had translated a psalm book into the Indian tongue and asked me to print it for him. He thought it would be useful for his preaching among the Indians.

"You alone among printers today have experience in printing in Algonquian," he said.

I laughed out loud at his words. "Oh, you are very wrong there, Master Mayhew," I said. "There is one printer who has more ability than I, one who reads and writes in Algonquian. He is the right printer for your job."

So it was that I rode out one fine fall morning in search of James Printer. At the end of a long day, I came to the town of Grafton, where I stayed at a little inn. The keepers there knew of James and directed me to his house. The next morning, I found it, not far off a large road, a fine, three-storied house with many gables.

And there inside was my old friend and teacher.

When I reached for his hand, he grabbed hold of me and pulled me to him. "I have heard much of your success, Bartholomew," he said.

We talked awhile of old times, but then I told him my purpose. "I have a commission for you," I said. "A job of printing in the Indian tongue and in English."

He seemed surprised. "It is so long since I have been a printer," he said. "I am now a printer in name only."

"Your skills have not faded," I said.

"Oh, they have all but disappeared," he said.

"You'll remember them quickly," I said. "No one else but you can do this job. It is to be a book in two languages, English and Algonquian, side by side on each page. And who but you can set and read the Algonquian? It is but a little job. Won't you consent?"

"Only if we stand together side by side while the work is done," James said.

"And we will race against each other?" I asked.

"Of course," he said. "We must see if the pupil has at last surpassed the master."

So it was that James came to stay with me in Boston, and we worked on one last book. For weeks, James and I and Annie had all of our meals together and talked as we did of old. What anger there was in him after the war seemed to have left him. And he laughed now at the memory of the wounds I suffered when my brother Sam threw type at me.

Every day, we worked together at my shop, racing as we did years ago to see who could finish his column of type before the other. Soon, it was clear that he was as fast as I. And through this competition, we finished the book in a few weeks time.

Late one night, I wandered back into the shop alone to set the final page. By lantern light I did sew together the signatures of the first of the books in a jacket of vellum.

The next morning, Annie was there when I handed him this finished book, holding it open so he could see the title page.

He smiled at what I had done, just as he smiled often upon me when I was a boy in those days before King Philip's War began. For this is what I had printed, first in Algonquian: "Upprinthomunneau B. Green, kah J. Printer." And then in English: "Printed by B. Green and J. Printer."

"So at last," James said, now laughing with pleasure, "I am a real printer. For now these words do tell me so."

Annie and I, too, began laughing at the joke that only the three of us could understand.

Laughter has a way of using itself up. And when we had finished with it, tears ran from my eyes, for I knew I had righted a great wrong against him. I took hold of James's hands and said, "Truly there is no greater printer in all New England. And now, all the world will be able to read it, in English and Indian alike."

He tried to speak, but had trouble doing so. Suddenly, he looked like the old man he was, almost three score and ten, at the end of his allotted days. Yes, he was crying, but with pleasure, reading over and over those words in English and Indian, his name and mine on the same title page.

"Look," he said, "look at the magic that words can make. They bring us together for all men to see, Indians and English, now and ever after." I nodded my agreement.

"Oh, the magic," he said. "The magic of words, of black marks upon white paper!"

Afterword

I WAS SITTING IN THE RARE BOOKS COLLECTION at Harvard University, just a few steps from where James Printer once lived and worked. A librarian handed me the book I had asked for—presenting it to me in a box, as if it were a present. Inside was an old volume bound in deerskin, marred only a little by the centuries, with stains of ordinary handling and small holes left behind by long-dead insects. I turned the volume over carefully to admire the fine stitching that held it together.

This was one of the few remaining copies of the first Indian Bible, printed in Cambridge in the year 1661, when Charles the Second was king of England. James's name does not appear in its pages. Yet, I knew that by this time, he was an apprentice to printer Samuel Green, whose name is on the title page. And James had worked on this Bible, its words in the Algonquian language that he spoke as well as the English he learned as a boy. He had helped to set the type, feed the paper into the press, and sew the separate sections together. I could feel his presence in the book as I turned it in my hands.

James Printer is mentioned in passing in many diaries and histories of King Philip's War, written at the time or soon after. It is from these sharp, little fragments that I have tried to reconstruct some sense of a long, rich life and explain how he came to join a rebellion against the English he had known all his life.

As boys, he and a cousin were taken into the house of Harvard's President Dunster, where there was a print shop. Later, the press was moved to what had been an Indian college next to the main college. The brick building was torn down in 1698. I like to think that occasional bits of lead type can be found even now in Harvard Yard, including a few that Sam Green might have thrown at his young half-brother Bartholomew.

During the war, James fled from Cambridge and was brought back along with several others by Captain Samuel Moseley. One Indian, called Little John, was sentenced to hang on the Boston Common, but was killed instead by another Indian who stabbed him in the chest. James was released a few days later, along with the other captives. He found his way to King Philip's camp, where he served as a scribe and translator and played an important role in the release of English hostages. He is also thought to be the author of the note left on the bridge at Medfield, warning the English that "the Indians thou has provoked in wrath and anger will war this twenty-one years if you will."

Like all wars, this uprising of Indians against the growing numbers of English immigrants was full of violence and the worst sort of atrocities on both sides. It was almost impossible to remain neutral. James had to choose the side he did.

Although he is listed in several histories of early New England printers, James's name appeared on only a single publication, Master Experience Mayhew's 1709 book of psalms, in English and in Algonquian. It is there on the title page, alongside the name of Bartholomew Green, where it properly belongs.

— Paul Samuel Jacobs
July 1, 1996
Davis, California